Night of the Fourth Moon

COLD BLOOD
IV

Edited by
Peter Sellers

MOSAIC PRESS
Oakville-New York-London

CANADIAN CATALOGUING IN PUBLICATION DATA

Cold blood IV

ISBN   0-88962-513-1 (bound)   0-88962-512-3 (pbk.)

1.   Detective and mystery stories, Canadian (English).*
I.   Sellers, Peter, 1956-

PS8323.D4C65 1992   C813'.087208   C92-094968-1
PR9197.35.D48C65 1992

Published by MOSAIC PRESS, P.O. Box 1032, Oakville, Ontario, L6J 5E9, Canada. Offices and warehouse at 1252 Speers Road, Units 1&2, Oakville, Ontario, L6L 5N9, Canada.

Mosaic Press acknowledges the assistance of the Canada Council and the Ontario Arts Council in support of its publishing programme.

Copyright © Peter Sellers, 1992
Design by Patty Gallinger
Cover Illustration by HENRY VAN DER LINDE
Typeset by Jackie Ernst

Printed and bound in Canada.

ISBN   0-88962-512-3 PB   0-88962-513-1 HC

MOSAIC PRESS:
In Canada:
        MOSAIC PRESS, 1252 Speers Road, Units 1&2, Oakville, Ontario
L6L 5N9, Canada. P.O. Box 1032, Oakville, Ontario L6J 5E9
In the United States:
        Distributed to the trade in the United States by : National Book Network, Inc., 4720-A Boston Way, Lanham, MD, 20706 USA
In the U.K.:
        John Calder (Publishers) Ltd., 9-15 Neal Street, London, WCZH 9TU, England.

For Daniel and Jennifer
Two challenging, rewarding short mysteries.

TABLE OF CONTENTS

INTRODUCTION

by Peter Sellers

When the first book in the Cold Blood series was published, back in 1987, it was subtitled "Murder in Canada." Not all the stories were about homicide, but it was close enough to give readers a pretty clear indication of what they could expect to find inside.

Two years later, the subtitle was gone. Replaced by Roman numerals. But this fourth book could make a strong case for the subtitle's reinstatement, for it truly tells stories of murder (or at least attempted murder) in almost every part of the country.

Jas. R. Petrin's serial killer, who fancifully dubs himself "The Creeper," takes a terrified government employee on a murderer's tour of Winnipeg. The search for a missing girl leads Mel Ames' private eyes Stu Blaze and Connie Wells through the orchards and along the backroads of the Okanagan Valley. Charlotte MacLeod returns us to bucolic Pitcherville, New Brunswick. Ted Wood takes us back in time for a murder at Louisburg, the French fortress on Cape Breton Island. And in William Bankier's "The Best of Birtles" an unexpected reunion begins and ends in Montreal.

However, much as the book contains a lot of murders committed close to home, several also involve Canadians abroad. So Cold Blood IV could just as easily be subtitled "Death Takes a Holiday."

Gregor Robinson offers us expatriates involved in a coup d'etat on an unnamed Caribbean island. Alison Cunliffe also features expatriate Canadians and murder off the Cayman Islands. Anne Stephenson relates the consequences of a weekend in Bermuda. Both Eric Wright and newcomer Eliza Moorhouse explore the consequences of chance meetings in foreign bars.

But no matter where the authors set their stories, Peter Robinson's Yorkshire, John North's Ontario golf course or at a resort on Cape Cod, the end result is always intriguing. And, like each of the previous books in this series, Cold Blood IV features a mix of new and established authors.

There is one difference about Cold Blood IV, however. It appears at a time when the short crime fiction scene in Canada is stronger than it has ever been. Both of the first two volumes came out in isolation, with neither competitors nor companions on the horizon.

So far, the nineties have been a much better time for short Canadian crime fiction. Cold Blood III came out in 1990, and captured all five places in the list of finalists for the Crime Writers of Canada's Arthur Ellis Award for Best Short Story. The same year, Oxford University Press published Canadian Mystery Stories, although this was mainly a reprint anthology (including stories reprinted from both Cold Blood and Fingerprints) it did include a few original stories. The following year saw the release of Great Canadian Mystery and Suspense Stories, published by Quarry Press. And 1992 marked the appearance, from Macmillan, of Criminal Shorts, the second Crime Writers of Canada anthology, plus this edition of Cold Blood. Compared to just five or six years earlier, this was nirvana for writers and fans of short crime stories.

Nineteen ninety-two is also the year that Bouchercon comes to Canada. Literally hundreds of mystery authors, editors, agents, publishers, book dealers and fans will converge on Toronto for the 23rd annual World Mystery Convention, named in honour of the legendary reviewer, anthologist, novelist and short story writer Anthony Boucher. It marks only the second time the convention had been held outside the United States, the first in Canada.

So the burgeoning of all forms of short crime fiction continues. And perhaps the dark night endured by the short crime story over the past years is ending. Here's hoping it isn't a false dawn.

Toronto, July, 1992

A Murder Story by *Jas. R. Petrin*

Jim Petrin's reputation as one of Canada's finest writers of short crime fiction grows steadily. In Cold Blood III, his Arthur-nominated story "Man on the Roof" was an exercise in pure suspense. Here, he combines humour with steadily mounting horror.

A MURDER STORY

by *Jas. R. Petrin*

"**I** confessed again today but they just won't listen." The Creeper struck his fist into the palm of his hand. "I tell 'em and tell 'em, but they just won't stop and turn around and believe me. What can I do about it, huh? Answer me *that!*"

"I don't know," Moskewitz said.

"I'm dangerous."

"Yes," Moskewitz agreed.

Moskewitz was a legal clerk in the municipal offices. A slightly plump, slightly balding man with wire-rimmed glasses that were forever riding down his nose to make him repeatedly thumb them back up again. Always last to lock his desk and leave the building, this time he had delayed too long and had been buttonholed here in the deserted parking lot by a madman.

"I'm a menace," the Creeper said. "They oughta lock me up." He stood on the asphalt in seam-burst sneakers, feet splayed wide, stooping over the car, the tips of his fingers leaving round sweaty dimples on the fake mahogany door panel. An acid odour of half-digested beer and something that might once have been a cheeseburger riding out on his breath. Moskewitz glanced around, feeling anxious. But the other employees of the offices - courtroom workers, city hall administrators - had all gotten into their cars and rolled home to their dinners and families a long time before. Except for an empty Slurpy cup rattling hollowly over the pavement on the wind, there was only Moskewitz - and the Creeper.

That's what he called himself: the Creeper. He said in a voice that was taut with subdued rage that he had written many letters to the radio stations and newspapers urging them to use that name, his

4

proper name, his rightful name, but they hadn't seen fit to take him up on it. They continued to refer to the Winnipeg serial killer as the Winnipeg Serial Killer.

Something he meant to put right.

"So how about a lift?" It wasn't really a question.

Moskewitz thought about the grim presence in his life, his mother, sitting waiting for him at home by the door, and a small panic took him.

"Well, Mr...ah...Creeper, no offense, of course, but the thing is I'm running a little late, and—"

"Sure."

The Creeper walked around the front of the car, opened the passenger's door and got in.

Moskewitz closed his eyes for a long-suffering moment, took a deep breath and reluctantly opened them again. Everything happens to me, he thought. He put the Celebrity in gear and backed out of his spot, away from the wooden cross-member with the stenciling that said CLERK and didn't say MOSKEWITZ. It was the only cross-member without a proper name on it; but then, Moskewitz had only held his position of legal clerk for thirteen mind-numbing years.

There was no justice in the world.

Not even in the courts.

*　　*　　*

In the passenger's seat the Creeper lit a cigarette, ignoring the sticker that the Grim Presence had pasted on the dashboard - two-inch high letters - YES, I MIND VERY MUCH IF YOU SMOKE! The Creeper didn't mind if anybody minded. Moskewitz noticed that. He wished he could be that assertive.

Moskewitz stopped at the exit to the street. There was no traffic. No one to honk or flash his lights at, no one to rescue him. It was as if the whole town had abandoned him. He waited for instructions. The Creeper offered none.

"I guess you want me to drive you home? If you tell me which way to turn—"

"Don't drive me home. I'll tell you when to drive me home. You're not driving me home. Not yet."

"But, I thought. . ."

"Drive us to a beer store. We need some beer."

We need some beer? Moskewitz drove to the only beer store he knew of, kitty-corner from the Brookland's Inn, where the Creeper plucked the keys out of the ignition and went inside and came out a moment later toting a twelve-pack of Molsons like a hunter with his kill. He slung it into the car, got back in and broke open the case. He popped a bottle open and tipped it to his lips. There was a gurgling sound, like water in a drain. Moskewitz stared as the contents quickly vanished.

The Creeper wiped his mouth on his fist, let out a volcanic belch, and then handed back the keys.

"Drive down by the creek. You know - that way." He pointed in no particular direction. "Out by the s-sentemary - cemetery. Out where the fishermen died. Take me there and I'll prove I done it, that I'm the Creeper, an' then you can tell the police, tell the newspapers, tell the whole damn world - they'll listen to you."

"But..."

"You'll be a hero."

A hero? Moskewitz had trouble with that concept. But he obediently made a left turn at Keewatin, then a hard right at Notre Dame, and after a few minutes driving and another beer for the Creeper they arrived at the narrow bridge spanning Omand's Creek. Moskewitz pulled off the road and stopped. The Creeper bullied him out of the car, and down the easy slope to the water's edge. It was a chill though peaceful fall evening: a dwindling sun drawing a purple skirt over the sky, cattails drooping in black silhouette, the water dark and vaguely solemn, recalling the violence that had occurred here.

There was a wide, flattened area of trampled grass about their feet. Looking down at it, Moskewitz's glasses slipped and he pushed them up again.

"People still come here," the Creeper said, sounding like an old soldier, "to look." With his beer he pointed north to where the creek emerged from under the chain link boundary of the cemetery. "See that rock? They were sittin' right there. Couple of dopes. Both of 'em."

Moskewitz frowned, trying to remember the press reports. He shook his head and turned to face south, towards the bridge. "But surely the papers said..."

"Don't tell *me*."

"Nevertheless..."

"Don't believe that media crap."

"No. No I won't. Sorry."

"You oughta be. Those jerks."

The Creeper went on to explain - to actually demonstrate - how he had stalked the lounging fishermen, "Guy A and Guy B", as he called them.

"Crept up quiet as a bunny, y'know, right in behind Guy A on this carpetty grass, and then—"

He made a sudden movement to show how he'd dispatched first one, and then the other. Two quick thrusts of their own sharp filleting knife.

"Guy A went down here, by this bush. Look, you can see the stain. Guy B dropped right here, had his big mouth open, turning around to learn what the grunting was about."

"I see."

"It's the truth."

"If you say so."

Moskewitz hoped they could now proceed to the Creeper's house so that he would be free to hurry home himself, to his cooling supper, his cold tea, and the Grim Presence. But the Creeper wasn't finished. He wanted to show Moskewitz how he had dealt with the stargazer. Made Moskewitz drive to Westview Park, a lonely wind-swept knoll above the town, a mound that had been changed from an octogenarian garbage dump into a modern-day park by official edict. Again the Creeper shooed Moskewitz out of the car and held forth about the crime.

"See this ragweed? Guy was flopped down here. Stargazer. Flat on his back, can you believe it? With a killer on the loose and all them mosquitoes? Hell, I did him a favour. Slipped up and blipped him with his own damn telescope."

"Binoculars," Moskewitz said, and shivered. The temperature was dropping fast, a keen norther lofting over the crest of the hill and cutting through his thin coat. "They were never found, but the press said that he always used binoculars."

"Binocs? Nope! No good for blipping. I'd of used a rock if he had those. But he had a telescope - and that's something else. Goddamn bludgeon, a telescope. That's what he had and I blipped him with it."

"It was never found."

"Course not. I tossed it in a dumpster."

"You told the police this when you confessed?"

"Absolutely. But soon as I said telescope, they sneered and said I was lying."

"Ah."

"Still don't believe me, huh? I'll show you another spot."

Moskewitz sighed. The Presence would be slumped in a chair by now, burning two holes through the face of the kitchen clock with her eyes.

They drove to the industrial park where the warehouse worker had been killed a year earlier, very late one evening, crushed to death in the garbage press beside his loading dock. Official reports had stated that his death had been an accident.

As the Celebrity bounced in over the railroad siding, empty beer bottles clinked and boinked under the seat. They reminded the Creeper of his manners.

"Oops. Wanna beer?" The Creeper explaining, "Us killers never say 'scuse me, we only say oops." He giggled and shoved a cold Molsons at Moskewitz, who hedged.

"I don't usually..."

In fact he had enjoyed a cold beer once. A long time ago, in his younger days, those days before the Grim Presence had rooted that particular short-lived vice out of him. The Presence being vehemently opposed to the consumption of alcohol. Especially beer. I MIND VERY MUCH IF YOU DRINK BEER!

"Lighten up. Enjoy," the Creeper urged.

I MIND VERY MUCH IF YOU ENJOY.

"Just 'cause I'm a murderer—"

"It's not that," Moskewitz said hurriedly, as though some of his best friends were murderers. He couldn't bring himself to speak about the Presence.

"Well then, break down an' have a brewski an' don't stop."

Moskewitz took the beer from the Creeper's hand. The bottle slid cool and weighty into his palm. Rigid. Cold. A thin and slightly bulging neck that you could close your hand around. A lot like the neck of the Presence.

He twisted the cap off.

"Strong hands," the Creeper cackled. "He's a killer!"

This time they stayed in the car. The Creeper gesturing at the loading dock, content to explain the mechanics of this crime with waves of his bottle and cigarette.

"Middla the night. Hotter'n hell. Eatin' his lunch. Hunka pizza. Hears me comin'. Musclebound guy. Jumps right up. Hell of a struggle. Trips and falls." The Creeper chuckled and pointed his cigarette. "Man, he was a good one. Swan dive straight into the goddamn trash compactor. All's I had to do was push the button. Ain't technology wonderful?"

Moskewitz shoved his glasses up.

"The police said he fell into the machine by accident."

"They would. One less murder on their books, isn't it?"

The Creeper had other murder scenes he wanted Moskewitz to see. As they drove about the city, he rambled on about them like a drunken guide explaining historic battles, describing each atrocity.

Moskewitz thinking.

Could there be substance to his claim?

Some of what he said was predictable enough: that he was the killer; that he alone knew all the facts. The police were idiots. The media were fools. To expose their collective stupidity, he was coming clean, but still the authorities would not listen. So Moskewitz - lucky Moskewitz - was elected to take the Creeper's detailed confessions to the public in person and explain how it could only be the Creeper and none other than the Creeper who was the arch-fiend and sole perpetrator of these numerous, brutish and odious crimes.

Weaving in detail after detail.

Insisting that the woman in the lane who'd been hit with the rock, had not been chased - that had been the girl in the field; that the drunk in the alley had been suffocated in his sleep, right enough, but the bruise on his head was from striking the ground, not from being clobbered with the fence post - that was the transient in the ditch. Explaining convincingly and clearly why all this had to be so.

More and more it seemed to Moskewitz that the Creeper knew what he was talking about. His babble made more sense than the smug rhetoric enunciated by the police and parrotted in the press. Could the authorities be wrong? It would not surprise Moskewitz. Thirteen years in the courts had taught him how easily facts could be misinterpreted.

He began to steal careful, sober looks at his drunken passenger, feeling subtle nudges of curiosity and respect.

*   *   *

The beer was beginning to tell. The Creeper announced a need to relieve internal pressures. "T.B.," he confided.

Moskewitz stared. "You've got T.B.?"

"Absolutely - tiny bladder." The Creeper sniggered. He directed Moskewitz onto a rough, secluded road that wound its way into a gravel pit. Before the car rolled to a stop, he was performing like a contortionist, leaning out the door. "Airplane beer," he shouted. "Drink two–P-38." He zipped up and slammed the door against the cold, settled himself more comfortably and turned the radio on loud to 92 CITI-FM. He groped between his legs for two more beers and wasn't gentle about opening them; they foamed all over the new lavender terry-cloth seat covers that had been personally selected by the Grim Presence.

"Oops!" the Creeper said. He giggled and grinned sheepishly. "That's the thing about us killers..."

But Moskewitz was staring at the dark, spreading stain, almost experiencing physical pain from it. Surely the Presence had sensed this transgression, surely her eyes had flown open wide, like a fiend whose nest has been dashed with holy water.

The Creeper going:

"...we never say 'scuse me, we only say oops."

"So you mentioned."

"Oops is what we say." The Creeper handed a Molsons to Moskewitz - who now had a beer in each hand - and added in a more confiding tone: "Oops is what I said the first time I...you know..."

"Yes...?"

"You know..."

"The first time you killed somebody?"

The Creeper slapped the dash so hard the speedometer needle leaped to sixty miles an hour.

"That's it! By Jeez, your honour, you're quick. I bet not many of them smarty-assed lawyers get by you."

This was something new. Somehow - Moskewitz had missed the exact moment - the Creeper in his Molson-muddled mind had elevated legal clerk Moskewitz to the bench.

He protested. "I'm not a judge."

"No?"

"No."

"You look like a judge."

"Well, I'm not."

"You wouldn't shit me, would you? I say you are. And I oughta know. I'm a killer, aren't I?" Frowning now. Worried. "Drink your beer."

Moskewitz drank. His glasses slipped down. He pushed them up again.

Neil Young's reedy voice wailed out of the radio - *Rocking In The Free World*. The Creeper turned the volume up several decibels and beat a sinewy fist against the dash, keeping time. Moskewitz bravely turned the volume down. He had decided he wanted to know if the Creeper was truly the serial killer, or if he was just another madman.

"Tell me about your first victim. Let me see, that would be the Ste. Mary's Academy teacher...?"

"Her? Hell no. Started long before that, your honour. Lo-o-o-ng before that. I'm a bo-o-o-orn killer, you know." He cranked the music up again. "Song's about me," he said, thumping the car. "I been rocking in the Free World a long time. With real rocks."

Moskewitz turned the radio down.

"Tell me about it."

"Sure. Jus' gimme a sec to get the ole head-kidney working." He knuckled the side of his skull causing another gusher of Molsons to erupt, this time inundating Moskewitz's console. The Creeper took a half-hearted swipe at the spillage with his cigarette hand, saying "oops", and grey ash feathered down to create a frothy scum. He tugged one ear reflectively, fingered something out of that bristly orifice and wiped it on the dash. "Guess I must of been about ten."

"Ten!"

"Must of been. Let's see, Mom locked Dad out of the house just before that, an' he slept under the porch an' froze his toe off. I remember that." He turned to explain. "See, he had this hole in his boot..." The Creeper closed his eyes again.

"Anyway, it weren't too long after that. Spring time. Guy got me started, he was a wino. Filthy ole bum. Disgustin'. Met him by the creek after school an' the two of us got to talking. This guy, you should of seen him. He'd swivel his eyes at you, like a crab, all the time grinning. Said he'd killed a hunnerd people, and each time he'd said oops."

"Oops?"

"That's it. That's what he said. Said he'd got started when he was a kid like me. Said what got him going on it was when he first of all took an' killed himself a stranger."

"He killed a stranger?"

"Yup."

"A complete stranger?"

"That's it. Said killing that stranger was the thing got him started." A look of extreme pleasure crept into the Creeper's eyes. "But now we're comin' to the best part. See, the guy's been sidling up on me all this time, closer an' closer, right? Thinks I don't notice. An' he suddenly leaps at me, long fingers wagglin', reachin'. But, hey, I was strong for my age. And quick. He'd got a tiger by the tail. I killed him, the sumbitch, right there by the water, with a rock. Pow. Blipped him a good one. Whadda you think of that?"

"Holy cow," Moskewitz said.

"You're darn right, holy cow. I got to thinkin' about what he'd said. I realized that *he* was *my* stranger. It was sort of like I was his apprentice, know what I mean? An' when they didn't come breaking down the door to arrest me, well then I seen how easy it was to... you know..."

"Kill somebody?"

"That's it."

"And he was your first."

"Yup. Number one. Numero uno. And right after him there was the second one, this woman lived across the road from us - Merviss...Derviss...Terviss... whatever the hell she called herself. Bad old broad, your honour. Real piece of work. Babysat us sometimes, an' I bet you'd of given her four hunnerd years in the gas chamber for what she used to do to us kids."

"That bad, was she?"

"Absolutely. She was the worst. Ghost of Ma Barker. Cruelty an' perversions, you can't imagine."

"I see."

"That's why I'm warped."

"That would explain it. Yes. So...what did you do about her?"

"About Merviss—Derviss—Terviss? Well, your honour, I fixed

her good. One day after she'd took an' put us through a whole bunch of hell, feelin' a bit cocky after that wino, I sneaked across the road to her place an' crept up on the shed where she was pickling beets. Hotter'n forty bastards that day. I'm telling you. Hell boilin' up in waves off the ground. I snuck up on that picklin' shack, creepitty-creep, took a boo in to make sure she was there—"

"And was she?"

"Oh yeah. Large as life."

"So then what?"

"She turned around an' saw me, an' yelled YOW."

"And what did you do?"

"Boom! I slammed the goddamn door on her. Yup! Jus' reached out an' slammed that sucker. An' then I latched it."

"Did she die?"

"Die? Pal, it was a hunnerd degrees that day, I'm telling you, with a hot stove and thirty gallons of boiling water in it. They didn't call it a pickling shed for nothing. She died all right. And when they finally got around to telling us kids about it, an' somebody asked me how I felt, you know what I said?"

"No."

"I said oops. That's what I said, I said oops." The Creeper took a long reflective pull on his bottle and picked his nose with his thumb. "Fact was, I was glad, your honour. Glad that I'd stifled that old horror. Glad! Figured I'd done the world a favour. So that was my second victim, an' it was that ole master murderer down by the creek that got me started. That ole wino."

"And since then I suppose you've killed, well, a lot of people?"

"Dozens. Hunnerds—almost." He suddenly spun in his seat and grabbed a handful of Moskewitz's coat, his eyes wild, pupils madly staring. "That's why I gotta be stopped!"

They sat for a moment. The Creeper quiet again, reliving some previous atrocity, sucking at his beer and his cigarette. Filling the car intermittently with unpleasant sounds and odours. He finished his cigarette, lit another one. He finished his beer, opened another one. Finally he said:

"So, your honour—your turn. Did you ever kill some jerk?"

"Good heavens, no!"

"No, huh? Ever think about killing someone?"

Moskewitz sucked in a lungful of air and exhaled. Think about it? Oh yes. Out loud he said, "I suppose *everybody's* thought about it. I suppose *I've* thought about it."

"Goody," the Creeper said. "Who? Who'd you think about killing?"

Should he tell this madman of his personal miseries? Explain to him about his mother, a woman who by anybody's reckoning deserved to become more intimate with a pickling shed?

The Grim Presence.

She who waited up to sniff for cigarette smoke on his clothes. She who wore strapless sandals that snick-snicked against her flat heels when she paced. She who slept in her chair with her mouth wide open and her yellow teeth bared, like a marmot. Yes, you could certainly find good reasons to make a big batch of Polski Ogorkis out of her. You only needed a barrel. And an ax.

Still, he couldn't share these thoughts and feelings with a man like the Creeper.

"Nobody in particular," he mumbled.

"Too bad," the Creeper said.

There was a real regret in his tone. Moskewitz looked at him, puzzled. The Creeper clapped him affectionately on the knee.

"I mean, it's too bad I'm turning myself in. Else I could sort of take you in hand a while, see, an' show you the way it's done."

"What do you mean?"

"Well, I could teach you how to...you know..."

"Kill people?"

"That's it."

"Become a sort of apprentice myself?"

"You got it."

A macabre thought.

"See, I was the wino's 'prentice. you could be mine. I'm slowing down, y'know. Gettin' tired. It's hard work, all this murdering. You could take over."

"Take over!"

"Absolutely. I'd get you started, see. I mean, you stop an' think about it, I couldn't of killed ole Merviss-Derviss-Terviss without that wino, could I? It was that man taught me confidence." He gave a big owly wink. "Do it my way, the way I'd show you, the cops'd never touch you. Not even if you walked right up and confessed to 'em. Listen, I *know.*"

There was still something Moskewitz had to understand.

"But why, if you've been trying to turn yourself in all this time, would you all of a sudden want to get somebody else started?"

The Creeper lit a cigarette before he answered. Shook out his match and tossed it out the window.

"Teach 'em a lesson, that's why. Other night, fer zample. I had a new confession all worked out, spent the whole night on it. An' you know what? Those damn cops wouldn't even let me in the door. Teed me off. But did I kill a cop? Oh, no no no." He touched his head. "I got kidneys up here. Didn't want to make it too easy on 'em. So what I did, I went out an' murdered the telephone man the papers all went wild about."

"The telephone man? That was you?" Moskewitz pushed his glasses up.

"Yours truly. Followed him right up the ladder. With him all the way. Bop! Down he went. Oops, I said. Us killers don't say 'scuse me—"

"—you only say oops," Moskewitz finished for him, and the Creeper cackled, nodding appreciatively at Moskewitz.

Moskewitz's thoughts wandered. He thought of cranky judges, arrogant lawyers, parking stalls without names on them - a Grim Presence...

Oops.

It was that easy.

"Were you ever almost caught?"

The Creeper answered without removing his cigarette, and it wagged in his lips as he spoke, grey ash showering down his shirt.

"Once I almost got caught. It was out the west end, see. Just past midnight. I'd gone for this woman, see, but then she screamed. I took off running. There was this band heading home, high school band, that J.T. Band, on a bus. They seen me an' stopped, an' Jesus H. Christ, next thing I know they're jumping all over me, your honour. Man, I was in a world of pain. All trombones an' clarinets, cymbals an' trumpets. I broke free finally an' run like a deer. You ever been whacked with a slide trombone?"

Moskewitz shook his head.

"Hurts like the devil."

The Creeper rummaged in his beer box.

"Brewski?"

Moskewitz took one.

"Smoke?"

Moskewitz took that too.

The Creeper cackled.

"You'd make a wunnerful 'prentice. You learn quick."

"Thank you."

"Don't mention it." He belched. "Know what I think? I think you an' me, we oughta go pick us up some burgers. Know jus' the place. Cockroaches size of cats, you got to beat 'em off with your fork—but good solid food. Real filling. Nice greasy onion rings. Sit in your stomach for days..."

*   *   *

The twilight had failed completely and a gibbous moon was pushing through shredded cloud by the time they finally drew up on the north side of town, near the railway yards, a block away from the Creeper's little house.

The burger Moskewitz had eaten was filling all right. It was solid, too. It sat in his stomach like a brick. He was sure it would still be there in a week.

"S'matter?" asked the Creeper. "Can'tcha drive us right up to the goddamn door?"

Yes, he could. The way he was feeling, Moskewitz could drive them *through* the goddamn door. But a sixth sense told him it was a bad idea to let his vehicle be seen in proximity to the Creeper's house.

"Never mind. We'll walk," the Creeper said, shouldering open the door. "We'll get some air." He farted. "You're comin' in, ain't you? Have a nightcap?"

Moskewitz, under the effects of the beer—it *had* to be the beer, there was no other explanation—was actually beginning to enjoy the Creeper's company, the only socializing he'd done in months. But still the Grim Presence shook her forbidding finger. He saw her still waiting up for him by the door, a hard, cutting woman with a hard, cutting mouth, a clock in her hand with two smoking holes in its face.

A woman who had hijacked his life, arranged it with the unflagging single-mindedness she always applied to his world. The girl he had met? She had to go. The clothes he dared to buy? Too frivolous, gone. A few furtive nights out with a friend? She'd brought that part of his life to a shuddering halt with one stamp of her cloven hoof.

"Comin'?"

There was a lot of grunting, but the Creeper had managed to off-load himself to the boulevard, and now squatted on a fireplug like some nefarious garden gnome. Thumbs hooked in his pockets, large hands splayed out on his thighs. An enormous Sears sign towered into the night behind him.

Moskewitz wanted to leave and yet he didn't. He thumbed his glasses up.

"Your wife..." he faltered.

"Don't worry about her."

"No? Where is she?"

"She went out for a whiz an' the crows got her."

"I beg your pardon?"

"Naw. But listen. She's gone. Wanna know where?" The toothy grin lengthened. "Six carboys." He drew their shapes with his hands. "Sulfuric acid. Glug-glug. Bathtub." He pulled an imaginary plug and made a glurping, tub-draining sound. "All gone. Now, come on, grab that beer an' let's go."

Moskewitz swallowed. Could this man actually have committed such an abominable crime? Ridding himself of a human being in such a crude and grotesque way? He thought of the Grim Presence. She was a thin, fleshless woman. Four carboys ought to do it.

"The beer is all done," he told the Creeper.

"Done? Shit. Well, that don't matter—I got more." The Creeper pressed a finger against one nostril and emptied his nose onto the grass. "I even got snacks," he said.

They went down an alley, their own shadows cast by the Sears sign lengthening in front of them. Moskewitz had to help the Creeper keep to a straight course, and had to support him when they stopped at a sagging back-yard gate. They went through it and into an overgrown garden, then up the back steps to the door of a slumping, slant-roofed shanty. The Creeper, beer rolling like a high tide inside him, had some trouble with the lock, but he eventually got his key into it and let them both inside.

The place smelled musty.

"I got to...you know..."

"Relieve yourself?"

"That's it," the Creeper said, and went off to do it.

The house seemed even mustier, now Moskewitz was left alone to smell it.

A tiny kitchen, with paint in garish pinks and greens as if it had been chosen by a cake-decorator. And a bedroom—Moskewitz saw glancing through a door that another kind of decorator had been at work in there: a paper-hanger. Newspaper clippings of the murders stretched from ceiling to floor, most of them front page headlines hacked from that paragon of paperdom, the Winnipeg Sun.

The Creeper reappeared and exhumed two beers from the bowels of his fridge. Banged them onto the table. "Li'l nightcap to top off the evening, your honour?" He belched and looked glum. "Jeez, I wish I hadn't eaten that goddamn burger."

Moskewitz accepted one of the frosty bottles—getting over his own burger now and beginning to feel mellow. He pushed his glasses up with his thumb and followed the Creeper on a tour of the house.

Not a lot to see, the place nearly devoid of furniture. What furnishings there were appeared to have been scavenged from trash bins and nuisance grounds. In the bedroom, a legless box-spring flat on the floor. Beside it cases of empties from previous nightcaps climbing like an escarpment up the wall beside the photographs. Teetering. They'd seek their own level one night to the discomfort of the Creeper below. Crumpled clothing and newspapers scattered virtually everywhere.

They came at last to the basement. The Creeper had saved this place for last, as if he were particularly proud of it. A dark, forbidding place, open-beamed, earthen-floored. A cellar, really. And in the middle of the room, a disaster. A marine corps might have done their fox-hole training here, then marched away with their entrenching tools, leaving the mess.

There was a deep, dark pit there in the center of the floor.

The Creeper passed Moskewitz a cigarette. Took one himself. Lit them both. He gestured at the pit with his bottle.

"In case of emergency," he said mysteriously.

"Huh?"

"This hole. Dug it in case I had to get rid of a...you know...real quick."

"A body?"

"Absolutely." He blew a cloud of smoke out his nose. "Course, I wouldn't plant a...you know...here in my own house unless I had to. But since they won't believe me anyway, I don't suppose it matters a hell of a lot, do you?"

The Creeper's eyes were watery, bulging and red. His speech becoming more and more slurred.

"I hate to make it too easy for 'em. First time I confessed, they sorta b'lieved me. Drove straight out here, the S.O.B.'s, and snooped around." The Creeper hawked and spat into the hole. "Asked me how come, if I was the murderer, all I had in my cellar was a great big patch of undisturbed dirt."

He kicked dirt into the pit with his shoe.

"Made an issue out of that, did they?" Moskewitz said.

"Absolutely. I was su'prised. Bring a body home? Bury it here in my own house? No way, I tole 'em. Think I'm loopy? Well, they said, if you want us to believe you're the Killer, you're gonna have to at least show us a hole in the ground, or somethin', don't you think?"

"They must have been teasing you."

"They musta been idiots," the Creeper said.

He made a dismissive gesture. Beer slopped out of his bottle and ran in an amber-white stream down his arm. Then he turned and looked solemnly at Moskewitz.

"Know what I was thinkin' to do? Kill myself. Kill myself, an' not leave them stupid police no letter. Make sure those murders stayed on their goddamn books forever. They hate that, y'know, unsolved murders. Drives 'em wild." He dropped his empty bottle into the pit, fumbled in his pocket and held something out. "See what I got? A gun."

Moskewitz flinched. He'd never had a close-up look at a handgun before.

"Shoot myself, that was my idea." He narrowed his eyes. "Now I got another one. How about this? How about I give the goddamn cops what they're askin' for? A goddamn body in this goddamn hole."

He peered at Moskewitz to see how he was taking this. Then hobbled to the stairs, took hold of the railing and eased himself down onto the step.

19

"I was goin' to kill myself. That was the plan. But then I met you."

Moskewitz felt a warm glow spreading through him, sensed he was becoming intoxicated. He took another puff on his cigarette, beginning to enjoy it. What was the Creeper hinting at? Did he truly mean to kill him? It was, he decided, quite possible.

So why didn't he feel afraid?

He burped. The beer coming back on him.

Maybe, he thought, in some precognitive part of his mind he had guessed why the Creeper was inviting him in. Guessed what the Creeper was planning to do. Could it be that he, Moskewitz, actually wanted to destroy himself? Was he really as unhappy with his life as that?

Adrenalin coursed in his veins.

He glanced about. Cardboard blocked the windows. Anything might happen here. Could he escape? Should he even try? Or would it be more interesting to wait and see if some outside force would intervene. Who could tell? The J.T. Band, at the last moment, trampling down the door to cymbal and saxophone the Creeper into submission, beat the lost chord out of him with a trombone and rescue Moskewitz?

Anything could happen.

"What's funny?" the Creeper wanted to know.

Moskewitz shrugged. He realized he had been smiling. He thought he saw hilarity in the Creeper's eyes, too—hilarity of a wild, insane kind. A mad, reptilian grin on those thin, hard lips.

Suddenly the Creeper blurted out:

"What if I killed you? Splang, right now?"

Killed. Splang. Now there was a notion. To be or not to be. Very amusing. Moskewitz took another puff on his cigarette, pushed his glasses up, and sat down on an upended pail. They were both seated now. Studying one another. Maybe the Creeper did intend to kill Moskewitz, but they were chums now, weren't they? They could talk to one another. He tried to probe deeper into the Creeper's real intentions.

"Why would you want to do that? Kill me? I couldn't straighten the authorities out about those murders then, could I, if you killed me? I couldn't tell them all the things you explained to me."

The Creeper smiled, and Moskewitz decided that his teeth looked false—too straight and too dazzling white. Moskewitz tried to imagine the Creeper in a dentist's chair, just like an ordinary person; but he couldn't do it. Had the Creeper maybe plundered them from a victim? That was a terrible thought.

The Creeper said, "Walked up an' down an' all aroun' that cop shop today, wonderin' how to make 'em b'lieve me." His eyes had hardened into small glassy orbs. "Desperate. Ready to blow my brains out. Do it right there on their damn front step, make a hell of a mess. Then along you come, like God's answer, an' climb into your car. I says to myself, look at that. A real live judge."

Moskewitz giggled. "I'm not a judge."

"Course you are."

"No, I'm not."

"Don't try an' kid me."

"I'm not kidding."

The Creeper cocked his head to one side.

"Not even a lousy ole notary public?"

"Not even."

"What are you then?"

Moskewitz told him. The Creeper made a face.

"A crummy clerk?" He looked unhappy. "I thought for sure you were a judge, with that big cranium of yours. I *need* you to be a judge. See, they'd pay attention to a judge. Specially a dead one."

"You need a dead judge?"

"Don't really *need* one, I guess. Take a clerk if I have to, I mean if that's all I can get."

They locked eyes. Each took a swig of beer. This is crazy, Moskewitz thought. It's me we're talking about. But when the Creeper started laughing, Moskewitz burst out laughing too, beer shooting up his nose in a jet, forcing tears to his eyes in large drops. Watching this, the Creeper laughed even harder, toppled slowly forward onto his knees, pawing at the dirt floor, roaring. He spluttered:

"You're—not even scared."

Moskewitz cackled.

"I'm in a basement—with an open grave and a murderer—why should I be scared?"

The Creeper howled. Moskewitz howled with him. The Creeper brayed and hooted, and Moskewitz slapped his thigh in convulsions. The Creeper wandered about on all fours giggling and grunting.

"Why be scared? Why be scared?"

"Just don't say boo! or anything," Moskewitz warned.

"Boo! Boo to you! Hoo! haw!"

Hands and knees wouldn't support the Creeper now. He fell in the dust, rolled on his side, clutching his stomach and making loud whistling noises. Moskewitz laughed along with him. They laughed together until the breath was gone out of them, and then the Creeper dragged himself back to the steps, and sat down again, still holding his stomach. He had not once let go of the gun.

He picked his cigarette up off the ground, had a big puff from it, then took a swallow of beer to wash the fun away.

"I like you. But you *know* why I gotta kill you."

"Yes," said Moskewitz.

"You know it's the only way I can make 'em believe me down at that station?"

"Yes." Moskewitz let out a snigger.

"You know I gotta do it?"

"I suppose so."

The Creeper lifted the gun. They looked at it together, then at each other. They laughed again.

The Creeper said, "I'm a killer."

"Uh-huh."

"I killed Mrs. Montague."

"I believe you."

"I killed the Trane sisters, muffled 'em in their beds."

"I know!"

"Mr. Jarlaharl, in the thicket, with a stick—that was me," the Creeper said.

"Yes."

"And the Deets. Ma and Pa. Out on the river. Paddled up, whacked 'em, and drownded 'em. Glug. Dead."

"Uh-huh."

Moskewitz had never felt so alive. This was why people did dangerous things—climbed mountains, jumped out of airplanes.

They did it to feel alive. The Grim Presence would have been furious: I MIND IF YOU FEEL ALIVE!

The Creeper motioned Moskewitz to his feet, then backed him up toward the pit. Moskewitz picked his way carefully. Didn't want to trip and hurt himself. Ha ha. The light was poor. A bulb on a wire. He stopped at the brink of the pit, a place of blackness and undisturbed cobwebs in the shadow of an octopus furnace. He felt like a paratrooper about to jump. He pushed his glasses up.

"Here we are," the Creeper said.

"Here we are," Moskewitz agreed.

They both grinned.

"Guess I gotta shoot you now."

"I guess you do."

The Creeper raised the gun. His grin thinned out and lengthened as his finger tightened on the trigger.

Moskewitz thought, Wait a minute—I don't want to die. I just learned to live.

So he lunged.

The two men came together, closed and danced a jarring two-step in the dirt. The Creeper was stronger, but he'd been drinking more, beer dulling his perceptions, weighing his limbs. Moskewitz swung his open hand, felt it connect and saw the gun go skittering. He jumped after it, felt his glasses fly off, and managed to close his hand around the small automatic, still slick with the sweat of the Creeper's hand. He was bringing the gun up and around when the Creeper came down on him with a yell.

*　　*　　*

Moskewitz found his glasses and put them on. They slipped down his nose. He pushed them up again.

Somewhere in the house an old clock bonged. He glanced at his watch. Midnight. The Presence would be seething, reaching critical mass. He went to work. Throwing quick spadefuls of dirt into the pit, another one, and another one, filling the hole right up.

"What you gotta unnerstand," he said, scooping the last of the loose earth over the hole, "about us clerks..."

Patting it down flat with the back of the spade.

"Is we never say 'scuse me neither..."

Standing back and examining his handiwork.

"We jus' say oops."

He wiped his fingerprints from the spade handle with the cuff of his shirt sleeve, then threw the spade down.

And giggled.

* * *

The house itself seemed relieved. It echoed with gentle creakings as it settled upon itself. Moskewitz went up the stairs to the kitchen, washed his hands in the sink and dried them on a tea towel. He nudged the basement door shut, and wiped the doorknob. He wiped his prints carefully from everything he had touched. Then he let himself out into the night, under the gliding moon, a megacephalic little man who for the first time in ages felt very pleased and sure about himself.

"Absolutely," he said.

And taking a navigational fix on the forty-foot SEARS sign at the end of the block, he lurched down the alley for his car. Fished the Creeper's last beer out of his pocket, popped the cap off, took a healthy swallow and kept on going.

Pushing his glasses up.

Wondering if the Grim Presence might still be waiting up for him.

Anna Said. . . by *Peter Robinson*

Peter Robinson has garnered huge acclaim internationally for his popular Inspector Banks novels. He has also won praise for his short fiction. He has won Arthur Ellis Awards for both forms of writing. Here, he combines the two in the first Alan Banks short story to see publication.

ANNA SAID. . .

An Inspector Banks Story

by *Peter Robinson*

"I'm not happy with it, laddie," said Dr. Glendenning, shaking his head. "Not happy at all."

"So the super told me," said Banks. "What's the problem?"

They sat at a dimpled, copper-topped table in the Queen's Arms, Glendenning over a glass of Glenmorangie and Banks over a pint of Theakston's. It was a bitter cold evening in February. Rain beat against the amber and red coloured windows beside them. Banks had just finished a day of dull paper work and was anxious to get home and take Sandra out to dinner as he had promised, but Dr. Glendenning had asked for help, and a Home Office pathologist was too important to brush off.

"One of these?" Glendenning offered Banks a Senior Service.

Banks grimaced. "No. No thanks. I'll stick with tipped. I'm trying to give up."

"Aye," said Glendenning, lighting up. "Me, too."

"So what's the problem?"

"She should never have died," the doctor said, "but that's by the way. These things happen."

"Who shouldn't have died?"

"Oh, sorry, laddie. Forgot you didn't know. Anna, Anna, Childers is—was—her name. Admitted to the hospital this morning."

"Any reason to suspect a crime?"

"No-o, not on the surface. That's why I wanted an informal chat first." Rain lashed at the window; the buzz of conversation rose and fell around them.

"What happened?" Banks asked.

"Her boyfriend brought her in at about ten o'clock this morning. He said she'd been up half the night vomiting. They thought it was stomach flu or something like that, but paracetamol did no good. Dr. Gibson treated the symptoms as best he could, but. . ." Glendenning shrugged.

"Cause of death?"

"Respiratory failure. If she hadn't suffered from asthma, she might have had a chance. Dr. Gibson managed at least to get the convulsions under control. But as for the cause of it all, don't ask me. I've no idea yet. It could have been food poisoning. Or she could have taken something, a suicide attempt. You know how I hate guesswork." He looked at his watch and finished his drink. "Anyway, I'm off to do the autopsy now. Should know a bit more after that."

"What do you want me to do?"

"You're the copper, laddie. I'll not tell you your job. All I'll say is the circumstances are suspicious enough to worry me. Maybe you could talk to the boyfriend?"

Banks took out his notebook. "What's his name and address?"

Glendenning told him and left. Banks sighed and went to the telephone. Sandra wouldn't like this at all.

II

Banks pulled up outside Anna Childers' large semi in south Eastvale, near the big roundabout, and turned off the tape of Furtwangler conducting Beethoven's Ninth. It was the 1951 live Bayreuth recording, mono but magnificent. The rain was still falling hard, and Banks fancied he could feel the sting of hail against his cheek as he dashed to the door, raincoat collar turned up.

The man who answered his ring, John Billings, looked awful. Normally, Banks guessed, he was a clean-cut athletic type, at his best on a tennis court, perhaps, or a ski slope, but grief and lack of sleep had turned his skin pale and his features puffy. His shoulders slumped as Banks followed him into the living-room, which looked like one of the package designs advertised in the Sunday colour supplements. Banks sat down in a damask-upholstered armchair and shivered.

"I'm sorry," muttered Billings, turning on the gas-fire. "I didn't. . ."

"It's understandable," Banks said, leaning forward and rubbing his hands.

"There's nothing wrong, is there?" Billings asked. "I mean, the police. . .?"

"Nothing for you to worry about," Banks said. "Just some questions."

"Yes." Billings flopped onto the sofa and crossed his legs. "Of course."

"I'm sorry about what happened," Banks began. "I just want to get some idea of how. It all seems a bit of a mystery to the doctors."

Billings sniffed. "You can say that again."

"When did Ms. Childers start feeling ill?"

"About four in the morning. You can call her Anna. She complained of a headache, said she was feeling dizzy. Then she was up and down to the toilet the rest of the night. I thought. . .you know. . .it was a virus or something. I mean, you don't go running off to the doctor's over the least little thing, do you?"

"But it got worse?"

"Yes. It just wouldn't stop." He held his face in his hands. Banks heard the hissing of the fire and the pellets of hail against the curtained window. Billings took a deep breath. "I'm sorry. At the end she was bringing up blood, shivering, and she had problems breathing. Then. . .well, you know what happened."

"How long had you known her?"

"Pardon?"

Banks repeated the question.

"A couple of years in all, I suppose. But only as a business acquaintance at first. Anna's a chartered accountant and I run a small consultancy firm. She did some auditing work for us."

"That's how you met her?"

"Yes."

Banks looked around him at the fitted entertainment centre, the framed Van Gogh print. "Who owns the house?"

If Billings was surprised at the question, he didn't show it. "Anna. It. . .it was only a temporary arrangement, my living here. I had a flat. I moved out. We were going to get married, buy a house together somewhere in the dale, out of the town."

"How long had you been going out together?"

"Six months."

"Living together?"

"Three."

"Getting on all right?"

"I told you. We were going to get married."

"You say you'd known her two years, but you've only been seeing each other six months. What took you so long?"

"We were friendly, just business acquaintances, really."

"Was there someone else?"

Billings nodded.

"For you or her?"

"For Anna. Owen was still living with her until about seven months ago. Owen Doughton."

"And they split up?"

"Yes."

"Any bitterness?"

Billings shook his head. "No. It was all very civilized. They weren't married. Anna said they just started going their different ways. They'd been together about five years, and they felt they weren't really going anywhere together, so they decided to separate."

"What did the two of you do last night?"

"We went out for dinner at that new Chinese place on York Road. You don't think. . .?"

"I really can't say. What did you eat?"

"The usual. Egg rolls, chicken chow mein, a Szechuan prawn dish. We shared everything."

"Are you sure?"

"Yes. We usually do. Anna doesn't really like spicy food, but she'll have a little, just to keep me happy. I'm a curry nut, myself. The hotter the better. I thought at first maybe that was what made her sick, you know, if it wasn't the flu, the hot peppers they use."

"Then you came straight home?"

"No. We stopped for a drink on the way at the Red Lion. Got home just after eleven."

"And Anna was feeling fine?"

"Yes. Fine."

"What did you do when you got home?"

"Nothing much, really. Pottered around a bit, then we went to bed."

"And that's it?"

"Yes. I must admit, I felt a little unwell myself during the night. I had a headache and an upset stomach myself, but some Alka Seltzer soon put it right. I just can't believe it. I keep thinking she'll walk in the door at any moment and say it was all a mistake."

"Did Anna have a nightcap or anything?" Banks asked after a pause. "A cup of Horlicks, something like that?"

He shook his head. "She couldn't stand Horlicks. No, neither of us had anything after the pub."

Banks stood up. The room was warm now and his blotched raincoat had started to dry out. "Thanks very much," he said, offering his hand. "And again, I'm sorry for intruding on your grief."

Billings shrugged. "What do you think it was?"

"I don't know yet. There is one more thing I have to ask. Please don't take offence."

Billings stared at him. "Go on."

"Was Anna upset about anything? Depressed?"

He shook his head vigorously. "No, no. Quite the opposite. She was happier than she'd ever been. She told me. I know what you're getting at, Inspector - the doctor suggested the same thing - but you can forget it. Anna would never have tried to take her own life. She just wasn't that kind of person. She was too full of life and energy."

Banks nodded. If he'd had a pound for every time he'd heard that about a suicide he would be a rich man. "Fair enough," he said. "Just for the record, this Owen, where does he live?"

"I'm afraid I don't know. He works at that big garden centre just off North Market Street, over from the Town Hall."

"I know it. Thanks very much, John."

Banks pulled up his collar and dashed for the car. The hail had turned to rain again. As he drove, windscreen wipers slapping, he pondered his talk with John Billings. The man seemed genuine in his grief, but it didn't do to go by appearances. It had only been a couple of months since Banks had worked on the Caroline Hartley murder, and that had certainly taught him not to take anything for granted. Still, Billings seemed to have no motive for harming Anna Childers; but again, all Banks had to go on was what he had been told. Then there was Owen Doughton, the ex live-in lover. Things might not have been as civilized as Anna Childers had made out.

In the morning, Banks would have to arrange for a Board of Trade investigator to check out the Chinese restaurant, just in case.

Banks knew the place well and doubted they would find anything amiss. He and Sandra had eaten there often and were on friendly terms with Harry Wong, the owner, a second-generation Yorkshireman.

The marvelous fourth movement of the symphony began just as Banks turned into his street. He sat in the parked car with the rain streaming down the windows and listened until Otto Edelmann came in with "*O Freunde, nicht diese Tone. . .*" then turned off the tape and headed indoors. If he stayed out any longer he'd be there until the end of the symphony, and Sandra certainly wouldn't appreciate that.

III

Banks found Owen Doughton in the garden centre early the next morning hefting bags of fertilizer around. He was a short, rather hangdog-looking man in his early thirties with shaggy dark hair and a droopy moustache. The rain had stopped overnight, but a brisk, chill wind was fast bringing in more cloud. Banks asked if they could talk inside, and Doughton led him to a small, cluttered office that smelled faintly of paraffin. Doughton sat on the desk and Banks took the swivel chair.

"I'm afraid I've got some bad news for you, Owen," Banks started.

Doughton studied his cracked, dirty fingernails. "I read about Anna in the paper this morning, if that's what you mean," he said. "It's terrible, a tragedy." He brushed back a thick lock of hair from his right eye.

"Did you see much of her lately?"

"Not a lot, no. Not since we. . .We'd have lunch occasionally, if neither of us was too busy."

"So there were no hard feelings?"

"No. Anna said it was just time to move on, that we'd outgrown each other. We both needed more space to grow."

"Was she right?"

He shrugged. "Seems so. But I still cared for her. I don't want you to think I didn't. I just can't take this in." He looked Banks in the eye for the first time. "What's wrong, anyway? Why are the police interested?"

"It's just routine," Banks said. "I don't suppose you'd know anything about her state of mind recently?"

"Not really."

"When did you see her last?"

"A couple of weeks ago. She seemed fine, really."

"Did you know her new boyfriend?"

Doughton returned to study his fingernails. "No. She told me about him, of course, but we never met. Sounded like a nice bloke. Probably better for her than me. I wished her every happiness. Surely you can't think she did this herself? Anna just wasn't the type. She had too much to live for."

"Most likely food poisoning," Banks said, closing his notebook, "but we have to cover the possibilities. Nice talking to you, anyway. I don't suppose I'll be troubling you again."

"No trouble," Doughton said, standing up.

Banks nodded and left.

IV

"If we split up," Banks mused aloud to Sandra over an early lunch in the new McDonald's that day, "do you think you'd be upset?"

Sandra narrowed her eyes, clear blue under the dark brows and blonde hair. "Are you trying to tell me something, Alan? Is there something I should know?"

Banks paused, Big Mac halfway to his mouth, and laughed. "No. No, nothing like that. It's purely hypothetical."

"Well thank goodness for that." Sandra took a bite of her McChicken sandwich and pulled a face. "Yuck. Have you really developed a taste for this stuff?"

Banks nodded. "When I was in Canada. It's all right, really. Full of nutrition." And he took a big bite as if to prove it.

"Well," she said, "you certainly know how to show a woman a good time, I'll say that for you. And what on earth are you talking about?"

"Splitting up. It's just something that puzzles me, that's all."

"I've been married to you half my life," Sandra said. "Twenty years. Of course I'd be bloody upset if we split up."

"You can't see us just going our separate ways, growing apart, needing more space?"

"Alan, what's got into you? Have you been reading those American self-help books?" She looked around the place again, taking in the plastic decor. "I'm getting worried about you."

"Well, don't. It's simple really. I know twenty years hardly compares with five, but do you believe people can just disentangle their lives from one another and carry on with someone new as if nothing happened?"

"Maybe they could've done in 1967," Sandra answered. "And maybe some people still can, but I think it cuts a lot deeper than that, no matter what anyone says."

"Anna said it was fine," Banks muttered, almost to himself. "But Anna's dead."

"Is this that investigation you're doing for Dr. Glendenning, the reason you stood me up last night?"

"I didn't stand you up. I phoned to apologise. But, yes. I've got a nagging feeling about it. Something's not quite right."

"What do you mean? You think she was poisoned or something?"

"It's possible, but I can't prove it. I can't even figure out how."

"Then maybe you're wrong."

"Huh." Banks chomped on his Big Mac again. "Wouldn't be the first time, would it?" He explained about his talks with John Billings and Owen Doughton. Sandra thought for a moment, sipping her Coke through a straw and picking at her french fries, sandwich abandoned on her tray. "Sounds like a determined woman, this Anna. I suppose it's possible she just made a seamless transition from one to the other, but I'd bet there's a lot more to it than that. I'd have a word with both of them again, if I were you."

"Mmm," said Banks. "Thought you'd say that. Fancy a sweet?"

V

"The tests are going to take time," Glendenning said over the phone, "but from what I could see, there's severe damage to the liver, kidneys, heart and lungs, not to mention the central nervous system."

"Could it be food poisoning?" Banks asked.

33

"It certainly looks like some kind of poisoning. A healthy person doesn't usually die just like that. I suppose at a pinch it could be botulism," Glendenning said. "Certainly some of the symptoms match."

"Any other possibilities?"

"Too damned many," Glendenning growled. "That's the problem. There's enough nasty stuff around to make you that ill if you're unlucky enough to swallow it: household cleaners, pesticides, industrial chemicals. The list goes on. That's why we'll have to wait for the test results." And he hung up.

Cantankerous old bugger, Banks thought with a smile. How Glendenning hated being pinned down. The problem was, though, if someone - Owen, John or any undiscovered enemy - had poisoned Anna, how had he done it? John Billings could have doctored her food at the Chinese restaurant, or her drink in the pub, or perhaps there was something she had eaten that he had simply failed to mention. He certainly had the best opportunity.

But John Billings seemed the most unlikely suspect: he had no apparent motive; he loved the woman; they were going to get married. Or so he said. Anna Childers was quite well-off, and certainly upwardly mobile, but it was unlikely that Billings stood to gain, or even needed to gain financially from her death. It was worth looking into, though. She had only been thirty, but she may have made a will in his favour. And Billings' consultancy could do with a bit of scrutiny.

Money wouldn't be a motive with Owen Doughton, though. According to both the late Anna and to Owen himself, they had parted without rancour, each content to get on with life. Again, it might be worth asking a few of their friends and acquaintances if they had reason to think any differently. Doughton had seemed gentle, reserved, a private person, but who could tell what went on in his mind? Banks walked down the corridor to see if either Detective Constable Susan Gay or Sergeant Philip Richmond was free for an hour or two.

VI

Two hours later, DC Susan Gay sat in front of Banks's desk, smoothed her grey skirt over her lap and opened her notebook. As usual, Banks thought, she looked tastefully groomed: tight blonde curls; just enough make-up; the silver hoop earrings; pearl blouse with the ruff collar; and a mere whiff of Miss Dior cutting the stale cigarette smoke in his office.

"There's not much, I'm afraid," Susan started, glancing up from her notes. "No will, as far as I can discover, but she did alter the beneficiary on her insurance policy a month ago."

"In whose benefit?"

"John Billings. Apparently she has no family."

Banks raised his eyebrows. "Who was the previous beneficiary?"

"Owen Doughton."

"Odd that, isn't it?" Banks speculated aloud. "A woman who changes her insurance policy with her boyfriends."

"Well she wouldn't want it to go to the government, would she?" Susan said. "And I don't suppose she'd want to make her ex rich either."

"True," said Banks. "It's often easier to keep a policy going than let it lapse and apply all over again later. And they were going to get married. But why change it so soon? How much is it for?"

"Fifty thousand."

Banks whistled.

"Owen Doughton's poor as a church mouse," Susan went on, "but he doesn't stand to gain anything."

"But did he know that? I doubt Anna Childers would have told him. What about Billings?"

Susan gnawed the tip of her Biro and hesitated. "Pretty well off," she said. "Bit of an up-and-comer in the consultancy world. You can see why a woman like Anna Childers would want to attach herself to him."

"Why?"

"He's going places, of course. Expensive places."

"I see," said Banks. "And you think she was a gold-digger?"

Susan flushed. "Not necessarily. She just knew what side her bread was buttered on, that's all. Same as with a lot of new businesses, though, Billings has a bit of a cash-flow problem."

"Hmm. Any gossip on the split-up?"

"Not much. I had a chat with a couple of locals in the Red Lion. Anna Childers always seemed cheerful enough, but she was a tough nut to crack, they said, strong protective shell."

"What about Doughton?"

"He doesn't seem to have many friends. His boss says he's noticed no real changes, but he says Owen keeps to himself, always did. I'm sorry. It's not much help."

"Never mind," Banks said. "Look, I've got a couple of things to do. Can you find Phil for me?"

VII

"Did you know that Anna had an insurance policy?" Banks asked Owen Doughton. They stood in the cold yard while Doughton stacked some bags of peat moss.

Doughton stood up and rubbed the small of his back. "Aye," he said. "What of it?"

"Did you know how much is was for?"

He shook his head.

"All right," Banks said. "Did Anna tell you she'd changed the beneficiary, named John Billings instead of you?"

Doughton paused with his mouth open. "No," he said. "No she didn't."

"So you know now that you stand to gain nothing, it all goes to John?"

Doughton's face darkened, then he looked away and Banks swore he could hear a strangled laugh or cry. "I don't believe this," Doughton said, facing him again. "I can't believe I'm hearing this. You think I might have killed Anna? And for money? This is insane. Look, go away, please. I don't have to talk to you, do I?"

"No," said Banks.

"Well go. I've got work to do. But remember one thing."

"What's that?"

"I loved her. I loved Anna."

VIII

John Billingslooked even more wretched than he had the day before. His eyes were bloodshot, underlined by black smudges, and he hadn't shaved. Banks could smell alcohol on his breath. A suitcase stood in the hallway.

"Where are you going, John?" Banks asked.

"I can't stay here, can I? I mean, it's not my house, for a start, and. . .the memories."

"Where are you going?"

He picked up the case. "I don't know. Just away from here, that's all."

I don't think so." Gently, Banks took the case from him and set it down. "We haven't got to the bottom of this yet."

"What do you mean? For Christ's sake, man!"

"You'd better come with me, John."

"Where?"

"Headquarters. We'll have a chat there."

Billings stared angrily at him, then seemed to fold. "Oh, what the hell," he muttered. "What does it matter." And he picked his coat off the rack and followed Banks. He didn't see DS Philip Richmond at the window of the cafe over the road.

IX

It was after seven o'clock, dark, cold and windy outside. Banks decided to wait in the bedroom, on the chair wedged in the corner between the wardrobe and the dressing table. From there, with the door open, he could see the staircase, and he would be able to hear any sounds in the house.

He had just managed to get the item on the local news show at six o'clock, only minutes after Dr. Glendenning had phoned with more detailed information: "Poison suspected in death of Eastvale woman. Police baffled. No suspects as yet." Of course, the killer might not have seen it, or may have already covered his tracks, but if Anna Childers *had* been poisoned, and Glendenning now seemed certain she had, then the answer had to be here.

Given possible reaction times, Glendenning had said in his late afternoon phone-call, there was little chance she could have taken the poison into her system before eight o'clock the previous evening, at which time she had gone out to dine with John Billings.

The house was dark and silent save for the ticking of a clock on the bedside table and the howling wind rattling the window. Eight o'clock. Nine. Nothing happened except Banks got a cramp in his left calf. He massaged it, then stood up at regular intervals and stretched. He thought of Richmond, now down the street in the unmarked car. Between them, they'd be sure to catch anyone who came.

Finally, close to ten o'clock, he heard it, a scraping at the lock on the front door. He drew himself deep into the chair, melted into the darkness and held his breath. The door opened and closed softly. He could see a torch beam sweeping the wall by the staircase, coming closer. The intruder was coming straight up the stairs. Damn! Banks hadn't expected that. He wanted whoever it was to lead him to the poison, not walk right into him. As still and silent as he could be, he sat rigid in the chair as the beam played over the threshold of the bedroom, mercifully not falling on Banks in his corner. The intruder didn't hesitate. He walked around the bed, within inches of Banks's feet, and over to the bedside table. Shining his torch, he opened the top drawer and picked something up. At that moment Banks turned on the dressing-table light beside him. The figure turned sharply, then froze. "Hello, Owen," said Banks, getting up and walking towards him.

X

"If it was anyone, it had to be either you or him, John," Banks said later in his office at the station, while Owen Doughton was being charged downstairs. "Only the two of you were intimate enough with Anna to know her habits, her routines. And Owen had lived with her until quite recently. There was a chance he still had a key."

John Billings shook his head. "I thought you were arresting me."

"It was touch and go, I won't deny it. But at least I thought I'd give you a chance, the benefit of the doubt."

"And if your trap hadn't worked?"

Banks shrugged. "Down to you, I suppose. The poison could have been anywhere, in anything. Toothpaste, for example. I knew if it wasn't you, and the killer heard the news, he'd try to get it back. He wouldn't have had a chance to do so yet, because you were in the house."

"But I was at the hospital nearly all yesterday."

"Too soon. He had no idea anything had happened at that time. This wasn't a carefully calculated plan."

"But why?"

Banks shook his head. "That I can't say for certain. He's a sick man, an obsessed man. It's my guess it was his warped form of revenge. It had been eating away at him for some time. Anna didn't treat him very well, John. She didn't really stop to take his feelings into account when she kicked him out and took up with you. She just assumed he would understand, like he always had, because he loved her and had her welfare at heart. He was deeply hurt, but he wasn't the kind to make a fuss or let his feelings show. He kept it all bottled up."

"She could be a bit blinkered, could Anna," John mumbled. "She was a very focused woman."

"Yes. And I'm sure Doughton felt humiliated when she dumped him and turned to you. After all, he didn't have much of a financial future, unlike you."

"But it wasn't that, not with Anna," Billings protested. "We just had so much in common. Goals, tastes, ambitions. She and Owen had nothing in common any more."

"You're probably right," Banks said. "Anyway, when she told him a couple of weeks ago that she was going to get married to you, it was the last straw. He said she expected him to be happy for her."

"But why did he keep on seeing her if it hurt him so much?"

"He was still in love with her, I suppose. It was better seeing her, even under those circumstances, than not at all."

"Then why kill her?"

Banks looked at Billings. "Love and hate, John," he said. "They're not so far apart. Besides, he doesn't believe he did kill her, that wasn't really his intention at all."

"I don't understand. You said he did. How did he do it?"

Banks paused and lit a cigarette. This wasn't going to be easy. Rain blew against the window and a draught rattled Banks's faulty venetian blind.

"How?" Billings repeated.

Banks looked at his calendar, trying to put off the moment; it showed a woodland scene, snowdrops blooming near The Strid by Bolton Abbey. He cleared his throat and stubbed out his cigarette. "Owen came to the house while you were both out," Banks began. "He brought a syringe loaded with a strong pesticide he got from the garden centre. Remember, he knew her intimately. Did you and Anna make love that night, John?"

Billings reddened. "For Christ's sake—"

"I'm not asking whether the earth moved, I'm just asking if you did. Believe me, it's relevant."

"All right," said Billings after a pause. "Yes, we did as a matter of fact."

"Owen knew Anna well enough to know that she was frightened of getting pregnant," Banks went on, "but she wouldn't take the pill because of the side effects. He knew she insisted on condoms, and he knew she liked to make love in the dark. It was easy enough to insert the needle into a couple of packages and squirt in some pesticide. Not much, but it's very powerful stuff, colourless and odourless, so even an infinitesimal coating would have some effect. The condoms were lubricated, so they'd feel oily anyway, and nobody would notice a tiny pinprick in the package. You absorbed a little into your system, too, and that's why you felt ill. You see, it's easily absorbed through skin or membranes. But Anna got the lion's share. Dr. Glendenning would have found out eventually how the poison was administered from tissue samples, but further tests would have taken time. Owen could easily have nipped back to the house and removed the evidence by then. Or we may have decided that you had better access to the method."

Billings paled. "You mean it could just as easily have been me either killed or arrested for murder?"

Banks shrugged. "It could have turned out any way, really. There was no way of knowing accurately what would happen, and certainly there was a chance that either you would die or the blame would fall on you. As it turned out, Anna absorbed most of it, and she had asthma. In Owen's twisted mind, he wanted your love-making to make you sick. That was his statement, if you like, after so long suffering in silence, pretending it was okay that Anna had moved on. But that's all. It was a sick joke, if you like. We found three poisoned condoms. Certainly if one hadn't worked the way it did, there could have been a build up of the pesticide, causing chronic problems. I did read about a case once," Banks went on, "where a man married rich women and murdered them for their money by putting arsenic on his condoms, but they were made of goatskin back then. Besides, he was French. I've never come across a case quite as strange as this."

Billings shook his head slowly. "Can I go now?" he asked.

"Where to?"

"I don't know. A hotel, perhaps, until. . ."

Banks nodded and stood up. As they went down the stairs, they came face to face with Owen Doughton being led up in handcuffs from the charge room. Billings stiffened. Doughton glared at him and spoke to Banks. "He's the one who killed her," he said, with a toss of his head. "He's the one you should be arresting." Then he looked directly at Billings. "You're going to have to live with that, you know, Mr. Moneybags. It was you who killed her." The constable started to pull him away, but as he went, he half-turned and shouted over his shoulder at Billings. "Hear that? Mr. Yuppie Moneybags. You killed her! You killed Anna. You fucked her to death."

Banks couldn't tell whether he was laughing or crying as the constable led him down to the cells.

Bermuda Short by *Anne Stephenson*

Writer and film-maker Anne Stephenson lives in Ottawa and creates, both alone and in collaboration, three different series of mysteries for young adults. Bermuda Short is her first published adult fiction.

BERMUDA SHORT

by *Anne Stephenson*

Carolann Gravelle flew to Bermuda two days after Alex and his new bride.

Had it been any other Tuesday, she would have been at her desk in suburban Toronto, processing death claims for Parkwood Life and Casualty. But not today. Today, she was flying first class on Air Canada's Flight 942 to Bermuda, drinking champagne and dreaming of death and dismemberment amidst the bougainvillea.

Carolann had fantasized more than a few people to death over the years. Her favourite method, used countless times by the great Agatha Christie, was poison. Especially, the obvious ones. They made one feel decidedly superior.

She chatted with her seat companion as the plane flew over Manhattan and headed out over the Atlantic. He seemed pleasant, and she enjoyed his company until he began flirting with the flight attendant. If that was the way he was, Carolann decided, she'd rather read her book.

Allowing herself an anticipatory shiver at the thought of being with Alex again, she settled back in her chair.

The first time she'd met Alexander Wright, she'd been hovering around the mystery section in Mirvish Books, disappointed that there was nothing new from her usual authors, when a rather handsome man had asked her a question.

At first, she'd thought he'd mistaken her for one of the clerks. But when he'd engaged her in a spirited conversation about the state of mystery writing in Canada, she realized he'd wanted her opinion. Next thing she knew, they were moving towards the cash together and talking about structure.

"It's all in the plot. Don't you agree?"

"Oh, absolutely," Carolann had said. He had such beautiful blue eyes. "As long as there are strong characters driving it along." She'd hesitated, groping for the right answer to keep his interest and the conversation going. "But I do think it's just as hard to kill someone as it is to figure out who did it."

Alex had given her an appraising look. "You seem to be well versed in the subject."

Clutching her book bag hopefully against her chest, Carolann had told him all about her book club as they walked out of the store together. They'd had coffee in a little Hungarian restaurant on Bloor Street and afterwards, he'd walked her to her car.

The next six months were the most glorious in Carolann's life.

They'd gone bicycling on the Island, checked out the specialty book shops around town and spent Sundays exploring the surrounding countryside in Alex's leased Mercedes.

Much to her surprise, and secret pleasure, Carolann found herself haunting lingerie departments on her lunch hour. She even read Cosmo in the grocery line.

At thirty-two, Carolann had all but given up on the reality of a long-term relationship. It wasn't that she couldn't attract men. She was simply too possessive. After two or three dates they invariably backed away. Her social activities of late had been restricted to odd evenings out with other lonely, single women.

Not anymore.

Having Alex was a dream come true. He was even interested in her job, constantly asking her questions about the insurance business and how it worked. Carolann wondered if he might be planning a book. Sara Paretsky, the Chicago mystery writer, had worked in the insurance business and used that insider knowledge to her advantage. Why not Alex?

When his questions had become too complex for her to answer, she'd put him in touch with one of the sales reps and forgotten all about it.

Alex's job, buying and selling commercial real estate, was extremely idiosyncratic. More than a few times, Carolann had had to pick up the entire bill when they went out on the town. But she didn't mind; it was a small price to pay if she could be with him.

Their relationship continued to blossom until one blustery afternoon in late November when Alex had unexpectedly arrived at Parkwood Life and Casualty. A client had given him two tickets to *The Mousetrap*. If they went directly from work, they would just have time for dinner before the show.

With pre-season snowflakes melting on his dark hair and the shoulders of his cashmere overcoat, Alex could have posed for a Harry Rosen ad. Half the women in the office had surreptitiously had their eyes on him since the moment he'd walked in.

Having a beau was a unique situation for Carolann, and she had delighted in showing him off, especially to Judith Costello.

Executive assistant to the vice-president of claims, Judith Costello was the most vain, shallow and mean-spirited woman Carolann had ever met. She was also one of the most gorgeous. Judith's father, Victor Costello, was on the Board of Parkwood Life and Casualty. It didn't take a genius to figure out how she'd gotten the job.

Despite the sexy black lace and garters she now wore beneath her business suits, Carolann felt like a frump beside Judith and Judith knew it.

"You're a well-kept secret," Judith had purred. She'd taken Alex's hand in hers and turned her back to Carolann.

"We'll have to do something about that, won't we," Alex had answered prompting Carolann to intervene and whisk him away before any permanent damage could be done.

Rather than raise her stock around the office, Alex's visit had seemed to work against her. Conversations dried up in mid-sentence when she entered the staff lounge. People checked out the ceiling when she stepped onto the elevator. When Carolann had jokingly asked one of the clerks if she had the plague, he'd flushed alarmingly and mumbled something about a rush job down in photocopying.

Even Alex had begun to act strangely. He had the flu, he'd said, but when Carolann had offered to come over and nurse him back to health, he'd put her off.

Judith, on the other hand, looked radiant. Tall, with long chestnut hair, she had always been the best-dressed woman in the office, but lately, even Carolann had to admit, she'd outdone herself. Suits from Jones New York. Silks by Liz Claiborne. Sweater dresses which hugged her body in curves that Carolann could never hope to have.

A few times Carolann had spotted Judith eyeing her stealthily from across the room. She'd put it down to paranoia until an anonymous note, left on her desk one noon hour, had finally confirmed her fears. Alex and Judith were an item and nobody'd had the nerve to tell her.

The next few weeks were humiliating.

"I just want to be free to see other women," Alex had said when Carolann had stormed into his apartment in fury. He'd given her the usual routine of wanting to remain friends, etcetera.

Carolann planned to hold him to it.

After that, whenever they saw each other, Carolann was bright and cheerful and Alex had typically acted as if nothing had changed. He'd even gone home with her one night when Judith was out of town, convincing Carolann that he loved her still.

She was so sure that Alex would eventually see through Judith's superficiality and come back to her that she'd been totally unprepared for Alex's announcement.

He'd been in her living room, drinking her scotch and sitting on her couch when, after a few minutes of idle chitchat, he'd set down his glass and taken her hand in his.

"I'm marrying Judith and I want you to come to the wedding."

Carolann had been stunned.

"Don't say no right away," he'd said anxiously. "I want you to think it through first." Then he'd raised his glass to her, and said, "After all, you are my best friend."

Carolann had wanted to scream. How could he sit there and calmly announce his engagement when he knew she loved him? She told herself to calm down and think. She'd invested too much in him to lose him now.

When the day of the wedding finally arrived, she'd put on her best black dress. People would admire her for her strength, she thought, as she added a little black hat with a hint of veil across its brim.

The wedding had been a glitzy affair, three bridesmaids, twin flower girls and a camcorder, sit-down dinner for eighty and an open bar.

A videotaped recording of the ceremony, complete with close-ups, had played over and over again on a big screen behind the head table, forcing Carolann to frequent the bar more than she should have.

"Tell me you're having a good time," Alex had pleaded, when he'd come upon her standing alone, drink in hand, in the hallway outside the reception room.

"Not really." She'd gazed up into his eyes and saw what she'd always seen. Alex loved her.

He must have seen it too, because he had reached for her hand and given it a squeeze. "I've missed seeing you, Carolann."

"Then why did you..."

She couldn't finish. Her throat had been so thick with impending tears that they'd stood there in awkward silence until a rustle of organza told them Judith was near.

"There you are," she'd said as she walked up to them, and slid her arm through her husband's.

"I've been looking everywhere for you, darling. It's time to cut the cake."

"I was just chatting with Carolann," Alex had said and he'd winked at her.

Judith was not amused. "Daddy wants us at the head table now, darling," she'd said to Alex.

Then she'd fastened her claws on Carolann. "I'm sorry to steal him away from you like this, Carolann...but you know how it is...but, no, I guess you don't, do you?"

Bitch, thought Carolann. She hoped the baker had accidentally laced the cake with almonds. It would serve Judith right.

Everyone at the office knew about Judith's allergies. She'd actually bragged about them as though they made her even more special. Her wedding cake was to be made with no almond paste, no citron and no pecans. And no taste, Carolann had giggled as she'd watched the bride and groom, poised, knife-in-hand, for another round of pictures.

Later that night, depressed and overloaded on scotch, Carolann had taken the small doily and ribbon-wrapped piece of wedding cake from her purse, and amused herself by sticking it with a straight pin.

"He loves me, he loves me not...," she'd chanted over and over again. The more she poked at the cake, the more she thought about Judith. And the more she thought about Judith, the clearer her thoughts became.

By the time the light began to lift over the lake, Carolann had made her plans. But first she'd need a few hours sleep. She had stumbled into bed, somewhat unsteadily, and slid the cake under her pillow. Maybe it would bring her good luck.

*   *   *

Carolann breathed in deeply. The early afternoon air was salty and moist, with just a hint of hibiscus and oleander.

She passed through customs as Anita Johnston, using the birth certificate she'd saved from her late cousin's estate, and queued up for a cab.

Neither she, nor Anita, had ever been to Bermuda before, and as the taxi rattled across the wooden causeway linking the airport with the main island, Carolann was ecstatic that Judith had chosen the tiny island for her honeymoon. It was beautiful. Carolann kept a firm grip on her purse. Before she'd left Toronto, she'd withdrawn a large amount of cash from her savings account and booked a "Bermuda Short," the three-day holiday package named for the island's famous knee-length dress shorts. Carolann thought it most amusing.

Next, she'd purchased a new wardrobe, which, combined with a few supplies from the health food store and the pharmacy, would provide all the cover and ammunition she'd need.

The roads in Bermuda were much narrower than they'd appeared in the brochure. Carolann was dazzled by the way they twisted and turned along the hilly terrain, passing so close to the side of the road, that every now and then a palm frond would slap against the open window of the cab.

As the driver swung left around the traffic circle outside Hamilton, she anxiously rechecked her reflection in the rearview mirror.

Her hair was now a deep reddy-brown, almost mahogany, with a wisp of bangs trailing across her forehead. The green eye liner she wore in concert with a pair of tortoise-shell frames had changed her appearance so drastically she was sure neither Alex nor Judith would recognize her.

The moment the taxi rolled to a stop in front of the pink-stuccoed Chelsea Hotel, a bell hop stepped from the shadows of the front portico and opened the rear door of the cab.

"Welcome to the Chelsea, ma'am," he said as he helped her alight. "Is this your first trip to the island?"

Carolann nodded and followed him into the hotel.

The lobby was stunning. Butter-yellow sofas with matching wing chairs were scattered invitingly around the room, their colour complemented by dramatic displays of island flowers. With its panoramic view of the Great Sound, the whole effect was breathtaking and somehow very British, despite the tropical blues and greens beyond the glass.

The receptionist had everything in order, and if she was surprised that Carolann was paying in cash instead of using the ubiquitous credit card, she kept it to herself.

"Enjoy your stay, Ms. Johnston."

"Thank you," said Carolann. "I'm sure I will."

She followed the bell hop across the lobby and into the waiting elevator. They chatted about the island and the sights she should see as the mahogany-panelled lift slowly rose to the third floor.

"You must be Canadian," he said as he led the way down the corridor.

Carolann smiled. "How can you tell?"

He looked over his shoulder to make sure there were no stray Americans. "Canadians are more conservative," he whispered as he unlocked the door to her room.

Carolann tipped him five bucks U.S.

The room was a delightful mix of rattan and floral prints. Carolann did a quick survey of the amenities before she carefully unpacked her bag. The small glass vial of walnut oil was still intact, safely hidden inside the plastic case she normally used for her toothbrush. She left the walnut oil where it was and placed her toothbrush on the counter. No one would assume her case was anything but an empty container.

At precisely seven o'clock, Carolann went downstairs for dinner.

Tables for two lined the perimeter of the dining room. Their elegant linen settings and high-back chairs had been carefully placed to give solitary diners the illusion of belonging to the crowd.

Carolann had a table by the window, but she still felt conspicuous, sitting alone, drinking a glass of white wine. It was almost seven-thirty before Alex and Judith strolled in, arm-in-arm.

When the maitre d' showed them to the next table, Carolann nearly fainted.

She smiled stiffly in response to Alex's polite nod, and buried her face in the menu. A cold trickle of sweat rolled over her rib cage and found its way to the waistband of her silk pants. It was incredibly exciting sitting beside them. Almost sexual in its intensity.

Carolann ordered the pumpkin soup and amberfish and watched them out of the corner of her eye while the waiters wove in and out of the room, bearing trays of silver-covered dishes.

Unlike Judith who, judging by the colour of her nose, had had too much sun, Carolann would not be going home with a tan. Her boss at Parkwood Life and Casualty thought she was visiting an old college friend in Winnipeg. The last she'd heard they still had snow.

The evening dragged slowly by. Carolann chatted with a few of the other guests in the lobby, then retired to her room for the night.

By the next morning, she was anxious to get started. After a huge breakfast of hot cakes, fruit and rolls, she ventured down to the salt-water pool, being careful to sit in the shade.

While the other tourists greased themselves for the afternoon ahead, Carolann pulled out the mystery novel she'd purchased for the trip, and prepared to wait.

Palm trees chattered in the warm breeze. Across the lawn at the tennis courts, the hotel's resident pro was trying to drum up business with a demonstration of his serving skills. Carolann thought she saw Alex among the onlookers, but after a while, the heat and the rhythm of the ball put her to sleep.

She awoke with a start around 12:30, her book on the deck beside her, her feet rosy in the shifting sun. Alex and Judith were nowhere to be seen.

The entire patio was peopled with leather-skinned seniors, most of whom had been coming to the Chelsea for two or three decades. Carolann figured she could probably do away with half of them by simply sprinkling digitalis on their prunes.

When the afternoon wore on without even a glimpse of the honeymoon couple, Carolann started to worry. She only had one full day left.

She was lingering over a second cup of coffee when Alex and Judith finally brushed by her table in the dining room. It was after eight.

Alex gave her a polite nod and held out a chair for his wife.

"I don't see why we can't go shopping together," Judith whined.

"Because one of the reasons I came to Bermuda was for the golf." Alex signalled the sommelier.

"Scotch."

"And for Mrs. Wright?"

Alex stiffened.

"Let's have a litre of that lovely white wine we had last night," smiled Judith. "And could you have the waiter bring me a green salad? Oil and vinegar dressing."

As soon as the wine steward left with their order, Judith started back at Alex. "Considering I spent the day on the back of a motorbike while you played James Dean, you could at least go into Hamilton with me in the morning."

Carolann would have loved to stay and listen, but she'd heard all she needed to know.

After signing for her meal, she sauntered into the lounge and joined three old dears from Baltimore who had begged her earlier in the evening to make a fourth for bridge. They turned out to be sharks in pink polyester. After an hour of playing a penny a point, Carolann excused herself and headed for the bar.

She ordered something fruity and idly planned her day while she nibbled fish-shaped pretzels imported from the States.

It wasn't as though you couldn't accidentally murder anyone in Toronto. All she had to do was wait. Sooner or later, Judith would unwittingly leave herself exposed. Only Carolann would never have as good cover as she did right now.

When Alex's reflection appeared in the window alongside hers, she was momentarily caught off-guard.

Their eyes locked for a second and he seemed to hesitate. Then he sat down at the bar and ordered a scotch.

"Will your wife be joining you?" asked the bartender.

"No," Alex answered. "Her sunburn is bothering her."

Good, thought Carolann. She hoped it would wrinkle and peel. Judith should live so long.

As if on cue, Alex turned and smiled at her.

Carolann gave him a half-wave and glanced away. She knew if he'd sat down beside her, one of them would have had to tell the truth.

*   *   *

After breakfast, Alex and Judith went off to Hamilton with several other couples in search of tax-free deals on Wedgewood and Royal Crown Derby.

Carolann was ready. She tagged along behind them, watching and waiting for the right opportunity. But by the time they'd done the stores on Front Street, it was raining too heavily to loiter inconspicuously outside. Carolann caught the ferry back to the hotel.

By early afternoon, the rain had tapered off to a fine drizzle. Carolann borrowed a putter from the pro shop and joined the other die-hards on the course.

She was on the practice green when the Warwick ferry began its approach to the Chelsea's dock.

A few minutes later, when Judith appeared, alone, her arms laden with purchases, Carolann quickly returned the club.

Predictably, Judith headed for the entrance to the lower level where she could tidy herself before going upstairs.

Carolann crossed the lawn and entered the hotel as her prey disappeared into the women's lounge.

She waited a moment or two until she was sure the hallway was deserted, then she pushed open the door. Judith was seated at the mirrors, the entire contents of her purse strewn across the counter.

Carolann quickly scanned the hodgepodge of make-up, cheque books and billfold, looking for the small white plastic injector she knew Judith carried everywhere.

It was poking out from under a soggy tissue.

"You must have been caught in the rain," noted Judith.

Carolann nodded. "I was playing golf."

She set her peaked golf hat on the counter next to the tissue and asked the other woman if she played golf.

"No, but my husband does."

"I didn't notice him on the course today."

Judith paused, a new lipstick hovering in her hand. "I made him take me into Hamilton." She laughed. "I refuse to start my marriage on a budget...the last I saw him, he was on his way to the bank."

Good thing, thought Carolann as she surveyed the array of bags before her.

Judith was so thrilled with her purchases from Trimingham's Department Store, she treated Carolann to a mini-show-and-tell right there in the ladies' lounge.

Back home in Toronto, she wouldn't have even given the real Carolann Gravelle the time of day.

She hadn't missed anything, Carolann thought, as she cooed appreciatively at a cashmere sweater and a Liberty scarf. It was about as exciting as playing Barbie dolls.

They exchanged pleasantries about the hotel and Carolann asked Judith if she'd tried any of the restaurants in Hamilton.

"No, I have allergies. It's safer to eat at a place where I know the food."

"You're very wise," said Carolann, her eyes fixed firmly on the artificial adrenalin. Then she smiled and said, "I guess I'll see you at dinner tonight."

She grabbed the peak of her golf hat and scooped it up along with Judith's prescription. Then, bending down to tie her shoe, she flicked her ball cap and sent the hypodermic syringe under the counter and behind the waste basket.

Judith didn't even notice her leave.

Carolann hurried up the steps into the main lobby and around the corner to the dining room. The travel agent had assured her the Chelsea was unwavering in its routine. By noon each day, the evening menu was posted in a glass display case outside the dining room.

That night was The Bermuda Buffet. Billed as "a meal to remember," Carolann savoured the irony as she rode the elevator up to the third floor.

The digital clock on the bed table read two-seventeen. She lay down on the bed and forced herself to breath deeply. It would be supremely ironic if she had a heart attack now. She grinned at the confusion it would cause if Anita Johnston were to die twice.

The way Judith sashayed into the dining room that evening Carolann was sure she must be wearing one of the day's purchases. Even Alex was sporting a jacket Carolann had never seen before.

Carolann fingered the contents of her pocket gingerly. Guests were wandering in and out of the buffet room, filling their plates with hot and cold entrees.

Alex was on his second scotch when Judith got up. Carolann looked over and, for a moment, she could have sworn he knew exactly what she had in mind. She flushed, then dismissing such a ridiculous suspicion from her mind, got up and followed Judith's lead to the buffet.

After several days at the Chelsea, Carolann was counting on Judith sticking to what she knew she could eat without having to double-check on the ingredients.

Carolann filled her own plate with a generous helping of salad, then unobtrusively released the small vial of walnut oil into the house oil and vinegar and quickly moved on. She was halfway down the buffet line when Judith reached for the salad dressing.

Carolann returned to her table and tried to eat, but it was like waiting for someone to open a special gift on Christmas morning. The food felt strange in her mouth as she watched Judith pick at everything on her plate but her salad.

Alex was still nursing his drink when Judith forked the first piece of lettuce into her mouth. Then another piece disappeared. Carolann held her breath. In less than thirty seconds, Judith began to wheeze.

It was an awful sound.

She clawed at her purse. Alex leapt up, his chair crashing to the floor. The other diners had stopped eating and were staring at the commotion, not yet sure what was happening.

Alex grabbed Judith's purse and dumped it, frantically rifling its contents for her missing prescription. An elderly gentleman tried patting Judith on the back. Alex screamed at him to stop.

Carolann felt like she was watching a movie. Judith turned blue and fell heavily to the floor, her eyes screaming in panic. She thrashed amidst the chair legs, her limbs an agony of despair. Then with one last cloying gasp, she fell silent, her new dress swirled around her like a shroud. It was all over.

The other diners were quickly herded into the lounge and given a reassuring drink. Carolann ordered a scotch and tried unsuccessfully to dredge up some compassion for the woman she'd just killed.

Snippets of conversation floated by.

"Such a shame."

"And on her honeymoon, too."

"The poor man."

Nearly everyone had an anecdote from another time, another accident, another place. But no one mentioned murder.

Carolann drank a second scotch and watched the door for any sign of movement from Alex.

When he did appear, a few minutes later, his normally flawless complexion was pasty despite his light tan. As the ambulance attendants wheeled the stretcher through the lobby, the hotel manager stepped in front of Alex, blocking his progress.

Another man, who wore the bearing of authority along with the uniform, stopped the stretcher-bearers and discreetly lifted a corner of the white sheet covering Judith's body.

It was the Bermuda Police.

"Why are they here?" asked Carolann. "It was an accident."

One of the old dears from Baltimore was standing beside her.

"Just routine, dear," she said. "When my Henry had a stroke on the eleventh fairway, they came to make sure I hadn't bopped him on the head with my three iron...bridge?"

"No...no, thanks." Carolann shook her head and quietly followed some of the other guests out onto the terrace. Now that the police were involved, it was crucial she get rid of the evidence.

A small group was heading down the hill to catch the ferry into Hamilton. Carolann fell in behind them and boarded the boat in their wake.

As they cut across the harbour, Carolann wandered away from the others and let her right hand dangle over the side of the boat.

She felt sick. The police were probably giving Alex the once over and there was nothing she could do to prevent it. She was half-afraid that even though Alex was innocent, the police might think he "misplaced" Judith's adrenalin.

The spray from the prow of the boat beat a tattoo on her forearm as she slowly unclenched her hand. The empty glass vial slid from her grasp and disappeared beneath the waves.

*   *   *

After a restless night worrying about Alex, Carolann went down early for breakfast. The hotel workers, as usual, were the most well-informed people on the island.

The cleaning staff had found Judith's prescription under the counter in the women's washroom earlier that morning. The police had concluded that it had either fallen out of her purse and rolled out-of-sight or Judith had inadvertently kicked it to where it had lain undetected until the next day. Either way, Alex was off the hook.

Carolann breathed a sigh of relief and got on with her breakfast. She dawdled over her coffee, half-hoping Alex would appear, but given the circumstances, that was unlikely. She browsed in the lobby gift shop for a few moments, then went to her room to pack.

Bermuda no longer seemed so inviting. On her way back to the airport, the mingling scents of the island, which had so intrigued her on her arrival, now seemed cloying and cheap. Bermuda had begun to close in on her, and despite the charm of the pastel cottages lining its roads, she was in a panic to get off the island.

The flight home was uneventful, and other than a few routine questions to answer at Customs, Carolann had no trouble re-entering the country as Anita Johnston.

She took the airport limousine downtown and got out at the Royal York. Suitcase in hand, she dodged the traffic on Front Street and disappeared into the depths of Union Station.

After retrieving her change of clothes from the long-term locker, Carolann went straight to the women's lounge. When she reappeared a few minutes later, it was as Carolann Gravelle.

She'd left the suitcase behind in an empty stall.

The glasses had been snapped in half and flushed down the toilet.

Rush-hour was well underway. Carolann navigated her way against the stream of people heading for the Go Train and caught a northbound subway. By the time she'd changed trains at Yonge and Bloor, she felt certain someone would have already walked off with the temporary wardrobe of Anita Johnston and any evidence of her Bermuda Short.

Carolann had no idea when Alex would be returning, so she went out to the airport every afternoon in time for Air Canada's daily flight from Bermuda.

The family waiting beside her on Tuesday was so boisterous she almost missed him.

He was standing on the other side of the glass partition, holding the same suitcase he'd used on their weekends together.

His clothes hung on him as if he'd suddenly lost an enormous amount of weight, and there were purplish streaks beneath his eyes.

Carolann got to her feet.

The stress of dealing with the police and transporting Judith's body back to Canada must have been too much for him. He had stopped just outside the door.

Then he saw her. Their eyes locked, and for a single second, Carolann knew she'd done exactly what he'd wanted all along.

She smiled as she began to walk towards him.

She was only a few steps away from him when a young blonde woman appeared at his side.

Carolann froze.

The woman must have been on the same flight; her face was well-tanned, and she carried a large shopping bag from the Bermuda Railway Company.

"Let's share a cab downtown," she said, and when Alex didn't respond right away, she slipped her free arm through his solicitously. "There's no one here to meet you, is there Alex?"

Carolann started forward, then stopped in mid-stride.

Alex was looking right at her when he said no.

Coup D'Etat by *Gregor Robinson*

A frequent contributor to Alfred Hitchcock's Mystery Magazine, Toronto writer Gregor Robinson's stories are frequently set in the Caribbean. Coup D'Etat is a fine example, rooted firmly in the Graham Greene tradition.

COUP D'ETAT

by *Gregor Robinson*

For months there had been rumours of grumbling at police headquarters, complaints that the government was doing little to stop the training of malcontents in the hills, that the Americans were unhappy. Rumours of unauthorized purchases by the army - even some helicopters, which someone claimed to have seen in crates at the harbour. We discounted the rumours. They were the subject of less discussion in the office than the Deputy Minister's hobbies, particularly those involving his executive assistant, a young person who, it was said, had been runner-up to Miss Philadelphia during her days as a student in the United States. There was something you could believe.

As to the rebels in the hills, my wife and I had come across them once. It was a Saturday. We were out for a picnic. So were the rebels - as far as we could tell. The leader was a man of about nineteen, one of the cab drivers who worked out of the Saint George. I had often seen him lounging against his van in the plaza, smoking and talking with the other drivers. He lent me a bottle-opener and gave me a mango to share with Maria.

"Thank you," I said. "Long live the Revolution."

He was armed with a stick - a stout, sharpened stick, to be sure, but a stick all the same. It was hard to believe that the army could be concerned.

"Perhaps," said Rinaldo, my colleague at the office, "but, from small beginnings - remember Che."

I did not need to be reminded: as well as working together, Rinaldo and I were in an economics discussion group. The idea was to read and talk about the latest books and articles from the U.S. and England. It was a way of keeping up, despite the palm trees. Rinaldo was always trying to push the discussion towards politics. He even went so far as to occasionally wear a bandanna around his head. I believed that such behaviour could do nothing but harm to his career, although I never mentioned it to him.

"Che lived in a dictatorship," I said. "I thought the current government is exactly what you and your friends wanted. What next - a Peoples' Democratic Republic?"

Rinaldo said nothing to this. He had been strongly in favour of the Coalition. There had at first been much enthusiasm everywhere for the new government, but that was now dissipated. There had been a lot of bickering amongst the members of the cabinet. A lot of clucking by the Americans. Exports rotting at the harbour in clouds of fruit flies. Worst of all, no tourists. Rinaldo could see as well as I could that the thing wasn't working. We both had our careers to think of, and under the Coalition, the Ministry was in a mess.

"Where's that report we're supposed to be working on?" I asked, rather sharply. "Fishboy wants to see it."

Rinaldo and I were cooperating with Fishboy on a report on the development of an air freight service, an attempt by the government to breathe life back into our foreign trade. Fishboy's chapter of the report had been finished for weeks, and he and I were now both waiting for Rinaldo. We were all in the running for Section Head, an appointment about which there was much speculation throughout the Ministry.

"Fishboy will get it," said Rinaldo. "He sucks up the best. Always running upstairs to see the Deputy, long memos to the Minister. Plus *the Englishman* likes him." Rinaldo almost spat as he said this; like most nationalists, he was xenophobic.

The Englishman (Harbottle was his name) had originally come to the country to sell Fizzies, a kind of tablet which when dropped into a glass of water produced an effervescent orange drink unpleasantly reminiscent of fruit salts. The product had not been a success. All the same, Harbottle had been able to gull the government into believing he was an expert on trade matters. He had devised much of the structure and nomenclature with which the Ministry was burdened. He was our boss: Assistant Deputy Minister (ADM), Exports and International Trade.

"No one in the Ministry except Harbottle likes Fishboy," I said. "Carolina does the best work."

"A woman?" said Rinaldo. "They will never give Section Head to a woman."

Rinaldo had a point. The Coalition may have been left-wing, but they were also Latin - very macho. Both my wife and I secretly believed that this strengthened my own chances of getting Section Head. I said to Rinaldo:

"You think we're living in the age of chivalry? The Coalition wants to *help* women, Rinaldo. You ought to know that. They want to liberate women. They want to liberate everyone."

"But that particular woman is a fascist. If it comes to politics, I ought to get the job."

"Unfortunately, it will not come to politics. Your position on U.S. imperialism and the International Monetary Fund will not matter to the interview board."

"At least I have a position," said Rinaldo, with a sneer. "Not like you. The perfect bureaucrat."

Rinaldo could be rather shrill at times. I believed his political stance could only work against him; the government, after all, was trying to project an image of moderation. I did not mention this to Rinaldo. Instead, I reminded him of the deadline for the report on the air freight service.

The change of government occurred at two o'clock the following Tuesday. The Cabinet was lunching in the banquet room of the Saint George Hotel on the occasion of the anniversary of their first year in office when General Diaz arrived and announced that henceforth they would be relieved of their duties. He graciously offered to arrange transportation to the airport for those who wanted it, and suggested that those who chose to remain in the country - and, of course, they would be welcome - should stay in their homes for the next few days, where, for their own safety, they would be guarded by men with sub-machine guns until things returned to a state of normalcy.

Several of the guards at the Palace, surprised when soldiers arrived in armoured vehicles, had panicked and drawn their revolvers. One man was critically wounded. (It was this which attracted the attention of the international press corps, before they were escorted out of the country.) People were advised to stay off the streets, to keep to their houses. This they did not do: there was sporadic shooting throughout the city, most of it in joyous celebration.

"These are difficult days," said General Diaz, "when what is needed is a firm hand, resolve, a sense of national purpose and reconciliation. Together, we can look forward to a time of peace, of prosperity, above all, of order. The hour of our destiny is at hand!"

We heard this on the radio in Carolina's office, late in the afternoon. The broadcasting facilities had been seized immediately.

"The hour of our destiny? A bit much, don't you think?" I said.

"Our Lord Jesus Christ in heaven!" said Rinaldo. "What about the men in the hills? What will happen now? They are finished."

"Just the opposite," I said. "At last they have an enemy. The best possible thing that could have happened to them."

The national anthem was played. Carolina's eyes glistened. Fishboy entered the room, rustling papers which he held in his hand. His glasses glittered under the fluorescent lights. Speaking loudly to make himself heard above the stirring music now being played on the radio, he asked about the report.

At five o'clock, two army helicopters flew over the plaza. Jeeps and a tank rumbled on the pavement below, and soldiers with rifles slung from their shoulders patrolled beneath the arcades of the capital.

It was soon announced that, as a result of the excesses and inefficiencies of the previous regime, economic renewal would be the highest priority of the new government. The nation would re-enter the world of international trade. General Diaz himself, in addition to his presidential duties, would assume responsibility for Trade and Development. A great honour for the Ministry. Our Section would be particularly affected: certainly this was my wife's view, based both on my daily reports to her of what was happening at the Ministry and on her own sources of information at the tennis club. We were responsible for exports and special import licenses. Within a week there had been orders for Mercedes Benzes for the new cabinet, but so far nothing else.

A question frequently asked was, "Are the Americans coming back?" Yes, they were. They would buy our produce. They would sell us small computers and software. Also automatic rifles, the first of which were said to be already on the way. This was something about which the Americans wished to remain discreet. Selling weapons to a military coup to put down popular insurrection: it would not be difficult for the enemies of the regime to cast the policy in an unfavourable light.

There was even talk of going ahead with the air freight scheme - bad news for Rinaldo, for he had never finished his chapter of our report, and it had come to light. Things were not going well for Rinaldo. General Diaz had terminated the Peoples' Education Office, through which the Ministry had proselytised in the countryside about the need for self-sufficiency. The new government didn't believe in that sort of thing. It was a project in which Rinaldo had taken a special interest.

Also, there would be no more gatherings of our little discussion group. Regis Debray had been scheduled for the next meeting. We thought it just as well to dispense with that.

"Is that all?" my wife asked when I reported all this to her. "No promotions?"

A devout Catholic and the reason for my coming to this country, Maria is not spiritual when it comes to those elements of the material world which fall within her immediate ken. She had been expecting much more from the upheavals in the capital.

"They left the Englishman in charge," she said. "That means Fishboy will get Section Head. And you, with all your bloody degrees."

It was true: they had left Harbottle in as ADM. Very few officials had as yet been ousted. But the structures which Harbottle had so carefully put in place, the titles and positions - Section Head, Director, Assistant Deputy Minister - all seemed somehow not to matter as much as before. The government had placed a certain Captain Gonzales in the Ministry. He was present whenever the Minister - a white haired former ambassador to the U.S. who had been brought out of retirement - held a meeting, signed a memo, or spoke on the telephone. Liaison Officer was the title conferred upon Captain Gonzales.

"The same Captain Gonzales who plays tennis?" asked my wife, brightening a little. She leaned forward in her chaise, indicating that I might mix her another drink. "He comes from a very old family." She seemed to think it was a good sign. Maria has an instinct for these things.

One morning Fishboy came to my cubicle with a message from the switchboard. He was excited. He did not, as a rule, bring me my telephone messages.

"The Liaison Officer wants to see you, Mortimer. Immediately. Chop, chop."

Captain Gonzales was on the seventh floor, the highest in the building, where the Minister and the Deputy Minister had their offices. I saw that the Minister was not in when I reported to the officer at the reception area. This was not surprising because the Minister usually came to work for only two or three hours a day. But the Deputy's office was empty. The room had been cleared out.

Captain Gonzales rose and came around from behind his desk to introduce himself when I was ushered in. Very charming. Very polished. Like the Sam Browne belt he wore.

"Mr. Mortimer. I am so glad you were able to come and see me. You are busy?" His manners were what Harbottle referred to as 'continental'.

"Things are picking up," I said.

"A very important job, you have. A very important Ministry. There is much opportunity for a man like you. Especially now."

He offered me a little cigar from a silver case on his desk. Cuban. The man was broad-minded.

"You know, we are hoping for more exports in the future. Not only our traditional products, but industrial exports as well. Manufactured goods."

I nodded. I was in agreement with whatever the new government had in mind. It was a matter of principle with me.

"For these new products, we will need new factories. New machines. We will need investment from abroad. We do not have money enough in this country to finance our own development. Forgive me, Mr. Mortimer, I don't suppose any of this is new to someone with an education from - where was it?"

"The London School of Economics," I said.

"The LSE, yes. My brother was there. Perhaps you knew him? No, I think not. He is older; with our central bank. As I was saying, investors in our country will want some assurances. They are not going to be happy if we have riots in the plaza, like we had last summer. Or rebels in the countryside. Investors are like old women - very nervous people."

I nodded. We both chuckled.

"And we will be buying more from the Americans," Captain Gonzales continued. "Materials vital to the well-being of the nation. We will need aid. But the Americans will be reluctant to help if there are bandits in the hills. I think you have encountered some of these people. You were on a picnic?"

"You mean the fellows from the hotel?" I was taken aback. Did he also know about the economics discussion group? The office had grown suddenly warm. "That was nothing," I said, "boys with sticks."

"The hotel?" He took up his pen and noted something down. He was poised to write more. "Which hotel?"

"I thought I had seen one of them before at one of the tourist hotels. I don't remember which one exactly."

"Perhaps it will come to you later," said Captain Gonzales. "Perhaps."

"Also, there is a man in your unit, Rinaldo. What can you tell me of him?"

"Nothing," I said, perhaps a little too quickly. I shrugged and added, "A good worker."

Captain Gonzales' gaze remain fixed. "Keep an eye out, will you, Mr. Mortimer? Tell me anything you hear of that might, shall we say, discourage investment in our country."

He stood up to show me out. He was smiling again.

"By the way," I said, "where is the Deputy Minister?"

"He has left the country," said Captain Gonzales, "with his executive assistant."

"Where did they go?"

"Philadelphia. My kindest regards to your charming wife." He closed the door.

I was back in my cubicle only a moment when the large head of Harbottle appeared above the frosted glass of the partition. It was unusual for him to visit; normally, we were summoned.

"Good morning." He crossed the small space in front of my desk and stood gazing out the window, his hands behind his back. He was upset. Captain Gonzales had reached straight down to me. A break in the chain of command. The whole system was starting to crumble.

"So," he said, "you have met our Captain Gonzales."

"Yes."

"What's he like?"

"Oh, you know - foreign."

One of our little jokes. Harbottle laughed without amusement. "And what did you two chat about?"

"Oh, nothing really," I said. "This and that. You know. Tennis."

"Tennis?"

"It appears that he plays at the same club as my wife."

"Ah. Yes." He turned again to the window. "You know, Mortimer, governments come and go. But we - the professionals, the civil service - we remain."

"Do you think this government will go?" I asked.

He didn't answer that one. Instead he said, "I have been here many years, and I can tell you it is not a good idea to become identified with a particular regime." He turned at the door as he was leaving. "Could be bad for one's career."

"I see. A tricky situation," said Maria. We were drinking our evening cooler on the garden terrace. The air was filled with the rich scent of the white star jasmine. "The Deputy is gone. Captain Gonzales is running the Ministry. It is good that he likes you. But the Englishman is still in charge - he will pick Section Head. There is no getting away from that."

"Right, my dear, as always. On the other hand, if Captain Gonzales were to become annoyed with me, well. . ."

"But you can't go telling him things about Rinaldo, spying," said Maria. "At the convent, we were always taught that that sort of thing is simply not done."

"Quite right, my angel. But as of this afternoon, there will be nothing to tell about Rinaldo." And I told her the news that I had learned just before leaving the office: "Rinaldo has resigned. The man has his principles."

"One down," said my wife. "What about the woman, Carolina?"

"She has the right politics. But they have a very conventional view towards the place of women, the army. Fishboy remains the obstacle."

Maria placed her empty glass on the arm of her chair where I would notice it. She considered it bad manners for a lady to ask for, or indeed have anything to do with, the business of drinks. I rose and mixed her a fresh one at the glass table by the wall.

"With a big slice of lime, just the way you like it," I said, handing her the glass. Unlike most people, Maria has never lost her taste for cuba libre. "By the way, darling, did you by any chance happen to mention to any of your friends at the tennis club about that time in the hills?"

"Time in the hills? What are you talking about?"

"The picnic last summer, when we came across those fellows training, as they called it, armed to the teeth with sticks."

"I do not remember."

I will say this about Maria: she is a very ambitious woman. She gives me the confidence to do what must be done.

Two weeks later I received a message from Rinaldo asking if we could meet. I left the office a little early and strolled around to the Saint George. Rinaldo and I had frequently drunk there; the meetings of the economics discussion group used to be held in the downstairs bar. They made a particularly good frozen daiquiri. When I arrived, Rinaldo had already ordered his. He seemed rather intense, even for him. He did not bandy his words.

"What about the automatic rifles? From the Americans."

"Rifles? I don't know anything about any rifles," I said.

"We know for a fact the weapons are coming," Rinaldo said. "From Miami. We know that the Ministry is handling it. All I need to know from you is when. The date and the hour."

"From me?" I glanced around the downstairs bar of the Saint George Hotel - at the limp artificial palms in their immense pots, at the high barred windows. I was struck by what a sinister looking place it really was.

"Is this a good spot to be discussing this sort of thing?" I asked. "They have been asking about you. I hope we haven't been seen. I am still hoping to get Section Head."

An unpleasant expression crossed Rinaldo's face. "I came in through the kitchen. You do not have to worry. We are safe in the Saint George Hotel. We will be warned if anyone is coming."

This was worse than I had expected. Anyone capable of warning Rinaldo that the police were coming would also be capable of telling the shadowy officials in the basement of the Ministry of Justice that I had met with him.

"I know nothing about the rifles," I told him.

"Perhaps you can find out. The man who sells cold drinks from the cart in front of the Ministry. Tell him. He will get the message to me."

Rinaldo turned and left through the kitchen doors. I ordered another daiquiri, then a third. Then I returned to the Ministry, now empty. I ascended to the sixth floor, where Harbottle's office was located. I took the precaution of using the fire stairs rather than the elevator.

There was no oily charm the second time I was called into Captain Gonzales' office. I remained standing while he addressed me from behind his desk.

"You know that we have been expecting guns." I gaped in a way that I hoped conveyed puzzlement. "At the insistence of the Americans, the transaction was being handled by a civilian agency. I am speaking, of course, of the Ministry."

"The Ministry?" I rasped. "Guns?"

"They arrived last night. At the small airstrip north of the city. I am sure you know the place. It is no longer much used. That is why it was selected. But nobody was there to meet the airplane. No one from the Ministry. No one from the army. No one from the police. No one. It appears we had the wrong night." Captain Gonzales glared at me. "The pilot waited. He noticed men approaching in the darkness but was unable to take-off in time. The men disappeared into the trees with the cargo. By now the weapons are doubtless in the hands of rebels throughout the country."

"I suppose the thieves had been watching the airstrip," I suggested.

"You don't think someone could have tipped them off?"

"I very much doubt it."

As to the actual arrangements for the shipment, making certain that the plane was met when it landed and so on, well I told him, I really couldn't say. That wasn't my responsibility. "Just a foul-up, I'm afraid. There have been mistakes before. Very unfortunate."

"Who was in charge of this operation?"

"I'm not really sure," I said. "I think Mr. Harbottle may be able to help you there."

I arrived home early with a cold bottle of champagne. Maria was in the garden reading a paperback novel by Graham Greene.

"Good news," I said, "I have been promoted."

She rose from the chaise lounge. "Section Head at last," she said.

"Not Section Head."

"What, you mean Director?"

"Try again."

"You mean - ADM!"

"In an acting capacity only, but still."

"My darling! That's wonderful! But what happened to the Englishman?"

"Gone. Not clear where. England I think. Fishboy will be leaving too."

"You sit down," said Maria. "This time I will get the drinks!" She strode past me, through the french doors to get the champagne glasses.

General Diaz has drawn up a new constitution with a promise of free democratic elections three years hence. I expect that at that time I will vote Social Democrat, or perhaps even for the Front. I would expect a thorough shake-up of the administration, during which I might be confirmed as an ADM. Of course, if the Front comes to power, Rinaldo will certainly be a senior member of the Cabinet, and I would hope to make Deputy. In the meantime, I have assured Captain Gonzales that there will be no more foul-ups with the air freight service.

Murder at Louisburg by *Ted Wood*

Ted Wood has proven himself adept at the contemporary crime novel through the exploits of Reid Bennett and, under the pseudonym Jack Barnao, John Locke. This time, he turns his crisp style and lean prose to a crime committed in the last century at the French fortress of Louisburg, about to be put under seige by the British.

MURDER AT LOUISBURG

by *Ted Wood*

Two men stumbled out of the Hotel de la Marine, laughing, holding one another up. They turned away, up Rue Toulouse, lit for a moment by candlelight through the tavern window, then passing out of Corporal Lartigue's sight into the darkness.

Pecheurs, he though enviously, cod fishermen, making five times the money he made, able to drink rum every night if they chose. He straightened up and tilted his head to the left and then the right, letting the rain trickle off the corners of his hat. Then he put his musket in his other hand and walked on, around the corner to the waterfront and east, towards the end of the street where the pillory stood.

It was empty now. Lartigue and his guard of six men had taken the prisoner De Villiers out at sunset and carried him back to the cells in the bastion. He was only semi-conscious. P'tit Georges Santier had spent a drunken afternoon pulling out the man's teeth. And De Villiers still had to go back to the pillory for two more days. Served him right, Lartigue thought, with the same envy he had felt at the inn door. The rogue had stolen a bottle of rum from L'epée Royale. What right did he have to drink rum? He should drink sapinage, spruce beer, as the rest of the garrison did except on paydays four times a year.

There was no light from the sky and none on the street. All the windows were shuttered against the driving April wind with its needle-sharp rain. Lartigue shuddered and wiped the water off his face then felt automatically down the barrel of his Charleville musket until he reached the lock. He had primed it and sealed it with beeswax before he came on patrol but there was no guarantee that the flint would spark against the wet steel. He hoped that the rain had driven all the criminals indoors. Soon it would, he was sure of that much. By midnight the town would be asleep. The officers and merchants at ease in their curtained four-poster beds, fishermen sprawled in their cribs, and the off-duty soldiers snoring, two to a bed, in the barracks with its dripping wet walls.

His clumsy shoes, slopping through a puddle, checked suddenly against something soft. He stumbled and swore and then bent to touch the obstacle with his numb left hand. It felt like a bundle of wet rags wrapped around something heavy. And then his fingers found chill smoothness. A face, hairless and cold.

A shock raced up his arm to his brain. He gasped, then patted the cold face and said, "Come on. Wake up," in a harsh nervous voice that didn't sound like his own. There was no response and he crouched there, fearful, listening to the sounds of the night. He could hear only the wind and the creaking of the spars of some ship moored close to the shore, beyond the wall. And then, faintly, a splashing step further east along the street.

He leveled his musket and shouted, "Halt or I fire!" The splashing continued and he aimed at the sound and pulled the trigger. The hammer clicked forward but the flint failed to spark and he swore and got to his feet, racing after the sound which had stopped now as the invisible runner reached dry ground.

For a few minutes Lartigue hunted among the houses, stopping often to listen for footsteps. But at last he realised he was beaten. The man had gone. Slowly he felt his way back to the waterfront and edged back along the street, feeling with his feet for the body. It took him about ten minutes to find it, helplessly small in the width of the street. Lartigue felt downward from the face, checking the clothing. A woman. He hoisted her on his shoulder. Holding his useless musket in his right hand as he trotted to the Royal Bakery. The bakers were soldiers, one of them would help.

He pounded on the door until a sleepy voice from upstairs called out that they were closed. Go away.

"Corporal Lartigue of the guard. Come down and let me in. I have a dead body here."

A minute later a baker with a candlestick opened the door. He was barefoot, wearing only his shirt and trousers. The other three bakers were crowding down the stairs behind him.

"Get over to the Dauphin Gate and tell Captain Desrochers what's happened," Lartigue ordered.

"Me?" the man with the candle asked in horror.

"You," Lartigue told him firmly. "On the double."

The man swore under his breath, then lit a second candle from the flame of the first and ran upstairs to dress.

One of the other men was bending over the woman. "She's dead, corporal. Been stabbed. Look at the blood."

Lartigue crouched and checked the woman's dress. The front of it was soaked with blood. Low, at the gut. And there was a vertical cut in the front of her skirt, one finger wide, the kind of cut a filleting knife would make.

"D'you know her?" Lartigue asked.

One of the soldiers nodded. "That's Marie, the maid for Captain Desrochers." He gulped awkwardly. "They say she could be had."

"Who says?" Lartigue demanded impatiently. "Come on, man. Who says?"

The soldier shrugged. "Everybody, corporal. You know, I heard it at the tavern."

"For money? Was she a whore?" Lartigue insisted. Behind him the other soldier had come downstairs again, dressed, carrying a lantern. As he went out the gust of wind made Lartigue's candle flicker.

"For money." Another baker spoke now, a tall, lean man with the pallor that came from his lifetime spent indoors. "She wanted to go home to France."

Lartigue stood up and rubbed his wet face. "I never knew," he said disbelievingly. After nine years at Louisburg he had thought he knew everything about the fortress and its people. "Why did none of the men at the Crown Bastion know there was a new woman of the town?"

"She started only a little time ago."

"Why?" Lartigue wondered out loud. "She had a good position. Captain Lartigue keeps, what, four servants?"

"And a slave," one of the bakers said. "That African does all the heavy work."

"How long has she been here? Anybody know that?" Lartigue asked. But before the men could answer him the door flew open and Captain Desrochers burst in with six men, one of them carrying a lantern.

Desrochers was a man of about forty, slim even now, wrapped in the huge bulk of his cloak. He returned Lartigue's salute offhandedly and asked, "You found her?"

"Yes, captain." Lartigue volunteered nothing more. Desrochers was a hard man, for all his smooth-faced elegance. He doubled his military pay by lending money to his men at a rate of two-livres for one. The men, who needed money to replace broken shoes or to buy *surtouts* if they missed the biennial issue, had no choice but to pay.

"This woman is from my household," Desrochers said with surprise. He stood up. "Where did you find her, corporal?"

"In the roadway, east of the Frederic Gate about fifty paces, captain. I heard someone running away but my musket misfired and he escaped."

"Search the town," Desrochers ordered briskly. "If you see a light anywhere, knock and ask the people if they heard anything."

"Yes sir," Lartigue said but Desrochers held him back with an upraised finger. "Not you, Lartigue. You stay with me."

Lartigue said nothing. He rubbed his bristly face with his left hand. What now? he wondered.

The rest of the guard pushed back out into the rain, taking their lantern and Desrochers looked at Lartigue coolly. "You say she was dead when you found her?"

"Yes, captain. Lying in front of the Widow Montaigne's house."

"And you were alone at the time?"

"On patrol from the barracks, captain."

"And at what time did you leave the barracks?"

Lartigue shrugged. "When Sergeant Foret told me."

"Did anybody see you on patrol?" Desrochers had taken off his gloves and was slapping them slowly into his left palm, slap, slap, slap, like the rhythm of the lash when a man was being punished.

"There was nobody on the street on such a night, captain." Lartigue shrugged. Then he remembered. "I did see two *pecheurs* coming out of the Hotel de la Marine. Drunk they were. They went up Rue Toulouse. That was just before I turned the corner on the quay. Keeping the patrol, as ordered."

Desrochers gave his gloves a final impatient slap and held them in his left hand while he stretched out and touched Lartigue's *surtout.* "You are bloody, corporal."

"But of course. I carried her from the place where I found her."

"Let me see your musket," Desrochers demanded and the corporal ported arms and handed over the musket with its hammer down and the pan lying open.

Desrochers took it from him and laid it on the long baker's table where he could inspect it in the dim light of the candle. "Very clever, corporal," he said easily. "I see you wiped the bayonet after you stabbed her."

"Me stabbed her? No, captain. I swear it. I found her. I did not stab her. I chased the man who did."

The captain raised the candle and held it in front of Lartigue's face. "I arrest you for the murder of this woman, Marie-Louise Dupuis," he said coldly, then to the three bakers, "Hold this man until the guard returns. If he escapes you take his place in the cells."

"But captain," Lartigue protested, "I did nothing. I was patrolling and I found her. I did not stab her, as God's my witness."

"When the guard returns, have them bring the prisoner to the Dauphin Gate," Desrochers said and turned for the door.

The bakers stood at attention until he left then relaxed. One of them said, "Sit down, corporal. Would you like some bread?" Lartigue was not hungry but recognized the kindness. He took the crust and chewed it numbly.

*   *   *

Anne-Marie Gaspian tied a ribbon around the dead girl's face, supporting the sagging jaw, then slowly began to undress her. She was not perturbed by what she did, as the layer-out for the colony she had handled dozens of corpses, sometimes three a day when the smallpox raged. But this was the first time she had worked on a murder victim and her ritual Ave Maria had been said more fervently than usual.

As she stripped the clothing she measured it appraisingly. It would fit her own daughter well, once the blood had been washed away and that cut in the belly had been patched. A good dress, fine linen, too good to be put into the ground. As long as Claudette did not guess from whom it had come it would be excellent for her.

The soldiers who had carried the body to her house were standing looking on and she turned to scold them. "Shame on you. Respect the poor child's modesty. Go."

They left, grinning awkwardly and Anne-Marie went back to work. It was not until she tried to remove the dress that she realised the corpse was holding something in its stiff left hand. Gently she pried the fingers apart and found they contained a crucifix. Anne-Marie gasped, then turned her eyes to the ceiling and said another prayer. This was a good girl, even as she went about her evil work on the streets, work that all the women of the town had heard of. She had repented no doubt as she lay dying from that corporal's bayonet thrust.

The old woman removed the dress and the underclothes, stiff with blood, and looked at the wound. She had dressed many such wounds, knife wounds, she recognized at once. Not the triangular tear a bayonet would make, a neat flat cut that did not look big enough to have cost the life of this child, barely sixteen. Thoughtfully she got her wash cloth and began to bathe the body.

*   *   *

Judge Pepin's foot was aflame with gout. He eased it gently on the little stool under his bench and glanced across at the clock. Three hours of testimony and no closer to the truth. The stupid corporal had given his testimony, the same story Judge Pepin had heard already from Captain Desrochers at dinner the night before. Then the Captain had told his damning tale of the blood on Lartigue's surcoat and the corporal had protested that he had carried the woman to the bakery. It was frustrating. No doubt about it, the man would have to be tortured. See if he persisted in his lying when the executioner was driving wedges into the bones of his legs. Pepin's gout flared at the thought and he winced. "And the guard found nobody when they searched the town?" he enquired in an angry tone.

The captain answered that. "Nothing at all, your honour. There was nobody on the street except the corporal that night."

Pepin snorted. "Are there any more witnesses?"

The secretary of the baillage cleared his throat nervously. "One, your honour, Madame Gaspian, the layer-out."

"And she was there on the street when this happened?" the judge snapped.

"No, your honour, but she prepared the body for burial and has requested to speak to the court."

Pepin wrinkled his nose in disgust. "Very well, this is a court of law. Let her speak."

The clerk of the court left the room and came back with the old woman who bobbed her knee in a quick curtsey and took the stand.

"You have something to say, woman?"

"Yes, your honour. Three things. First, I saw the cut in the girl's belly. It was a knife cut. It was not made by any bayonet."

"And you have seen bayonet cuts many times before?"

"Never. But many knife cuts." She shrugged. "The *pecheurs*. They fight with knives."

"And?" Pepin wanted to be in bed with his foot swathed in bandages dressed in camphor. His impatience showed.

"And this was such a cut. It was flat, about as long as this." She held up her hands, right index finger indicating a length on the index finger of her left. "A bayonet is triangular." She shrugged. "A weapon of war, it has to hurt the enemy. A *pecheur's* knife, no."

"You said there were three things," the judge snapped. What did an old fool like this know of bayonets?

The old woman fumbled in her dress pocket. "She was holding this in her left hand," she said and held up a little wooden cross with an ivory Christ.

"Bring that here," Pepin ordered and the secretary took it from the woman's hand and brought it up to the bench.

Pepin considered himself a man of reason, not subject to the tyranny of the Church but he attended Mass as was appropriate to a man in his position and he knew what this was. "This came from a rosary," he said. He showed his proof to the secretary. "See the hook in the top there. This was part of a rosary, an expensive rosary."

The secretary took it from the judge, blessing himself as he did so. "Yes indeed, your honour," he said. "Such a rosary would cost perhaps thirty livres."

"Not the kind a serving wench would own," Pepin said. "No doubt she stole it."

"Perhaps from the man who killed her," the secretary ventured.

Pepin frowned at him and the secretary flushed and busied himself with his papers. He should have remembered how jealous Pepin was of his authority. Pepin snapped at the old woman, "You said there were three things."

"Yes, judge." Pepin frowned at her clumsiness but let her continue. "She was with child. Four months perhaps."

"Not surprising for a whore," Pepin said with a grim smile.

The old woman shook her head impatiently. "But she was selling herself for only a few weeks before this. Not four months."

"Are you sure of this?" Pepin frowned at her but she was not dismayed.

"Sure as I am that you have gout," she said. There was a ripple of suppressed laughter in the court from everyone except the accused corporal and Captain Desrochers.

Judge Pepin looked around angrily and the faces all straightened at once. "I shall think more about this," he said. "Take the prisoner to the cells."

*   *   *

Captain Desrochers sent the guard back to the Crown Bastion with Lartigue and hurried home, drawing his cloak around him against the rain. He should be at the bastion, he knew that. There was a rumour that the New Englanders had sailed north to invest the fortress and the officers were preparing for its defence, but he had a private worry of his own. His manservant Gregoire opened the door for him, bowing low. "The widow Flambeau is in the kitchen with her daughter, a strong girl, Madame says she would be a good housemaid."

"Later." Desrochers undid the clip of his cloak and let it slip. His manservant caught it and held it, waiting for the next command. "Where is my son?"

"In his room reading, sir," Gregoire said.

Desrochers said nothing but climbed the stairs to the second bedroom. His son was sitting at the little desk with his lawbook open in front of him. He looked up in surprise as his father opened the door without knocking. "Father. The trial is over so soon?"

"Where's your rosary?" Desrochers demanded.

"My rosary?" the boy stammered. "Why, father? Are we going to Mass?"

Desrochers snapped his fingers impatiently. He should have left all the children in France with their mother. What use was a dreamy fool like this one? Said he wanted to be an advocate but had not come to the trial today, preferring to sit with his lawbooks in this little room. "Your rosary, at once," he repeated.

"I don't have it, father." The boy's face was white now. "I noticed it was missing last Sunday when we went to Mass."

Desrochers strode over to the desk and whisked the drawer out, shoving his son aside impatiently. He flopped the drawer upside down on the bed and rummaged through the contents, papers, letters, a pen knife. No rosary.

"What are you doing?" his son asked in a croaking voice. "Father, what is the matter?"

Now Desrochers rounded on him, grabbing him by the shoulders. "When did you sleep with this girl?"

The boy looked as if he would collapse. "What girl?"

"The servant who was killed. When did you sleep with her?"

The boy still seemed shocked. "Me, sleep with a servant girl?"

"Come," Desrochers said impatiently. "Every young man does such things. When did you?"

The boy licked his lips nervously. "I suppose close to Christmas time. She came with my hot water one morning and I could not help myself."

Desrochers let go of him and sat on the edge of the bed. Christmastime. Yes. The old hag had said the girl was four months. Now it was April. Yes. That was it.

"And you gave her the rosary," he said carefully.

"Yes, father," the boy said eagerly. "I gave her the rosary then, that morning."

Desrochers looked at him and saw the lie in his eyes. He stood up wearily and opened the armoire next to the bed. As his son watched, helplessly, he searched the pockets of the boy's surtout. He found the rosary in the right hand pocket and drew it out slowly, dreading what he would see. The crucifix was gone.

Dangling the beads from his right hand he sat down on the bed, crushed. "How did it happen?" he asked in a tight voice.

The boy pursed his lips a moment, then clenched his hands together for strength and spoke softly. "She would not stop. I knew she was selling herself. There was no need. She could have had the child. I would have told you. She could have stayed here. But she was selling herself."

"And you followed her, with your rosary in one hand and a knife in the other?" his father asked softly.

"I wanted her to go to the Brothers, to confess and stop," the boy said. He checked himself a moment. "Forgive me father. I loved her."

"Loved a servant wench?" Desrochers shouted. "Men don't love servant wenches."

"I did, before God. I wanted her to stop what she was doing but she mocked me and I stabbed her," the boy said and burst into tears. "And now the corporal will be broken on the wheel for what I did."

"And when he dies, screaming, would you want to be in his place?" Desrochers raised his voice and then checked himself. The servants must not hear. They could suspect as they wanted but they must never hear proof.

"I am a coward," the boy said. "I will never be like you. I should have stayed in Lyons with maman."

That was when Desrochers slapped him. The boy turned to the window, sobbing, and the captain ran down the stairs, pushing the broken rosary into his pocket and calling for his cloak.

Gregoire brought it at once, coughing discreetly as he draped it over Desrochers's shoulders. "You are leaving, captain? What shall I tell Madame Flambeau?"

"Hire the girl," Desrochers said. "She will be paid four livres a month, like the last one."

"Yes sir," Gregoire said. Four livres and she would sleep by the fireplace and eat the household's food as the other girl had. Madame Flambeau would owe him a favour for this. He looked forward to collecting it later that night.

The captain strode on up the Rue Toulouse, making his plan. He would search the barrack room and find the broken rosary under the bed Corporal Lartigue shared with two other men, one of them always on duty of course. Yes, that would be best. Then he reconsidered. My God. That would be folly. Lartigue had not been back to his bed since the killing. The rosary could not have been broken if the man had not yet murdered the girl. No, he would have to go to the cells and find it in the straw of the corporal's cell. That would be perfect. Then the man could be executed and the affair would be over.

He was passing though the gates of the bastion when he heard the first dull cannon boom and realised that the rumours were true. The New Englanders were investing the town. Impatiently he returned the salute of the guard and hurried to the office of the commandant. For one happy moment he forgot completely the dead girl and the problems she was causing him.

*   *   *

The New Englanders were cunning. They did not attack from the sea, against the defensible sea wall and the enfilading cannon. Instead they marched overland to the heights beyond the fortress and cannonaded the town. By the third week of the siege their shots had damaged most of the houses in town and killed one hundred and seventy townspeople. On the twenty-sixth day a cannon ball hit Captain Desrochers's house, killing his son. In all that time, the captain had never left the bastion, never been able to rid himself of the broken rosary. Now, in mourning for his son, he went to the commandant with his plan. "We must sally out and attack them," he said. "I volunteer my company for the honour."

"Suicide," the commandant said automatically. "There are four thousand men out there. What can one hundred Frenchmen do to them?"

"We can capture and spike the cannon," Desrochers said in a harsh voice. "The men know it is our only chance. They will follow me."

The commandant looked at him for a long time before speaking. "Have a mass said for your troops," he ordered, then extended his hand. "You are a brave man, captain."

Desrochers shrugged, then voiced his last request. "One thing, sir. Two of my men are in the cells. One Lambert, a *voleur*. He stole money from a comrade, he has already been branded and flogged, he is awaiting transfer to the royal galleys in the Mediterranean. I think he would prefer the chance to fight."

"Take him," the commandant said. "And there is another, is there not? A corporal who murdered your serving woman."

"Lartigue." Desrochers nodded. "Him also. What is the death of one woman when the enemy have killed scores?"

"Very well." The commandant slumped in his chair. "It is our only chance. Food is low. We do not know whether the ship we sent to France has reached home. We do not know the government will reply in time." He shrugged wearily. "Go with the grace of God, Desrochers. I will put this in my report to France."

Desrochers saluted and left.

That night, after the men had attended Mass in the damaged chapel, they slipped out of the sallyport and climbed the hill towards the battery. A Micmac, fighting with the New Englanders, saw them almost at once and the enemy closed and cut them down. All of them. One of the last to fall was a tall slim officer. The New Englander who killed him with the butt of his musket could not believe the man's actions. Instead of defending himself he was tending to another fallen man, a corporal. He seemed to be arranging a string of Papist beads around the man's neck. Not that the beads were worth anything. The little figure of Christ which might have been worth money was missing. But for all that, the New Englander noticed in awe, the officer died smiling.

The Disappearance of Sarah-Sue
by *Mel D. Ames*

Mel Ames is most famous for the Cathy Carruthers novelets that appeared regularly in Mike Shayne Mystery Magazine, and continued in two volumes of Cold Blood. This time, he brings in former Mounties turned private eyes, Stu Blaze and Connie Wells, to search for a missing girl in B.C.'s Okanagan Valley. Himself an orchardist in the valley, Mel says of the story, "Every lake and town, street and backroad, cop and code, is scrupulously authentic. It's where I live."

THE DISAPPEARANCE OF SARAH-SUE

by *Mel D. Ames*

There was scarcely a doubt in anyone's mind that Sarah-Sue Prescott was a most precocious young lady. Her sprightly figure had become a familiar sight in Winfield, traipsing about the small British Columbia town where she had grown and blossomed, almost overnight it seemed, like an early morning flower. In any other venue, she might have been seen as something of a flirt, young as she was, but amid the pastoral environs of rural Winfield, her inherent innocence managed to dispel any sense of impropriety. To her peers and elders alike, she was the embodiment of inculpable youth and as such, she was perceived to be loved by one and all.

Little wonder that a chilling void was driven into the very soul of the small community when, one month to the day before her thirteenth birthday, Sarah-Sue suddenly vanished from the face of the earth.

The city of Kelowna hugged the eastern shore of Lake Okanagan, fifteen miles south of Winfield. The town and the city were linked by Highway 97 North, an oft-times congested stretch of road that was currently being widened to accommodate an ever increasing flow of traffic. It was in Kelowna where the Royal Canadian Mounted Police were headquartered, and it was there, in the squat administration building on Doyle Street, where Inspector John Warfield waited now with mounting impatience.

He punched the intercom button with an acerbic finger. "Any sign of Stu Blaze?"

His voice came through to Jan Thurston at the reception desk like the crackle of distant thunder.

"No, sir. Not yet." Jan, a civilian employee, was not intimidated. She knew the gruff voice to have a soft heart. Then, suddenly, "Sir?"

"Yes?"

"A black van has just pulled up in front. I believe it's him."

"About bloody time. Send him straight in."

"Yes, sir."

The pretty receptionist watched with thinly-veiled maidenly interest as Stuart Blaze emerged from the van. He was handsomely huge, six-four, with mountainous shoulders and a blond bristly head of hair that looked to have been tonsured by the Fuller-brush man. In a fur-lined parka, over a navy blue jacket and gray slacks, he looked trimly military, a bearing that was hard to shrug off after twenty years on the Force.

"Good morning, Sergeant Blaze," Jan smiled as he entered the reception area. She pressed the buzzer to open the door to the inner offices. "Inspector Warfield is expecting you."

"Let's make that *Mister* Blaze, Jan. *Sergeant* Blaze is history. I think we've been through this before."

"Oh, yes." She felt like a flustered little girl in the towering shadow of the ex-Mountie. "I keep forgetting – "

Blaze chuckled. "No big deal," he told her as he headed for Warfield's office, "I'm having a little trouble getting used to it myself."

John Warfield's deeply chiselled features could not disguise an obvious show of relief as Stu Blaze suddenly filled his office doorway. He came around his desk to grip the big man's hand.

"Thank God you're here," he said soberly, "we've got a real bummer on our hands." But he brightened in the next instant with an abrupt out-thrust of his chin, stepping back to give his favourite ex-Mountie the once-over. "So — tell me, Stu, how goes the proletarian pursuit of private policing?"

Blaze grinned at the friendly gibe. "You must have been up all night on that one, John. Still, if you're into measuring success in terms of dollars, my friend, I'd have to admit that we're making a hell of a lot more money now as P.I.'s than we ever did on the Force."

"We? Connie's still with you, then."

"You better believe it," a sultry voice informed him, in no uncertain terms. Connie Wells' happy face poked out from behind

Blaze's imposing bulk. Her abundant auburn hair tumbled loosely over one shoulder and her green eyes flashed like twin emeralds that had tapped into some inner light source. She stepped into magnificent view, dressed totally in white; a short denim skirt and jacket over a cotton turtleneck pullover. Her white car-coat was tucked under one arm. She was, to roundly understate the obvious, fetching.

"Connie, nice to see you." John Warfield had always found it difficult to reconcile that this lovely young lady had once been a seasoned policewoman. She had taken her 'purchase'[1] only recently to work full time for Stuart Blaze. "Have you tied a knot on this guy yet?"

"Not yet," Connie grinned, "but I'm working on it."

"Well," the inspector grunted as he resumed his seat behind the desk, "you know what they say: A Mountie always gets his man —"

"*Her* man," Connie interjected reprovingly.

"Yes, well, enough *deja vu* for one day. Let's get down to business."

"Your message said something about a missing girl," Blaze prompted. He and Connie had settled comfortably into the leather cushions of a settee that faced the desk. "Sounds to me like a case for Missing Persons."

"They've had the case for two months, Stu, working hand in glove with a team from G.I.S.[2]" John Warfield's craggy features betrayed uncharacteristic signs of deep personal concern. "They don't know any more today than when they started."

"Kids go missing all the time," Connie said, "what's so special about this one?"

"This kid didn't go missing, Connie, she *vanished*."

"There's a difference?"

"When kids go missing," Warfield replied gravely, "there's usually a reason: trouble at home, at school, some kind of discord among their peers — any number of seemingly valid provocations. And there are always the inevitable signs as to where they might have gone. In the case of Sarah-Sue Prescott, there was nothing. Absolutely *nothing*. She was simply here one day and gone the next, for no apparent reason."

---

1   Bought her way off the force.
2   General Investigation Section

Blaze shifted his weight uneasily. "Have you looked into foul play?"

"That was the first thing to come to mind, Stu, given the improbability of her taking off on her own, but, again, there was nothing to go on, nowhere to start. After two fruitless months of marking time, I pulled G.I.S. and Missing Persons from the case."

"They must have come up with *something*."

The inspector gave a weary sigh. "Nothing relevant," he said. "I went through the motions, of course, checking to see that proper procedures had been rigorously followed, that no avenue of investigation had been overlooked. They had, and there hadn't. I, too, drew a blank."

"At the risk of sounding heartless," Connie put in, "isn't two months of continuous investigation by four — uh, five badges a little excessive in a case of this kind?"

"Yes, and no. I'll admit it looks that way on the surface, Connie, but once you've been fully briefed, I think you'll see it differently."

"Speaking of being briefed," Blaze said, "is the Ghost still with you?"

"He's standing right behind you."

Ghost was Warfield's *aide-de-camp*; Sergeant Gary Goetze. He was well known in the Force as a veritable genius at gathering data, on any one and any thing. The epithet was chillingly apt. Goetze had the soul of a computer and the gray physical deportment of a living ghost.

Connie whirled at the sound of a ghoulish chuckle. "Ghost, you sure have a way of — sneaking up."

Blaze laughed. "Show yourself, you pussy-footing old zombie," he said without turning his head.

Ghost drifted into view like a puff of gray smoke. "Stu, Connie. Good to see you."

Gary Goetze's voice was as gray and weightless as his persona. The exposed flesh of his face and hands was the colour of cigarette ash and his balding pate was a diluted pallid grizzle. You had to get close to make out the faint dusty curve of his eyebrows, and the eyes that peered hollowly out from under them were the same smokey ethereal gray as the rest of him. Even the plain clothes he wore were nondescript and colourless.

"Ghost," Warfield said to his right-hand man, "I see you have the file with you, so give us a verbal on what you've got there. "It'll save time and, uh — money. These gumshoes don't come cheap, you know."

"John," Blaze interjected with mock indignation, "*you* called *us*, remember? Not only two months after the fact, I might add, but from what I gather thus far, with clues as scarce as coonshit and a trail as cold as carrion."

"Why, Stu," Connie piped up with a flutter of her magnificent green eyes, "that was positively poetic. I think we ought to up our fees – "

"Enough already." John Warfield kept his face grim but he could not hide the smile in his eyes. He gave Ghost a go-ahead nod.

Ghost opened the file and began to speak in his customary gray monotone. "The missing girl's full name is Sarah Susan Prescott, better known as Sarah-Sue. She was twelve when she went missing, but would have turned thirteen a month ago. We've pegged her weight at about eighty to eighty-five pounds. Her hair was long blonde and straight, her eyes blue and her complexion fair. She was the darling of Winfield, a small town fifteen miles north of here, and she was last seen November 27th, by everyone and no one. By that I mean, she was such a familiar sight in the town, no one could give us a last encounter that was either specific or verifiable."

Ghost flipped a page.

"The girl lived with her father," he went on, "Bernard Prescott, the town drunk. He was her sole guardian, but their mutual love and respect, in spite of his alcoholism, engendered a kinship that was 'sighed upon', yet tentatively accepted by the entire community. Truly a bizarre situation. Prescott did not report his daughter missing until the morning of November 28th, having passed out the night before. He's been bombed ever since, I was told, for seemingly obvious reasons.

"The girl's mother, Madeline Myers, her maiden name, moved out on them almost nine years ago. She is currently in Vancouver, living common-law with a Jonathan Winthrop, a commercial traveller. Lingerie. Neither Myers, nor Winthrop appear to be in any way connected to Sarah-Sue's tragic absence, nor, I gather, particularly aggrieved."

He paused to turn another page.

"A local orchardist," Ghost continued, "by the name of Nels Grimstad was known to be a devoted friend and mentor of the missing girl. This rather uncommon accord was looked upon as a sort of grandfather/granddaughter relationship that had evolved and nurtured, quite innocently, over the years. He's sixty-one, unmarried and unattached, and he gives every outward sign of being genuinely devastated by the girl's sudden disappearance.

"That is not the case, however, with a sixteen year-old dropout, Billy Sanford, who had been 'coming on' to Sarah-Sue for some time. He and a couple of his friends, uh — Jake Wilmans and Sly Farquat, had been seen accosting the girl on a few occasions."

"Accosting?"

"Mostly verbal ribaldry, I gather, which did not seem to upset her unduly, nor cause any serious concern to those who witnessed it."

Ghost drew a weary breath.

"And, finally, there is a Michel Oddette, an itinerant fruit worker from Quebec, in his early twenties. His name popped out of the CPIC[1] computer as a known potential sex offender; peeping, exposing, flashing, nothing too threatening — yet. He did some part-time orchard work for Grimstad during the summer, which could have put him in contact with Sarah-Sue, who, coincidentally, also worked for Grimstad, after school and over the summer holiday. Oddette is still in the area, pruning fruit trees in a neighbouring orchard."

He closed the file with a conclusive snap. "And that is it."

"After two bloody months, *that's it*?" Blaze drew a heavy breath. "Who gets the easy ones?"

"Stu," Warfield broke in, "I'm not about to inflate your ego by recounting your superb record while on the Force. However, it is precisely because of that record that we would even consider calling in a private investigator, ex-Mountie notwithstanding. In my opinion, Stu, this case is special. I can smell it. *Something* happened to Sarah-Sue Prescott and I want to know *what*. So — will you take the case?"

Blaze snared the file from Ghost as he got to this feet. "Can I have this apparition as my liaison?"

"You've got him."

"Our usual team rates, plus expenses?"

---

[1]   Canadian Police Information Centre

"You've got it."

"Our rates have gone up since that Ogopogo caper last summer, John."

"Spare me."

Blaze beckoned Connie with a jerk of his head and made for the door. "You, too, Ghost. Let's start with a guided tour of Winfield."

They took the van, with all its let-down, fold-out, home-away-from-home accoutrements securely anchored down in back. Connie had made coffee and they sipped from earthenware mugs as they headed north on Harvey Avenue with Blaze behind the wheel.

The heavily-peopled confines of the city soon fell behind, giving way to open snow-quilted farmland, then, eventually looming up on their right, the hustle-bustle of the Kelowna Airport. A passenger jet was just lifting off with a pervasive roar.

"It's the third largest airport in B.C.," Ghost volunteered, leaning forward from his swivel seat behind the driver. "They've just finished lengthening the runway to over seven thousand feet to accommodate long-distance charters from the East and the U.S. of A."

"Progress," Connie muttered disparagingly with a curl of her upper lip.

Blaze laughed at her facial contortions. "Progress is here to stay, Connie, like it or not."

The airport was replaced a few miles down the road by a scene from the past; a round shallow lake, frozen over and caked with January snow. A few oblongs of clear ice were peopled with a smattering of brightly coloured skaters and future NHL hopefuls.

"Duck Lake," Ghost informed them, "we're almost there." 'There', being Winfield, hove into view around the next bend. To their left, leafless fruit trees began to climb the easy slopes in orderly rows, while on their right, an old land-locked fishing boat marked the entrance to a sprawling mobile-home complex. Low mountains under their seasonal camouflage of snow rolled pristinely up and away on either side. And directly ahead, an earth-bound swarm of mechanical monsters impeded their progress.

"They're pushing the four-lane highway right through the centre of town," Ghost explained. "Some kind of compromise between dollars and common 'c-e-n-t-s.'" He spelled out the last word.

Connie held her nose. "But can't you just picture the beauty of this place," she mused, "B.P.?"

"B.P.?"

"Before Progress." She smiled smugly at Blaze, sure she had gotten in the very last word.

"Progress in Winfield, Connie, and in the next small town, Oyama, begins and ends with the highway," Ghost said, unwittingly relegating her 'last word' gambit to history. "Virtually the whole area is in the A.L.R.[1] which compels land owners to stay 'green'. There are a few head of cattle and some hay fields, but it's basically orchard country. And that is the way most people want to keep it."

Blaze swore as he dodged the first of a hundred and one road construction signs, weaving the traffic over and around half-finished stretches of blacktop and concrete curbing. The road-building equipment was covered with a dusting of snow, silently waiting out the winter months before resuming work in the early spring.

"For Chrissake, Ghost, get us out of here." He swerved to miss a truck swerving to miss another car. "It's Prescott, the girl's father, I want to talk to first."

Ghost pointed ahead. "Turn left at the light," he said. "Prescott lives in a pickers' cabin on an orchard about a mile and a half from town."

Blaze caught the sign, BERRY ROAD, as he swung left on a green light, leaving behind a few miles of bad road and a disorderly mix of machinery that seemed to have already given up on the questionable pursuit of progress.

The cabin was perched on the edge of Al Greene's old cherry orchard (a weathered sign informed them) overlooking Wood Lake, an elongated body of iced-over water that separated Winfield from its northerly neighbour, Oyama. They parked the van under a cherry tree and approached the cabin on foot. The cabin's plywood door opened as they drew near and Bernie Prescott moved into the narrow opening. He confronted them with a puzzled half smile.

"You from the police?" he asked, his eyes lingering on Ghost in vague recognition. There was a slight but noticeable slur to his words.

He was a little man, lean and wiry, but he seemed to exude an expansive inner presence that belied his modest stature. It was

---

[1]   Agricultural Land Reserve

not difficult, seeing the man, to understand why he and his daughter had been so warmly embraced by the community.

"Just a few questions, Mr. Prescott," Blaze told the man pleasantly. "May we come in?"

Prescott stepped back to let them enter, but as Ghost crossed the threshold, he placed a tentative hand on the Mountie's arm.

"Have you found her, officer? Is she all right?"

Bernie Prescott's eyes were glazed with a moisture that was not totally alcohol induced. His chin quivered as he spoke.

"No," Ghost said gently, "we haven't found her yet. But we haven't given up either." He introduced Blaze and Connie. "They've come to help us with the investigation," he added with a note of optimism.

The cabin was small but meticulously clean and comfortable. A wood-burning stove gave off a heady aroma and a cosy warmth. Two cubby-hole bedrooms egressed off a larger area that served as a living-room-cum-kitchenette. Among the modest furnishings were a TV set, a recliner and a small settee, and a fibreglass shower stall was squeezed into an alcove between the bedrooms, partly hidden behind an opaque plastic curtain. The toilet was outside, at the end of a path in the snow, a half-moon vent cut into its solitary door.

Prescott found his chair at the table and sank into it. Except for a half-empty bottle of rye whisky and a two-ounce shot glass, the table was bare. He reached unsteadily for glass and bottle.

"Isn't it a little early in the day for that?" Blaze asked. His voice carried no hint of censure.

Prescott levelled a look of pained forbearance at the big ex-Mountie. "You find my little girl, Mr. Blaze, and I swear to all that's Holy, I'll never touch another drop as long as I live. Until then – "

Blaze backed a wooden chair up to the table and sat down opposite Prescott, his heavy thighs straddling the seat, his arms folded across the backrest.

"What can you tell me, Mr. Prescott," he asked softly, "about that last day, November 27th—the day your daughter disappeared?"

Prescott took a tug at his shot glass. "Nothing," he said with a show of pent-up hostility. "Nothing I haven't already told a dozen bloody people a dozen bloody times before."

"Mr. Blaze and Miss Wells are here to help," Ghost reminded the man in solemn gray tones.

Prescott looked up and fixed the big P.I. with a long appraising stare. "You really think you can find her?"

"We can try."

"But it's been so Goddamn long."

"I know. That's what makes your testimony so important to us. Why don't you start with the morning of the 27th? Just talk about it. The things you remember. The little things — "

Prescott's sudden spate of anger seemed to have dwindled slowly into self-pity. "Well," he began finally, "as I recall, Sarah-Sue wasn't feeling too spry that morning. Matter of fact, she'd been feeling poorly for about a week. Said she thought she had a touch of the flu; but it'd take more than a tummy ache to put a damper on *my* little girl. We were planning for Christmas, you see," a wry smile flitting across his lips, "me and Sarah-Sue. I told her I was going to run a string of coloured lights along the path from the cabin to the john. Well, sir — Sarah-Sue, bless her heart, she just thought that was hilarious. I told her she'd be able to ascend to her 'throne' in style, like the Princess she was." He choked back an involuntary giggle. "We laughed about that till we cried." The giggle dissolved into a whimper.

Prescott straightened then, defiantly, wiping the moistness from his eyes with the back of his wrist. "She left here about eight-thirty," he recalled thoughtfully, "after she'd washed up the breakfast things. Told me she was headed for town, but that she might drop in on Old Nels on the way. That was the last I saw of her — " His words faded to a sob as he buried his face in his arms.

"And did she?"

Prescott looked up with a blank stare.

"Did she drop in on Old Nels?"

The distraught man shrugged his shoulders. "I told you, that was the last I saw of her. Christ, man, she could have gone anywhere — "

Blaze pointed to the two small bedrooms. "Which one was hers?" he asked.

Prescott indicated the room that had a curtain drawn across the doorless opening. A similar curtain on the other room was drawn aside revealing a slept-in, unmade bed, with a scattering of clothing that obviously did not belong to Sarah-Sue.

"Has anything been removed? Or altered?"

Ghost shrugged as Prescott shook his head. "That room, Mr. Blaze, is just the way she left it."

"Mind if I have a look?" Blaze's chair scraped noisily across the plank floor as he got to his feet. Without waiting for Prescott's response, he drew the curtain and entered. Ghost joined him.

The room was tidy, the narrow bed neatly made-up with gray army-type blankets. The one small window was covered by a flowered cotton drape, giving the room a sombre hue. On the wall where a headboard might have been, a half dozen snapshots had been carefully arranged. Two, Blaze noted, were of the girl and her father; the rest were shared with an unshaven white-haired man, wearing western garb and a brightly coloured headband.

"Old Nels," Ghost said to Blaze's raised eyebrows. Then, as his gray eyes swept the room, "What do you think?"

"As cold and cheerless as a nun's cell," Blaze muttered, more to himself than in answer. He flipped through a few school books that occupied a shelf over a small desk. The bed, the desk, a waist-high dresser and a wooden chair were the room's sole meagre trappings.

An old Sears catalogue caught Blaze's eye, resting just inside the desk top. Certain pages were thumb-smudged, as though having been pondered over many times; girls and ladies of all ages, modelling lingerie and dresses, sportswear and underclothing — even a few depicting assorted mens' and boys' wear.

"A young girl's wish list?" Ghost speculated over his shoulder. He reinforced the point by rattling through the few hangers in the room's one small open closet. The clothing that hung there was near-new and of good quality, if somewhat on the practical side for a girl as young and as pretty as Sarah-Sue.

"No frilly dresses?" Blaze asked. "No skirts?"

Ghost rummaged. "Uh-uh," he said flatly, "nary a one."

Blaze opened a drawer in the dresser, then held up an undergarment that did not seem to conform to the Spartan simplicity of the outerwear in the closet.

"She was twelve years old, for Pete's sake," Ghost said almost defensively, "going on thirteen."

Blaze continued to rummage silently through the drawers but other than the customary toiletry one might expect of a growing young girl, there was little out of the ordinary.

Ghost drew the curtain behind him as he and Blaze rejoined the others in the outer room. Connie had a comforting hand on Prescott's shoulder. "Tell me," she was saying, "did Sarah-Sue have any close friends?"

Blaze paused to listen.

"Yeah." Prescott straightened, blowing his nose into a crumpled handkerchief. "Her and Old Nels was pretty close."

"No, no. I mean another girl, or a boy. Someone her own age."

Prescott gave that some thought. "Not really," he said finally. "At least, not that I know of."

"She never brought other kids home with her? After school, or on the weekends?"

"No, she never did."

"Didn't you find that rather odd?"

Prescott gazed tearfully up at Connie, "No, I don't think so," he said. "She was always so, well — independent. Didn't seem to need no one else. She was old for her age; know what I mean? Why that little Miss had the get-along smarts of a full-grown girl." He paused to drain his glass in a single gulp. "Still, when I stop to think about it, there never ever was anyone else but me, I guess — and Old Nels. She was a happy one, though. Bright and sparky as a chipmunk." A tearful titter cut into his reverie. "I been calling her that, *Chipmunk*, since she was knee-high to a seedling. Oh, you bet. *Hey, Chipmunk*, I'd say, *wanna see what Daddy's got in his back pocket* — ?"

"Point us in the direction of Old Nels," Blaze told his colourless cohort. They were back in the van, along with Connie, buckling up. "I'm beginning to find this May/December togetherness of an old man and a young girl a little hard to swallow."

"Oh?"

"You don't accept the disparity of half a century in their ages as being — unusual?"

"It's been said," Ghost responded evenly, "that people in the declining years tend to revert to their childhood quite naturally. They have a known propensity for relating rather well to children. I would think the girl felt quite comfortable with the old gentleman."

"To the exclusion of all other peer-level relationships?" Blaze turned to Connie. "That was a good tack in there, love. It tells us more about the missing girl than Ghost and his gang were able to uncover in two months. Remind me to put a letter of commendation in your pay envelope."

"Given my druthers," Connie cooed artfully, "I'druther commendate in my own quaint way. Legally, that is." She left no room for doubt in what she meant with a flirtatious flutter of her emerald eyes.

Blaze chuckled. And Ghost gave his impression of what a laugh might sound like in an all-gray world. This unlikely spate of levity left his two companions agog.

"Okay," Ghost reluctantly conceded, "I'll buy the 'unusual' concept, given their ages and Connie's astute questioning about the girl's somewhat divided propensities, but I must take issue, Stu, with your reference to 'me and my gang,' as you so couthlessly put it. My involvement in this case, I hasten to clarify, began no earlier than yesterday morning, and only then for the sole purpose of compiling a concise and accurate file for *your* perusal and edification. I trust my efforts in this explicit regard have thus far met with your approval — *sir*."

"Couthlessly?" Connie echoed incredulously. "Is that word for real?"

"About as real as his trumped-up indignation," Blaze told her. To the current couthful butcher of the Queen's English, he said, "That raucous display of hilarity, Ghost, has left you glowing like a June bride."

Connie began to croon: *"The object of my reflection, Has changed his complexion, From wan to rosy red — "*

"On the Ghost," Blaze laughed, "wan is wonderful."

The gray Mountie treated his tormentors to a Bela Lugosi leer. "Turn onto Seaton Road," he said stonily, thereby stemming the flow of verbal abuse, "next right — *sir*."

Blaze dutifully followed directions, piloting the black van down Seaton Road, then left, onto a gravel driveway. He slowed to a crawl as they rounded an old country-style mailbox, balanced precariously atop an upright length of welded chain and bearing the name, NELS GRIMSTAD, in bold seriffed letters.

"That's our man," Blaze muttered as he followed the driveway for a hundred yards or more into the hidden heart of a large apple orchard, and there, in a cluster of well-kept outbuildings, a small shabby bungalow vied vainly for homey accord.

"Typical farmyard," Blaze noted dryly, "the house and the head are always the last to see a coat of paint."

"But what are all the buildings for?" Connie wondered.

"Cold storage," Ghost pointed out, fingering each building in turn, "machine shop, pickers' quarters, showers, garages, dry storage — "

"Ghost, I get the picture."

Blaze surveyed the yard expectantly. "So where do we find this granddaddy of eternal youth?"

"Listen." Ghost held up a cautionary hand. The muted rumble of a tractor could be heard drifting out from behind one of the buildings. "It sounds like he's over there, in back of that dry storage unit."

They found their man after a brief search, off-loading fifty pound sacks of fertilizer from a pallet behind the tractor. He looked up as the three detectives approached, recognizing Ghost from his previous visit.

"So," the farmer muttered apathetically, "it's you again."

Nels Grimstad was a poor-man's Willie Nelson. He had a hungry-looking leanness about him that was not unattractive, and behind the week-old white stubble on his cheeks and chin, his blue eyes held the glint and clarity of a man half his years. A multi-coloured headband on his too-long white hair rounded out the startling resemblance to the popular country singer. The only possible distractions from the Willie Nelson illusion were two parallel scars that descended down the length of his left cheek and were clearly visible even through its bristly camouflage.

"What can I do for you folk?" Even his voice had a subtle country twang. It was not too difficult to see how an impressionable young girl could be attracted to this aging caricature of the romantic Old West.

"Just a few questions, Mr. Grimstad," Blaze said after Ghost had made the necessary introductions. "We won't keep you long."

"So, what do you hope to turn up?" the old man asked, eyeing Connie with a barnyard candour that brought the blood surging to her cheeks. "I done told my piece so many times now, I'm beginnin' t'sound like a bloody parrot."

Blaze made an effort to smooth some hackles. "Mind if I call you Nels?"

"That's my name."

Blaze responded with a good-natured disarming smile. "You could have fooled me."

Grimstad broke the tension with a quick laugh. "The Willie Nelson bit, eh?"

"Well, there *is* a resemblance."

"Maybe so, Blaze, but I looked like me long b'fore that critter was knee-high to a cow's tit. *I* don't look like *him*, y'understand, *he* looks like *me*."

"Gotcha," Blaze acceded with a chuckle, "Nels, it is."

"Sing better'n him, too," Old Nels mused, "you just ask lil' Sarah—" He broke off abruptly and reached for a sack of fertilizer. When he straightened, his eyes had a blue sheen to them. "Say, let's get this over with, eh? I gotta lot more t'do than stand here jawin' with you bunch."

"Tell me about her," Blaze said gently.

"Sarah-Sue? She just popped up one April like a black-eyed Susan, 'cept her eyes was blue. She brightened up an old man's life for a time, then one day she went the way of the summer wind. Like as not, she'll just pop up again next spring, blue-eyed'n'sassy as ever." He groped angrily for a sack of fertilizer, fumbling through the film of moistness that had suddenly veiled his eyes.

"How old was she?" Blaze asked, "back then, back in April—?"

"Five — eleven — sixteen — "

At that moment, a muted growing clamour from the depths of the orchard swelled suddenly to such a crescendo that Grimstad's addled grief was lost in the din. All heads turned toward the offending tumult.

"That'll be Peaches," Grimstad stated flatly. "Silly old bitch."

A contrivance that vaguely resembled an old orchard tractor emerged from the fruit trees and advanced toward them. A loose pile of rusted metal seemed to be cradled between four wobbly wheels and powered by nothing more potent than the final heaves of its own death throes.

"It looks like something out of an old Rube Goldberg cartoon," Blaze muttered.

"With a little help from Dr. Frankenstein," Connie added. "Look what's driving it."

As the weird assemblage finally shuddered to a welcome, if reluctant standstill, the resulting chaotic blur slowly gave shape to a little old lady sitting astride the still idly tottering bucket seat.

Connie gawked in awe. She could not recall ever having seen anyone quite so old. Had Grimstad told her, then and there, that a week-old cadaver had been exhumed that very morning and propped up on the seat of the old tractor as some grim and tasteless joke, she would have believed him. But 'Peaches', as he had called her, was far from dead.

"Who's this bloody lot, then? Eh?" The old woman looked them over, each in turn, then singled out Blaze with a mindless cackle. "You're the law, aincha?" Then, to Ghost, "You too,eh? Them plain clothes don't fool me. I can spot you lot a mile off, eh?"

Her sunken eyes sought out Connie, looking so pristinely out of place in her all-white ensemble. "So the old fart's got hisself a new darlin', eh? Best keep an eye on that one, child, he's got the diddly-itch of a two-pronged goat."

She turned back to Blaze. "Lock the bugger up, I say. Best place for the likes of him, eh?"

Grimstad's jaw tightened beneath the white bristles. "Don't pay her no mind," he said with quiet vehemence, "she's about as hung together as that pile of junk she's squattin' on." He circled his right ear with a meaningful finger. "The old crone's head been empty as a dry well for nigh on twenty years, but she still keeps droppin' the bucket."

The old woman ignored him.

"That's why you're here, ain't it?" she persisted to Blaze, "'bout that l'il girl, Sarry-Sue, went missin' couple months back—" She pointed a bony finger at Connie. "Or have y'all caught'm fawnin' an' pawin' at this one now? Jeeze Christ, can y'cotton it? And Sarry-Sue at that, scars'n all?" She wagged a gnarled old finger at Connie. "It'll serve y'bloody right,mind, dressing yur body parts up like y'aint wearin' much else'n a coat a white paint."

Connie drew her car coat together and edged back behind her partner's burly shoulder.

Grimstad turned to Blaze and Ghost, neither of whom had uttered a word. "Do I gotta listen to this shit?" he seethed. "The old witch is a certified flake. Can't you see that?"

Blaze shrugged a noncommittal eyebrow.

"Look." Grimstad calmed himself with effort. "*You* know, and *I* know," he said evenly, "and Miss Wells most certainly knows, that I ain't done no fawnin' or pawin' at her, now or never, as this old hag is lettin' on, and my relationship with Sarah-Sue has been common knowledge from Duck Lake to Kalamalka, ever since she first come to visit me. I ain't got a friggin' thing to hide, I tell you, and this old bitch knows it better'n anyone."

The old lady wilted under the weight of Grimstad's sudden wrath. "No need t'rant'n'rave," she said with surly but cautious constraint. "Just come t'buy a sack of 34, is all."

Grimstad tossed a sack of fertilizer on a small pallet that hung by a twist of haywire behind the old tractor. "Won't do you no good till the frost comes outta the ground," he told her, "but least now you got no excuse to be comin' back. No charge, y'understand, just take it and go. And get that pile of junk offa my place b'fore I truck it off to the dump."

Without another word, the old woman coaxed the old machine into motion and turned it back, wheezing and clanking, into the maze of trees from whence it had come.

"Who is that woman?" Blaze asked when the sounds of her retreat had subsided sufficiently for his words to be heard.

"Name's Wanda Ballicks, truth to tell." Grimstad raised his right hand in solemn oath as Connie rolled her eyes. "Lost her old man 'bout twenty years ago, along with any moxy she mighta been clingin' to at the time. Sticks to herself, mostly; hardly ever opens her mouth. Got something in her craw now, though. Christ, never heard her spout off like that b'fore."

"You called her, Peaches," Connie reminded him. She felt his eyes on her again.

Grimstad walked the few paces to the centre of the clearing behind the storage shed, motioning them to follow. He pointed along the gentle south slope of the orchard to where an unpainted old shack squatted like an ugly wart among the trees. Even in their dormant leafless stage, it was quite apparent that these trees were of a different variety than those populating the orchard at large.

"That's my peach block," Grimstad told them, "'cept for that one overgrown acre that the shack sits on. That, in fact, is what Wanda Ballicks calls home. Y'can see a ring of peach trees round it, even from here, about a dozen of 'em now, I guess, all stole and replanted from my peach block."

"How can you be so sure?"

"Every year or so, we find a tree missing, same time as she ends up with a new one. Y'see, up here on the bench, peach trees have a way of frosting out, so every now and then they have to be replaced. Fortunately, peach trees, unlike apples or pears, are quick to come back and fruit-up again. Oh, she been takin' them all right."

"You don't try to stop her? Catch her at it?"

"Cagey old bitch'd make it more trouble'n it's worth. 'Sides, a new tree's only worth 'bout six or seven bucks, the way we buy 'em. I just call her Peaches to let *her* know that *I* know what's goin' on. As if she gave a damn."

"And 34?" Connie asked. "What's a sack of 34?"

"Short for 34-0-0; ammonium nitrate, used by most orchardists as a source of nitrogen. Fertilizer; the stuff I been off-loadin'. Costs about five loonies a sack. Cheap enough way t'get shed of her, wouldn't y'say?"

"When was the last time she stole a tree?" Blaze asked.

"Uh — late last fall, as I remember. We'd just done a fall plantin' and when we went back next day to water 'em down, sure 'nough, one was missin'. And lo'n behold," the old man raised both arms in mock conjuration, "a new tree had sprung up overnight in Peaches' garden."

"But you never saw her take one."

"Didn't have to."

"And you never confronted her with the theft."

"No." Grimstad began to show signs of annoyance. "So what's the big deal? You come all the way out here to arrest an old hag for stealin' a peach tree? Let it go, man, it don't make no never mind to me."

Connie adroitly changed the subject. "What about Sarah-Sue, Mr. Grimstad?" she asked quietly, "What did *she* think about Peaches, as you call her."

Grimstad shrugged his shoulders. "Most kids steered clear of the old hag. They figured she was some kind of witch. Only time anyone goes near that old shack is to get eggs."

"Eggs?"

"Yeah. Peaches raises chickens; sells off the eggs. Damn good eggs, too. Lets the chickens run free. And for a buck and a half a dozen — ?"

"You buy them yourself?"

"Not a chance. Not if I gotta go and pick 'em up. When Sarah-Sue'd ride over and get some for her pa, I'd get her to pick some up for me."

Connie scanned the open areas behind the buildings. A couple of brown horses grazed idly in one of two small corrals. "You keep horses, then?"

"Couple." He glanced toward the corral. "Kids like to ride 'em. Young girls, mostly. Sarah-Sue was a natural."

"There were other girls? Come to, uh — ride?"

"Some."

"Was there any other girl that Sarah-Sue was friendly with? Anyone special?"

Grimstad scratched his scalp thoughtfully. "Nope," he said finally, "Sarah-Sue rode with me, mostly, or by herself. She was kind of a loner; know what I mean?"

"Just one more thing, Nels, and we'll let you get on with your day." Blaze rested a huge friendly hand on one of Grimstad's wiry shoulders. "Did you notice anything, well — different about Sarah-Sue, before she disappeared?"

"Different?"

"You know; her hair, her clothes, her moods — "

"Nope, can't say's I did. She was growin' up, mind, gettin' to be quite a young lady — "

"You mean physically?"

"Yeah." He uttered what Connie thought to be a low satyric chuckle. "Used to kid her about it. 'Gettin' too big for your britches,' I'd tell her." He laughed outright. "Just the week b'fore she went missin' — she actually split her seat gettin' up on old Mawd, there. Had to lend her a pair of my old jeans to get home with."

Then, strangely, Connie thought, his eyes misted with genuine tears.

The van was parked in a pull-out along Highway 97, midway between Winfield and Oyama, overlooking Wood Lake. The three investigators were lounging in the back, sipping coffee and munching on sandwiches that Connie had fashioned from a fresh loaf of French bread, a can of salmon, chopped green onions and a generous splash of mayonnaise.

"Delicious," Blaze was saying. "Never knew anyone who could make something out of nothing taste so good, like good old Con."

Ghost concurred. "You missed your calling, Connie."

"Like making some jerk a good wife?" Connie quipped.

Blaze reached for another sandwich. "These things are good, my love, but not that good. Still, no sense letting them go to waste."

"Don't worry, Connie," Ghost said without conviction, "he'll come around. Give him time."

"Time's up," Connie chirped as she snatched the last sandwich out from under Blaze's big fist. "Maybe I ought to starve him into submission."

"Starve," Blaze repeated softly, "*starve*." He seemed suddenly to be in another world. "That's it, Connie. You're a genius. Don't you see? The kid was starved."

"Sarah-Sue?"

"Not physically," Blaze mused, "emotionally, perhaps; or maybe *psychically* would be even closer to the truth."

"Never a child; not yet an adult," Connie said, pursuing his train of thought. "You mean she was living her life in a kind of limbo, somewhere between a bug and a butterfly?"

"Something like that," Blaze agreed, snatching the half-eaten last sandwich from her startled grasp, "but time has a way of catching up. No one can long deny the metamorphic miracle of puberty."

"Beast," Connie pouted as she watched the sandwich disappear in a single gulp.

"But there was no one else in her life," Ghost reminded them, "apart from her father, of course, and Old Nels."

Connie shivered. "Talk about being visually undressed," she reflected. "I wouldn't trust that bogus cowboy any further than I could throw the glutton who just gobbled up my last sandwich."

"Enough, enough," Ghost protested. "You two act like you're married already. And I feel obliged to remind you both that we're not here to psychobiologically dissect the missing girl; we're here to *find* her."

"Too true," Blaze replied softly, "but wouldn't it be easier to find a needle in a haystack if the needle was threaded, and we knew the colour of the thread?"

"Oh, oh," Connie sighed knowingly, "he's on one of his hunches."

Blaze nodded. "Let's just call it a working hypothesis. But I'm going to have to go it alone for a while."

Ghost moved at once toward the radio. "We'll need another car," he said matter-of-factly, "and what else?"

"Some answers." Blaze waited until the Mountie had given their location to a P.C. that was in the area on General Duty. "I'd like you and Connie to work together on this," he said as Ghost hung up the mike. "I want *answers*, and I don't care who you get them from, Prescott, Grimstad, H.Q., or even *N'Ha-a-itk*." Connie recognized the Indian name for the Okanagan's legendary lake monster, Ogopogo, from a case they had worked on a few months back.

"Give," Connie said simply, pad and pen in hand.

"Okay. How long have the Prescotts lived in that cabin? Where did they live before? What made Madeline Myers leave as she did? And look beyond the obvious travelling salesman scenario. And I want Sarah-Sue's medical and dental records — "

"You think she's dead?" Ghost asked, then added a little defensively. "Not having found her, you understand, we didn't think we needed them for an I.D."

"We might need them to prove she's *not* dead," Blaze said cryptically, "and, I want a total on Wanda Ballicks, before and after the death of her husband. I want a prior and an update on our local Willie Nelson. I'm particularly curious as to how he came by those two parallel scars on his left cheek."

"We have most of this stuff at H.Q. in Kelowna," Ghost put in, "but we'll still have to make a few calls."

"I'll meet you in John's office at, say — five o'clock."

"10-4."

"And where will you be while we're doing all the work?" Connie wondered, arching a quizzical eyebrow.

"I'll be touching base with the Quebecois and the three 'juvies' who'd been giving Sarah-Sue a bad time."

"The high shool, George Eliot Secondary, is east of the highway," Ghost told him, "just below the Berry Road turn-off. You can't miss the big sign, GESS, on the front of the main building. The kids get out around three."

"And our francophone friend?"

"Pruning apple trees at Frank O'Hara's place, the next orchard down Seaton Road from Grimstad's."

"You really think you've got a handle on this?" Connie asked, recognizing the subtle but all too familiar signs of a possible *denouement* in the offing.

"I'm not looking for a handle, Connie, just a piece of *arriere-pensée* to thread a needle."

Blaze watched Connie and Ghost being chauffeured away in a blue'n'white before heading the black van back toward Seaton Road. Frank O'Hara's orchard was well marked and Blaze had no difficulty in locating the itinerant pruner, Michel Oddette. He was up a three-legged aluminum ladder, hacking away at a huge old apple tree with a pair of long-handled shears.

"You Oddette?" Blaze said, beckoning the man down with a jerk of his head.

Oddette descended the ladder slowly, then nodded. "You a cop?"

Blaze flashed his long-expired badge in the interest of breath and brevity. "I want you to tell me what you know about Sarah-Sue," he said. The acrimonious tenor of his voice left no room for misunderstanding.

"Sarah-Sue? The girl what went missin'? I keep tellin' you guys, over'n'over, I hardly knew the kid. She never talked to nobody, least of all, me. Old Nels'll tell you that."

Oddette had small shifty eyes and a skinny little body that barely seemed to exist beside and beneath the towering ex-Mountie. Blaze knew Oddette's type well: petty crime and pot. He'd be well known to local members of the Force as a Puker, or a Shit Rat. And in this case, a potential paedophile to boot.

"What'd she look like without her panties on?" Blaze growled, prying up the man's chin with a beefy finger.

"Huh?"

Blaze's voice took on the force of a violent act. "Listen, punk, you come straight with me, right now, or I'll put you where the sun don't shine and you'll stay there till the cockroaches begin the look good enough to peek at. Do you get the message?"

The little man nodded almost eagerly.

"Give," Blaze told him bluntly.

"We were picking apples at Grimstad's," Oddette began nervously, after a slight hesitation. He was finding it hard to speak with his chin being forced up against his nose. "She wouldn't give me the time o'day, man, I never made a move on her. Old Nels saw to that. But — "

"But?"

"There was an outside john near a hollow on the north side of the pear block, and — well, you guys already know I been nailed before for, uh, you know — lookin'."

"Peeking," Blaze prompted, "exposing — "

"Okay, okay. So that's what I did. I peeked. And that's *all* I did. And what's more, I wish I bloody hadn't."

"Meaning?"

"She weren't like a ordinary girl, man. She'd been burned or somethin'. Messed up. Know what I mean? Just lookin' at her, man, almost made me lose my cookies — "

"Why didn't you say anything about this before?"

"You kiddin'?"

Blaze lifted the man bodily by one arm and placed him half way up the ladder. With the other hand, he gave him the shears. "Go back to work," he said tiredly, "but don't even think about leaving town without seeing me first, you got that?"

Oddette nodded numbly, but as Blaze walked away, the *emigré* from Quebec had no cognizance of the depth of sorrow that had crept into the big man's heart.

By the time Blaze had found his way back through the Berry Road intersection to the high school, hordes of kids were already ambling away toward home in loose groups and clusters, causing vehicular traffic to halt and honk its way through a human maze of teenage insouciance. He pulled over to the curb to watch and ruminate.

By and large, the kids were a delight to watch but the flagrant disregard of the dissident few to any kind of authority seemed, to Blaze as he sat there, to be a symptom of a deeper, more lingering disaffection; it was in its finality, he decided, to be the loss of youth itself. He heaved a sigh in idle reminiscence of happier times.

But how did Sarah-Sue fit into all this? Had she, by some tragic anomaly, unwittingly fallen into the lure of the lunatic fringe? How had she been so badly burned? And where was she now?

He spotted the three misfits he was after, cruising slowly back and forth in front of the school yard, in a beat-up old Ford. They were whistling and taunting the other kids above the din of too-loud rock, and yet, for all their caterwauling, Blaze was gratified to see that they were largely ignored by the majority of students. On one of their sorties, Blaze manoeuvred the black van in behind the Ford and delivered a resounding jolt with his front bumper. The effect was immediate and gratifying.

The car stopped. The music died. And three irate young males popped out of the vehicle like corks out of a bad batch of beer. The air turned suddenly blue from more than a badly needed ring job.

"What in hell y'tryin' to'do, man?" That, Blaze guessed from Ghost's briefing, would be Billy Sanford; black T-shirt, black jeans, and a pockmarked face that, at the moment, had taken on the colour and lustre of a thick-skinned orange.

"Yeah, what'n hell y'tryin' t'do, eh?" And that would be Sanford's echo, Jake Wilmans; skinny as a rake without the claws and about as threatening.

"Hey, mister — what'd you go do that for, huh?" And that, of course, would be Sly Farquat, awkwardly large, pea brained, and probably just a well-meaning mindless lout were it not for the influence of his surly cohorts.

Blaze met their puerile intimidation with a wide grin.

"Pleasure's all mine," he said as he flashed his bogus I.D. "Roll that tin can you call a car over there, into the parking lot. We're going to have a little chat."

"Shit. Not another cop — "

"We already tol' you all we know — "

"That couldn't have taken long," Blaze said, backing off the van. "Now move it."

"Listen, guy," Billy Sanford whined, "we got rights, too -"

Blaze grabbed a handful of black T-shirt. "I said, *move it!*" His voice heralded the wrath of God.

In the parking lot, Blaze invited them into the van. They sat around the fold-out table as he tossed them each a cold Pepsi from the fridge. They accepted the pop with a hint of caution. This was something new.

Blaze turned first to Billy Sanford. "Tell me about Sarah-Sue," he said.

"What's to tell?"

"How about the time you took her for a ride?"

"Hey," Sly Farquat blurted out, "how'd you know — "

"Shut up, you brainless tit," Sanford cut in, then, to Blaze, "So we took her for a ride, so what?"

"Where'd you take her?"

"We just drove around, no big deal."

Blaze put a hand the size of a twenty-ounce T-bone on Sanford's shoulder, then squeezed. The kid yelped with pain. "I want to know *when, where and what,*" the big ex-Mountie said quietly, "and you are going to tell me — one way, or the other." He emphasized the last word with another squeeze.

"Okay, okay." Sanford rubbed his shoulder. "We got nothin' to hide. There's a deserted pickers' cabin up off Middlebench Road in Oyama, 'bout five miles from here, back of Nywoods Orchard against the mountain. No one ever goes there, 'cept us guys, sometimes, you know, to shoot the shit — "

"And share a toke," Blaze added.

Sanford glanced warily at his two companions. "Look, we didn't force her to come with us. It was like she wanted to, well - - fool around. Know what I mean? When we got to the cabin, me and Jake decided to oblige, that's all. She never said a word. She never tried to stop us. She could've got up and walked out at any time — "

"Got up?"

"There's a bed with an old mattress in the cabin. She just lay back with her arms across her face and let us do whatever we wanted. She was enjoying it, too, till we tried to take her jeans off."

"And did you?"

"No way, man. We just got 'em down enough to see the way she'd been burned, or somethin'. Hey that was enough for me."

"Me, too," Jake joined in. "Put me right off, know what I mean? Me and Bill, we went out and sat in the car. We lit up a smoke and waited for her and Sly to join us."

"And?"

Billy Sanford turned to Farquat. "This is your gig, big guy. You was the only one in there with her. *You* tell him."

Genuine tears misted the big lug's eyes. "She was like a little puppy," he said softly, "she was cryin' and whimperin' and I just cuddled her, that's all. I just cuddled her and stroked her like a little puppy. Honest to God, man, I didn't do nothin' — it was *her* what did it to *me*. Somehow, she got me inside her jeans and — ''

''And?''

''And it happened. That's all. It just happened.''

Farquat began to cry openly. He reminded Blaze of John Steinbeck's pathetic character, Lennie, in *Of Mice and Men*.

''Whatever did happen didn't take long,'' Billy Sanford volunteered. ''They both came out before we'd even finished our cigarette.''

''Then what?''

''Nobody said nothin' to nobody,'' Sanford said. ''I just drove her back to Al Greene's place where she lives.''

''And when did all this happen?''

''Christ, I dunno. Sometime in late August, I guess.''

''Yeah,'' Wilmans recalled, ''it was just before we started back to school.''

''Did it happen more than once?''

''No way, man.'' All three were adamant in their denial. ''She went right back to treatin' us like we didn't even exist, like she always used to. That was one weird kid, man, with or without her pants.''

''She just didn't have no one to love her,'' Sly Farquat said sadly. He turned to Blaze. ''How'd she get all burned like that?'' he asked with feeling. ''I just felt so sorry for her. She was so pretty — ''

''Why didn't you tell all this to the police?'' Blaze asked as he opened the van's sliding side door.

''Nobody asked,'' Sanford said with sarcasm, then, after a thoughtful pause, ''You mean you ain't a cop?''

''Nope.''

''Whyn't you tell us, f'Chrissake?''

Blaze echoed the boy's response to his own question only moments before. ''Nobody asked,'' he replied with mock innocence.

Connie and Ghost were waiting in John Warfield's office when Blaze arrived back in Kelowna.

''Did you find her?'' Warfield asked without fanfare.

Blaze shook his head. ''But I will,'' he said, ''if that's any consolation.'' He turned to Connie and Ghost. ''What did you two come up with?''

"Plenty," Connie responded, "but it's all so, kind of — disconnected. Still, if I were a betting girl, I'd put my money on that lecherous old cowboy."

"But can you prove anything?"

Connie rolled her emerald green eyes in frustration.

"Too pat," Ghost put in. "Connie's understandably upset at being ogled, but that doesn't make the man guilty of anything more serious than bad manners. There is more here, Stu, than flotsam and jetsom."

Connie perked. "Flotsam and jetsom?"

"He means," Stu volunteered, "that there is more to this case than can be seen floating on the surface. And I tend to agree. Did you get the info I asked for?"

"That, and more," Ghost assured him. "I think your little analogy about the needle in the haystack possibly having a thread attached, got us looking a little deeper. You know, beyond the obvious — "

A light tap on the open door heralded the sudden appearance of Jan Thurston. "I've made reservations at the *Fintry Queen* for four, as you requested," she told Warfield, "for six o'clock. I'll be leaving shortly. Is there anything else, sir, before I go?"

"Thank you, Jan." Warfield glanced at his watch. "Now, if you'll just pour us an *aperitif* from my, uh — private 'medicine chest,' you'll be free to leave. And, Jan, if you'd care to join us – ?"

"Thank you, sir, but no. I'm driving."

"Wise choice, my girl," Warfield said as the pretty receptionist meted out their pre-dinner libation. To the others, he said, "We'll be walking. The *Fintry* is only a few blocks from here."

"The *Fintry Queen*," Connie reflected. "Isn't that the old paddlewheeler that's moored at the entrance to City Park?"

"The same," Ghost affirmed. "Actually, it's a floating restaurant. If this was July instead of January, we could have taken a dinner cruise around Lake Okanagan."

"No time for cruises," Warfield barked.

"With respect, John," Blaze announced ominously, "I don't think time is a factor anymore."

"Oh, God. You mean the girl is dead?"

"I believe she is."

"But when you came in, you said you would find her."

"And I will, believe me. But as Old Nels reminded us, black-eyed Susans only resurrect themselves in April," he said soberly. "This is January."

They were shown to a corner table that provided a modicum of privacy. The interior of the *Fintry Queen* was tastefully nautical and the menu offered a Captain's Plate the appealed to all four of them, with Blaze ordering a half dozen raw Pacific oysters on the side.

"Well, well," Connie mused esoterically, "this promises to be an eventful night."

Blaze grinned. "Down girl," he cautioned softly.

Warfield seemed oblivious to the inside banter. "I would like to remind you people," he said with a tempered show of authority, "that this is a working dinner. And, Stu, you've got some explaining to do. I want to know what makes you think that Sarah-Sue is about to show up dead after going missing for no apparent reason."

"John, there was a reason."

"Oh?"

"She was pregnant."

All eyes focused on the big ex-Mountie.

"I'll explain," Blaze said quietly, "but first I'd like some input from Connie and Ghost. Let's start with how long the Prescotts have been living in that pickers' cabin."

"Ten years," Ghost said, "give or take."

"And before that?"

"Calgary, Stu. And there's more."

"Madeline Myers," Blaze prompted, "was not Sarah-Sue's biological mother."

Ghost drew a tolerant sigh. "Okay — so how did you know that?"

Blaze bowed his head and placed his palms together. "Confucius say: mother rarely leave young without cause."

"Mmmmm." Ghost creased his dusty eyebrows. "Sometimes, my friend, I wonder whether your revelations are insight or insult. I mean, it's obvious, isn't it? After it's been said."

"Columbus and the egg," Blaze added dryly.

"Okay. So do you want to hear the rest?" Ghost asked with mild chagrin.

"Shoot."

113

"Sarah-Sue's biological mother was Susan Dilworth. She and Bernie Prescott were married about a year before the birth of Sarah-Sue. They lived in wedded bliss until Sarah-Sue was about three. Then tragedy struck."

Ghost paused while their dinners were placed before them.

"Yuck," Connie muttered as she watched Blaze wolf down a whole raw oyster from an upturned half shell. "How can you *do* that? They're still alive, you know."

"Beats eating a corpse," Blaze chuckled as he sent another bivalve to the great ocean in the sky. "Listen." He turned his head attentively. "It's like putting a conch to your ear. I can actually hear the sounds of the sea."

"That's called the collywobbles," Connie told him.

"Collywobbles?"

"Gas," Connie affirmed, "and little wonder — "

"Enough," Warfield interceded, "let's get on with it. Ghost, you spoke of a tragedy."

Ghost swallowed, coughed into a gray fist, then continued. "It was during a power outage. Prescott had lit one of those white-gas lamps you often see in camping sites. Then, a few bizarre coincidences: Susan took a bath with a candle for company, Bernie went outside to see if the outage was local or city-wide, and Sarah-Sue, left alone for only a few moments, inadvertently toppled the gas lamp into her lap."

"Oh, wow," Connie breathed.

"The lamp fell from her lap to the floor," Ghost went on, "but not before spilling enough gas to inflict second and third degree burns to her lower abdomen, pubic area and the fronts of her thighs. Bernie smothered the flames on Sarah-Sue with his own body and got her out of the house just as the broken lamp sent a surge of fire flashing across the room. Bernie managed to get his wife out, as well, but by then the house was totally engulfed. She died, later, in hospital. Bernie, too, was hospitalized for a time. He had acted quite heroically."

"Sarah-Sue," Blaze said. "Was there no attempt made at plastic surgery?"

"She was too young, too weak — in the beginning. And when she was finally released from hospital, Bernie began to run into problems with the authorities regarding his ability to care for the child on his own. In a desperate move to get the social workers off his back, he married Madeline Myers, but it soon became obvious that the cure was going to be worse than the malady. His subsequent move out of the province, to Winfield, was just another attempt to distance himself from the bureaucracy."

"Talk about Murphy's Law," Warfield muttered, "anything that could go wrong, did go wrong."

"Well," Ghost countered, between forkfuls of seafood and sips of local wine, "to both Bernie and Sarah-Sue, the departure of Madeline Myers was a relief and a blessing, rather than a loss. Still, it did resurrect the threat of intervention by a new conspiracy of social do-gooders, a concern that was unexpectedly nullified by the caring, sensitive, rural community that now harboured them. This new low-profile security, however, meant that any corrective surgery for Sarah-Sue had to be put on hold."

"Low profile?" Connie exclaimed. "The man was the town drunk."

"Who's perfect?" Ghost said dramatically. "Prescott blames himself, not kismet, for the death of his wife and the cross he feels *he* has given Sarah-Sue to bear. The whisky is his way of diluting his inner grief and guilt."

"And no one locally apparently knew of the girl's disfigurement," Warfield added. "It all fits, except why and how she went missing. Stu?"

Blaze had polished off his oysters and was well into his Captain's Plate. "Let's hear from Connie first," he said. "I think she may have more of the answers."

"I have?" Connie looked bemused. She pushed back her plate and opened a small black notebook. "Force of habit," she confided, then, "Okay, let's start with medical records. For Sarah-Sue, there are none; they terminated in Calgary. Dental? Yes, a local dentist in Winfield, where she paid cash for a few porcelain fillings and one extraction. They have x-rays on file, if or when we need them."

She looked up with a disdainful curl of her upper lip. "Willie Nelson. It's all in his head, thank God. He's a eunuch, or as good as. He's been functionally impotent since being kicked by a horse in his early teens. He lived with his parents (who originally owned the orchard) until their deaths about fifteen years ago. The mother went first; the father ten months later. He never married (understandably) but just because he can't, uh—you know, does not let him off the hook—"

Blaze cut her short. "Just the facts, ma'am."

Connie took a deep count-to-ten breath. "Peaches *aka* Wanda Ballicks was widowed twenty years ago. Her husband had been a well-liked and highly respected M.D.-cum-veterinarian, serving the greater Winfield area. He'd make a house call for a foaling mare as quickly as he would for an ailing child. Wanda has been his 'gofer', receptionist, bookkeeper, nurse — whatever. She even assisted him in minor surgery, to man and animal alike. Ballicks was sorely missed by the community when he died and Wanda was devastated. She appeared to decline mentally as well as physically almost overnight, and she drifted quickly into the life of a recluse, rarely leaving that old shack. She'll be ninety-two in June."

"What about those two parallel scars on Grimstad's face?" Blaze asked. "Anything there?"

Connie shook her auburn head. "They were inflicted years ago by a pitchfork, wielded by his father. An accident. He was lucky not to lose an eye."

"Mmmmm."

Connie closed her notebook. "So what's this about Sarah-Sue being dead?"

"A hypothetical hunch," Blaze mumbled around a mouthful of seafood, "nothing more." He then recounted his meetings with Michel Oddette and the three teenage misfits, leaving out nothing but his strong-arm tactics and the outdated bogus badge.

"You certainly manage to get a lot out of people when we're not around," Connie noted suspiciously.

"Is that little huddle with the Farquat boy," Warfield asked, "all you have to suggest the girl was pregnant?"

"Nope." Blaze cleared his mouth with a sip of wine. "But it does add weight to a few former observations. Prescott told us that Sarah-Sue had been 'feeling poorly' just before she went missing, 'tummy aches' that she had shrugged off as a touch of the flu — "

"Morning sickness," Connie speculated, "and the timing does fit in with her trip to the cabin."

"Agreed," Blaze went on, "and you'll recall that both her father and Old Nels drew attention to her recently burgeoning young body, not to mention the splitting of her jeans when she tried to mount one of Grimstad's horses." Blaze yielded to a thoughtful pause. "It just seems to me to be somewhat excessive, even given the normal post-pubescent metamorphosis she was obviously going through, and, well, everything considered, not a little coincidental."

"You may be right, Stu," Warfield allowed, "but the girl being pregnant doesn't get us any closer to her sudden disappearance."

"It puts a thread in the needle," Blaze suggested as he turned to Connie. "Tell me, what would *you* do if you were Sarah-Sue's age and you suddenly found yourself pregnant?"

Connie coloured in spite of herself. "Well," she pondered, "I guess I'd consider my only alternatives; to have the baby or abort it."

"Would you think of leaving town? Go somewhere you weren't known?"

"An older girl might, but Sarah-Sue wasn't yet thirteen. And I can't see her leaving her father without telling him."

"Nor I," Blaze agreed, "which means she'd either try to abort herself or seek out help."

"Someone she trusted?" Connie's tone was dubious. "A stranger?"

"Where is all this going?" Warfield growled.

"They are hypothesizing on the still unverified premise," Ghost announced dryly, "that something extraordinary must have happened to Sarah-Sue to bring about her sudden disappearance. From their investigations thus far, and I tend to concur, pregnancy is a credible postulate. It has many ramifications."

"Do go on," Blaze urged his pallid friend.

"If an abortion did occur," Ghost continued, "and it was successful, it would be immaterial whether it was self-induced or not, seeing that Sarah-Sue would then still be among us and we would not be here looking for her."

"On the other hand, if Sarah-Sue had made an unsuccessful attempt to abort herself (given the propensity of severe and often lethal haemorrhaging that is synonymous with botched abortions) we surely would have found some sign of her by now. That leaves us with only one possible conclusion."

"Somebody else botched it for her," Connie softly spelled it out, "and then disposed of the body."

"Sounds plausible," Warfield conceded cautiously, "but it's still only a theory."

"And who would risk — ?"

Blaze cut Connie off in mid-sentence. "Ghost, we'll need a search warrant. Tomorrow morning will be soon enough."

"Wanda Ballicks?"

"Who else? And, John, I'll need the go-ahead to do a little digging on the old woman's property."

"A couple of men with shovels?"

"In January? How about a back-hoe?"

"You call that a *little* digging?"

"A good man with a back-hoe could dig up that entire acre and leave it as smooth as a ballerina's belly."

"And I know just the guy," Ghost told me. "Lives on Okanagan Centre Road, near the Fire Hall, no more than a mile from Peaches' Palace."

"Set it up for about ten o'clock tomorrow morning. That'll give us time to make it legal."

"As if that ever bothered you." Warfield looked at Blaze warily. "I hope you know what you're doing."

"That makes two of us," Blaze responded with a boyish grin.

"Three," Connie added impishly.

It had all the earmarks of a parade, winding up the narrow snow-covered driveway towards Wanda Ballicks' tumbledown shanty. The black van led the way with Blaze at the wheel, Connie at his side and Ghost leaning forward attentively from the swivel. A blue'n'white followed closely behind, bearing a uniformed driver and Inspector John Warfield lounging comfortably in the back seat. The back-hoe came next, looking like a huge praying mantis with its front appendages curled up under its yellow body. And bringing up the rear, a battered old Chevy pickup, as though umbilically attached to the back-hoe, hauling in the 'infantry', so to speak, the shovels, picks, pipes and wrenches, to 'mop up' after the high-tec onslaught of the mammoth earthmover.

The time was 10:07 A.M.

"Hold it right there." The door of the shanty had opened and Wanda Ballicks stood in the darkened opening, a double-barrelled shotgun cradled unsteadily in her emaciated old arms. "This here's private property."

The van was about thirty feet from the old woman as Blaze brought it to a halt. "Stay inside," he said to his companions as he opened his door and stepped out, standing behind the cover of the door.

"We're here on official police business," Blaze told the woman calmly. "Put down the gun, please."

"So, it's you." Peaches sounded a little less belligerent at the sight of Blaze. "Why'nt y'wearin' yur policeman's duds?"

John Warfield emerged slowly on the same side and joined Blaze behind the cover of the door. He was in uniform, majestically bestowing flesh and bone to the immutable concept of law and order.

"Put down the gun," he said evenly, "we're not here to harm you, Mrs. Ballicks."

The old woman hesitated, but only momentarily. The sheer weight of jurisprudence that now confronted her was overpowering. As the gun went down, Connie, Ghost and the uniformed driver alighted from their vehicles as though on signal and all five converged on the wizened old woman.

Connie confiscated the gun and handed it back to the constable who had driven the blue'n'white. Ghost handed the bemused old crone a folded document, which she accepted without giving it a glance.

"That is a warrant," Ghost told her, not unkindly.

"It is our legal authorization to search your premises, as well as the property on which it stands. We will cause as little disruption to your home as possible and still achieve our purpose, and any disturbance to your land will be refurbished as necessary. Now, kindly cooperate by remaining close to Miss Wells and we will endeavour to be as brief as circumstances will allow."

As Warfield and Blaze exchanged droll glances over Ghost's pontifical dissertation, Connie led the now totally confused woman to the van and ensconced her comfortably on the built-in leather settee. She poured a cup of coffee which the woman had difficulty getting to her mouth without spilling. Since giving up the gun, Wanda Ballicks had not uttered a word.

The interior of the shack was a veritable graveyard of junk. Dust coated everything and cobwebs claimed the shadows in every corner. Warfield stood watching the search from just inside the door, not willing to dirty his hands in so lowly a pursuit.

"What do you hope to find?" he asked with a disdainful twitch of his aquiline nose.

"We'll know when we find it," Blaze responded ambiguously, then, a moment later, from the depths of a dresser drawer, he extracted a pair of frilly laced panties, almost identical to the pair he had held up in Sarah-Sue's bedroom when going through her clothes. "Bingo," he muttered softly.

"But can you prove they were Sarah-Sue's?"

"No," Blaze admitted tentatively. "But they sure as hell don't belong to Wanda." He placed them with care into a cellophane bag, then slipped bag and panties into an inside pocket. "The Forensic Lab has been known to get a conviction on a lot less than this," he added, "and now with the help of DNA — "

"You're reaching," Ghost said from the small adjoining kitchen, "besides, that would take time. We need something *now*, something more incriminating. Something like this, maybe." He held up a highly-polished tubular instrument that was open at one end and had a scoop-like aperture at the other.

"And what, pray tell," Warfield asked, "is that?"

"It's a curette, a medical instrument for performing curettage, usually with the help of suction, or, in lay terms, the extraction of unwanted tissue from certain body cavities — "

"Such as the uterus?" Blaze suggested hopefully.

"The uterine procedure to which you refer," Ghost said authoritatively, "is commonly known as a D and C, Dilation and Curettage, or the 'scraping' of the interior lining of the womb."

"An abortion, in other words."

"Not necessarily; but, yes, if performed in the early stages of pregnancy."

"How come you know all this, Ghost?" Blaze asked as he examined the instrument.

"My father, like Wanda Ballicks' husband, was, and is, a doctor; a practising gynecologist, in fact, in Vancouver."

"Yes," Warfield acknowledged, "I've met the gentleman. Where did you find this thing, Ghost?"

"In with the kitchen cutlery."

"Sweet Jesus," Blaze breathed incredulously. He straightened suddenly and fixed Ghost with a long enlightened look. "I *knew* she had a hand in this thing, Ghost, but it didn't click together until just now."

Ghost raised a dusty eyebrow. "You *knew*?"

"Think back," Blaze said reflectively, "to when she was screaming away at Grimstad from the seat of that scrap heap she calls a tractor. *Jeez Christ,* she told him, *can y'cotton it? And Sarry-Sue at that, scars'n all*? I thought at the time, as we all did, that she was referring to the parallel scars on Grimstad's face. But, as we found out later, he'd had those scars for years; they'd be as much a part of him to the old hag as his Willie Nelson image."

"You think she was referring to — "

"What else? And how could she have known about the scars on Sarah-Sue, unless — "

"It's still only conjecture," Warfield put in dubiously.

"Maybe it is," Blaze agreed, "but the panties are real and so is the curette. And together, they do give us enough to assume probable cause. That's all we need to dig up a few peach trees."

It took less than three hours to transform Wanda Ballicks' overgrown acre into a microcosm of Flanders' Field. The eleven once-proud peach trees that surrounded the house now lay flat against the snow, their naked upturned roots seemingly appalled at having been so rudely torn from their earthy haven. A black bodybag, sealed and tagged, hunched ominously beside each yawning cavity, except for one.

The Forensic Team and the Coroner had been called to the scene after the first tree had been uprooted, then stayed on to oversee the other ten exhumations. Each tree had been a living tombstone to some grisly find beneath its roots. Sarah-Sue Prescott, still reasonably well-preserved by the frozen soil in her shallow grave, had been the third to be unearthed. Her fragile remains had been reverently but hastily whisked away for immediate postmortem scrutiny.

A horde of ghoulish looky-loos had gathered on the perimeter of the property to ogle and speculate on the impromptu disinterments. Fluorescent tape barriers had been strung to keep the crowd well back, but extra police had to be called eventually to hold them at bay. Flashbulbs exploded to preserve the scene for posterity, media cameras whirred and news gatherers jostled with the mounting police presence for best advantage. It was a scene that the erstwhile peaceful community of Winfield would not soon forget.

Stu Blaze, from the relative isolation of the van, caught a peripheral glimpse of Bernie Prescott and Old Nels Grimstad being haplessly jostled among the crowd of onlookers. He shouldered his way through to them and plucked them bodily from the rabble, then escorted them back to the van where Connie plied them with coffee that had been liberally laced with Remy Martin. Both men were numb with shock and grief.

"I wish it could have ended differently," Blaze told the distraught father.

"You did say you'd find her, Mr. Blaze, you did promise me that."

"Leastways," Old Nels added sadly, "we can put her peacefully to rest now. Them months of not knowin' was just pure Hell."

"Yeah." Prescott looked a little stronger after a belt of fortified coffee. "But I really still don't know what happened, even now, 'cept my little girl is dead — and old Peaches been carted off to jail. Was it her what did it, Mr. Blaze?"

"It'll take time to sort it all out," Blaze told the two men. "We do know, however, that each tree hid the remains of one of God's creatures. Sarah-Sue was the only one who could be identified on the spot. The other ten had become no more than skeletal fragments: three obviously human, two dogs, one cat, a goat and four beyond immediate recognition. An eventual lab report will undoubtedly give us a full list."

"Three human?" Old Nels echoed softly. "You mean that Sarah-Sue wasn't the only poor tyke — ?"

"Look," Blaze interjected, "why don't I drive you two home right now? There's nothing you can do here. I'll send a car for you sometime tomorrow. We should have the whole story for you then."

Old Nels seemed to find something interesting in the bottom of his coffee cup. "Want some company tonight, Bernie?"

Prescott hesitated, but only briefly. "Sure," he said. He gave Blaze a wary glance. "All right if we pick up a bottle on the way?"

Blaze grinned inwardly. "My treat."

"Don't have a bed, though," Prescott said to Old Nels as the van eased out through the crowd, "if you've a notion to stay over- 'cept'n Sarah-Sue's."

After a prolonged silence, Old Nels said, "Think she'd mind if an old friend saddled up in it, this once?"

Bernie Prescott's face sagged into a tearful smile. "You know? I think Chipmunk'd like that, Nels. I purely do."

It was two days before Blaze and Connie were able to get back to Bernie Prescott. They found him at Old Nels' place, busily moving into the spare room in the bungalow, on a permanent basis.

"This orchard is gettin' to be too much for me t'handle," Old Nels explained. "Me and Bernie, we been settin' up a share-crop arrangement that'll give Bernie a personal stake in the place. It'll make things a lot easier for me, too. 'Sides, neither one of us got any family to fret on — " he drew a deep breath before adding, "'cept Sarah-Sue, bless her heart."

"Sounds like a great idea," Blaze said with feeling. "I think Sarah-Sue would be pleased."

"Where you got her?" Prescott asked abruptly.

"She's at a Kelowna mortuary," Blaze responded. "Ghost will be in touch later to help you with the funeral arrangements."

"Can you tell me now what happened to her?"

Blaze and Connie had joined the two men at an old country-style table. The room was rustic and friendly, if a little untidy, with a large stone fireplace that claimed one entire wall. The heady aroma of wood smoke and fresh coffee permeated the room.

It was Connie, in her delicate womanly way, that told of Sarah-Sue's pregnancy and the way it came about. "How and why she sought the help of Wanda Ballicks is not clear, but the old woman's attempt to abort the pregnancy caused a haemorrhage that resulted in your daughter's death. Sarah-Sue's suffering would have been relatively minimal," Connie added commiseratively, "and of short duration."

"The bloody old butcher," Bernie breathed vehemently.

"Two of the other three human exhumations," Connie went on, "were identified by dental records as local girls in their early teens. Their disappearances date well back and were thought at the time to have been runaways, to have left home of their own volition. Regrettably, the third one is still a Jane Doe."

"What about them damn roughnecks what messed with her?"

"The three boys," Connie continued, "will be charged, of course, but due to the lack of any apparent forceful confinement on their part and an obvious element of compliance by Sarah-Sue, it would seem more than likely that all three will be severely reprimanded and given suspended sentences. Possibly some form of community work effort."

"And I suppose Peaches'll be let off, too, 'long with the others," Bernie muttered.

"My guess," Blaze cut in, "is that her lawyers will plead insanity, and that, coupled with her advanced age, will likely see her incarcerated in some mental institution for the remainder of her life."

"She took my little girl," Bernie seethed. "She should be sent titless into eternal torment."

"Well," Old Nels reflected, a little more generously, "we do have our memories, Bernie. We'll always have those."

Connie Wells leaned forward from the swivel seat behind her favourite ex-Mountie as he idly wheeled the black van north on Highway 97, out of Kelowna, Winfield, Oyama — enroute to Calgary. Her arms circled his neck and she nibbled an earlobe before pressing a velvet cheek to one of his own. Blaze caught her mischievous wink in the rearview mirror and responded with an unabashed sigh of contentment.

"Glad it's all over?" he asked.

"Glad, but sad," Connie replied. "But, you know, I just can't understand why Sarah-Sue would go for help to that crazy old woman when she had two of the most caring people in the world to confide in."

"You've changed your mind about Old Nels?"

Connie chuckled. "I still think he covets my bod — "

Blaze grinned. "The man should be horse whipped."

" — but who can deny what a true-blue friend he was to Sarah-Sue. And now to her father. They're going to be a great comfort to each other."

"Kind of warms the heart, doesn't it?"

"But that horrible old woman," Connie persisted. "Four kids that we know of, and God only knows how many more innocent creatures — put to death. Why, that filthy acre was little more than a cemetery with peach trees in place of tombstones."

"Maybe," Blaze said, waxing suddenly philosophical, "Wanda Ballicks truly believed she was perpetuating the life cycle by providing her victims with a living symbol of reincarnation."

"You really believe that?"

"Well, life must go on."

Connie pondered the idea a moment. "You know, I kind of like that thought," she purred against his ear. "Especially the bit about perpetuating the life cycle. So why don't we pull over, love-of-my-life, and do some perpetuating of our own?"

"You want to plant a tree?"

"Well," Connie giggled, "I wouldn't have thought to put it quite that way — "

Why the C Was Boiling Hot
by *Charlotte MacLeod*

In 1992, Charlotte MacLeod adds another to her long list of accomplishments when she will be honoured with Lifetime Achievement recognition at Bouchercon XXIII. This story is a fine example of why she is so highly regarded. Richly comic, with vivid characters and a clever plot, it marks the third Cold Blood appearance of her reverend Stongitharm Goodheart.

WHY THE C WAS BOILING HOT
by *Charlotte Macleod*

"**P**apa, I'm going to be an oyster!"

The reverend Mr. Strongitharm Goodheart, pastor of the Deliverance Church in Pitcherville, New Brunswick, still unwearied after a long day of welldoing, picked up his golden-haired little daughter and swung her high over his head, laughing with her as she crowed with delight. "And is an oyster a wonderful thing to be?"

"Oh, yes, Papa! We're all going to be oysters, and the walrus is going to eat us."

Smiling, comely Mrs. Goodheart came to kiss her husband's cheek and relieve him of the child. "Give Papa a chance to take his coat off, Betsy. Mr. Card is getting up a pantomime, dear, for the children to perform at the Harvest Festival. He's going to read The Walrus and the Carpenter while the Sunday School children act out the story. The whole baby class will be the oysters and Billy's the Walrus. He's out in the woodshed right now, whittling himself some tusks out of corncobs."

"And I'm going to be one of the seven maids with seven mops," said the eldest daughter, a bonny lass of twelve or so, named Rachel. "It will be such fun, Papa! You'll have to think up a way to make the oyster shells, you're so clever. Aren't you glad Mr. Card has moved back to Pitcherville?"

"I don't think he's moved back, exactly." Strongitharm was always careful to speak the exact truth, though not always the whole truth, for that might have meant hurting somebody's feelings, and a faithful shepherd did not willingly cause suffering among his flock. "Mr. Card visited the farm once or twice as a little boy, as I understand it, but had never actually lived in Pitcherville until dear old Mr. Card passed to his heavenly home. This Mr. Card inherited the property because he was the only living relative."

"Rather a distant one, I believe." Mrs. Goodheart set a steaming bowl of mashed turnip on the table and added a dollop of freshly-churned butter, the gift of a grateful parishioner. "Come, Betsy, let me tie your pinafore. Rachel dear, please go tell Billy that supper is ready."

Mr. Goodheart washed his hands to set a good example, took his place at the head of the table, gazed fondly from his beloved helpmate at the opposite end to the merry-eyed blessings on either side of them, and bowed his head in heartfelt thanks, not forgetting to put in a polite request for enlightenment on the subject of oyster shells.

It was in fact Mrs. Goodheart who got the message about starching chicken-feed sacks and slitting holes in the sides and bottoms for the children's heads and arms to poke through. The resourceful Billy painted out the advertising and decorated the sacks oysterly enough to fool any Carpenter, though of course not a Walrus. No matter, Billy was confident enough of his dramatic powers to sustain the illusion for the duration of the pantomime, especially since he wasn't really going to eat the oysters anyway.

The Harvest Festival was, as all agreed, a total success. The chicken shortcake supper not only delighted all palates but also netted a tidy sum for the Steeple Fund. The pantomime afterward was truly the end of a perfect day, even if one of Billy Goodheart's tusks did come loose while he was holding his pocket handkerchief before his streaming eyes and sorting out the biggest oysters for his personal (though of course only make-believe) consumption.

Before the applause had quite died down, Mr. Card stepped forward to make an amusing little speech. Despite his having become a gentleman farmer, he looked far more the gentleman than the farmer in his natty brown suit with green windowpane checks, his high starched collar and voluminous russet-coloured cravat, his brown boots polished bright as horse-chestnuts and his equally bright brown hair plastered down with patent stickum. Mr. Goodheart noticed several young ladies gazing upon this dashing bachelor much as they had eyed the coconut layer cakes at the Harvest Supper. To his regret, he also observed sundry lowering scowls among the young fellows looking at the young ladies who were looking at Mr. Card. It might, the minister thought with a certain apprehension, take some fairly brisk shepherding to keep Mr. Card from becoming a focus of disharmony among this normally united congregation.

However it was not as a bone of contention that Mr. Card showed himself at the parsonage door early the following morning. Mr. Card was perturbed. He said so himself.

"Mr. Goodheart, I beg your pardon for delaying you in your daily round of welldoing, but I am perturbed. Strange things have happened at Card Castle."

Such was the whimsical name that old Mr. Card, who had himself been something of a card, had attached to his relatively modest farmhouse, the great barn that loomed behind it, and the indeed somewhat palatial pigpen that was situated behind the barn. In former years, a Card pig or two would have been among the main exhibits at the Harvest Fair. This year, the new Mr. Card had not seen fit to show any of the prize porkers he had so recently inherited, perhaps because he had felt diffident about hogging the show. But such speculation was not germane to the issue at hand, Strongitharm went directly to the point.

"What strange things are these, Mr. Card?"

"You won't believe me if I tell you. Come and see for yourself."

It would not have occurred to Strongitharm to doubt anybody's word without ample cause, but he was soon given reason to perceive with his own eyes why Mr. Card might have thought him a doubter. Although the distance from the parsonage to the farm could easily have been covered in ten minutes brisk walk, Mr. Card had elected to drive the elegant black-lacquered wagon with the bright red wheels that had been part of his inheritance. The high-stepping Morgan chestnut had just reached the road and begun to hit its stride when a dishevelled figure in a well-worn leather apron rushed into the road, waving his arms.

"Mr. Goodheart! Mr. Goodheart! I've been robbed!"

Mr. Card pulled the horses to a halt. "Aha!" he cried before Mr. Goodheart had a chance to speak, "and what have you been robbed of, Mr. Stitch?"

"My shoes! Some gol-durned - I mean blessed," the town cobbler amended, for, despite Card's taking it upon himself to reply, Sam Stitch was still addressing his friend the minister, "cuss has broke in and stole every - er - blessed shoe in my shop; your Billy's boots among 'em, Mr. Goodheart. I never seen such a boy for eating up shoe leather. Now how am I going to make good to my customers? Answer me that."

"Easily," cried Mr. Card with some hint of merriment in his voice. "Climb aboard, Mr. Stitch. You'll have to perch in back, I'm afraid. Ready, Mr. Goodheart?"

"Drive on, Mr. Card."

Strongitharm's interest was by now thoroughly piqued, as well it might have been. The Morgan covered the distance to Card Castle in jigtime. There, what to its passengers' wondering eyes might appear but a great heap of shoes and boots of all sizes in various stages of dilapidation or repair, dumped higgledy-piggledy on the granite slab in front of the farmhouse door. In a trice, Mr. Stitch had leaped down from the wagon and begun sorting out pairs from the jumble, his professional instincts alert even though his mind was still befuddled.

"There is more to be seen," cried Mr. Card. "Through here, Mr. Goodheart."

He hustled the minister through the ell that was connected to the house, and on into the vast barn that was connected to the ell. "What do you make of this?"

Next to the ample woodpile stood a neat stack of paraffin slabs, the kind that housewives melt to seal their jelly jars. Surrounding these was a carefully disposed ring of wood chips. Strongitharm could not repress a smile.

"Shoes and chips and sealing wax, eh? Your skit last evening must have made an even greater impression than you realized. Only someone seems not to have heard you quite right."

"Or else there's a punster among your congregation," Mr. Card added with a rueful smile. "I suppose 'ships' and 'chips' do sound much alike to an illiterate bumpkin. And of course chips are easier to come by than ships in such backwaters as Pitcherville. But this is not all. Look here."

He pointed to the nether side of the barn door, where were affixed four playing cards: respectively the kings of hearts, spades, diamonds, and clubs. On the floor beneath them lay several particularly large, handsome heads of cabbage; Strongitharm recognized these latter at once as having come from his own garden.

This was going too far. Strongitharm never balked at sharing the fruits of his toil to comfort the afflicted and succour the needy, but to waste good food on a wanton prank, not to mention putting a worthy shoemaker to needless dismay and extra work, was going too far.

"So what shall I do about it, Mr. Goodheart?" Card was urging. "One hardly likes to call in the constable over some yokel's rude jape, but I can't have my property invaded and my barn broken into just because certain people don't like my hired man."

"Joe Minnow?" Strongitharm was amazed. "But everybody likes Joe. Where is he now?"

Card shrugged. "Who knows? Slopping the pigs, perhaps. Joe does have an affinity with pigs. Now what's this great iron cauldron doing here? I hadn't noticed it before. What do you make of it, Mr. Goodheart?"

"Why, this is the pot that the late Mrs. Card used to make her lye soap and apple butter in. I carried it up to the loft myself, after she passed away. Mrs. Card set a lot of store by that pot, her husband didn't want the neighbours borrowing it after she was gone and maybe not treating it with proper respect to her memory. He wouldn't even let Mrs. Plott use it, not that she'd have had time, poor soul."

Mrs. Plott was the neighbour who had been helping out at Card Castle ever since Mrs. Card was taken poorly. For years she had been the sole support of an invalid husband and her blind old mother. Both had not long since crossed the bar, now Mrs. Plott had nobody but herself and the present Mr. Card to look after, not counting Joe Minnow, who still occupied the hired man's room behind the kitchen. Ever since he'd come to the Cards as an orphan boy some forty years ago, Joe had been accustomed to eating in the kitchen with the elder Cards. He still ate in the kitchen, but the new Mr. Card took his meals from the plush-covered round table in the back parlour.

Mrs. Plott had been giving the neighbours an earful of late about her new employer's citified ways, she seemed to feel that his snobbery cast a certain reflected dignity upon herself. Strongitharm had so far felt no parsonly urge to reprove the penurious widow for such harmless gossip, Mrs. Plott had not been able to find much dignity in her life so far. But she was no snob. Lately Mrs. Plott had taken to inviting Joe to share a meal now and then in her own shabby little cottage, and Joe was finding these visits much pleasanter than his solitary evenings at Card Castle.

"What has Mrs. Plott to say about all this?" asked the minister.

"Nothing to me," Card replied. "I was rather short with her just now about the amount of starch in my collars while she was harnessing the horse, and she seems to have taken umbrage, though I can't think why. I doubt whether she noticed either the shoes or the rest of this nonsense, come to think of it. Mrs. Plott uses the back door, needless to say, and the horse was in the pasture so all she had to do was catch the beast and hitch it to the wagon. I suppose it would be a kind gesture if I ordered her to help Stitch carry his shoes back to the shop, now that I think of it."

"It might be an even kinder gesture for you to help Mr. Stitch load the shoes into the wagon and drive him back to the shop yourself," Strongitharm suggested gently.

"Do you really think so? I'd have to change my suit first, I never seem to have the right clothes for these bucolic pursuits. But about this pot, Mr. Goodheart. You say you put it in the loft? Then how did the pot get down here? And what's that odd-looking piece of wood doing inside? Careful, there might be a spider."

Strongitharm was as amiably disposed toward the insectivora, generally speaking, as he was to the mammalia. He reached in without fear and picked out the object in question, an eight-inch wooden carving of the letter C. "Here you are, Mr. Card, another ancestral relic. When Clegg's Drugstore was torn down about five years ago, these big letters were salvaged off the sign and given to various people who had the right initials."

Mr. Goodheart himself had been offered a G for his front door, but hadn't felt right about taking it since the parsonage was only his pro tem by the grace of God and the Board of Deacons. "Mr. Card was going to have the C regilded and mounted on the barn door, but he never did. I supposed he dropped it into the pot for safekeeping and forgot where he'd put it. But how the pot got down from the loft, I'm afraid I can't tell you. I'd stuck it back in the far corner so it wouldn't interfere with putting in the hay."

"Then Joe Minnow must have known where the pot stood, at any rate," mused the new owner. "That's something to think about. Well, Stitch is no doubt itching to get back to his stitching, I may as well go and give him a boost. Thank you for coming, Mr. Goodheart. I'm afraid I've made more of this affair than it's worth."

Strongitharm was not so sure about that, but refrained from saying so. He helped Sam Stitch to load his shoes into the wagon while Mr. Card stood around giving helpful advice; then he went off on his pastoral round, wondering just why he was finding this odd start to his day so bothersome.

Late in the afternoon, Strongitharm dropped in to see a little girl with a twisted leg who had been too ill to attend the pantomime. He'd brought her a big piece of coconut cake, and was reciting The Walrus and the Carpenter to cheer her up when light dawned. The time had come, the Walrus had observed, to talk of many things including why the sea was boiling hot and whether pigs had wings.

Pigs! That was the word which had been tugging at the coattails of Strongitharm's mind ever since he'd left the Card place. He hadn't seen the pigs. That was understandable since the pigsty was out behind the barn and he hadn't got that far; but why hadn't he heard them? The Card pigs had always been sociable pigs, as pigs went. Normally their sty would have been a lively place so soon after feeding time, with lots of grunting and slurping and Joe amiably exhorting his charges to enjoy their mash. Sometimes he even played his concertina for them, producing quite piglike squeals and wheezes for his and their mutual enjoyment. This morning they hadn't emitted a single oink or squeak. Why not?

After having gently wiped the last vestige of frosting off the little girl's nose and presenting her with a toy walrus that clever Mrs. Goodheart had contrived from a wornout sock, a wisp of yarn, and a couple of buttons, Strongitharm hurried out to his buggy and explained to his faithful horse that they had yet another pastoral visit to pay. Old Balaam was quite willing to oblige, having enjoyed a refreshing nap while waiting for the minister and knowing a good supper would be his reward back at the parsonage; for the labourer, quadruped, or triped, was worthy of his hire.

Nobody was around Card Castle's dooryard. Strongitharm found Mrs. Plott in the kitchen, wholly surrounded by brass candlesticks, pen trays, bookends, figurines, thingamabobs, and doodads. Old Mrs. Card had been a great one for brass. Mrs. Plott clearly was not, she greeted Mr. Goodheart with some asperity.

"Well, I must say it's a change to see a human face around here. You've missed Mr. Card. He went off quite a while ago, all shieked up in his blue serge suit."

"And where is Joe Minnow?"

"Don't ask me, Mr. Goodheart. I haven't laid eyes on him all day. He didn't even show up at noontime for his dinner. I had pea soup all hot and waiting, Joe's always like my pea soup."

Had Mrs. Plott been the crying kind, Strongitharm might have suspected she was close to tears. His perturbation grew. "Mrs. Plott, have you been out to the pigsty today?"

"I have not. The pigs are Joe Minnow's business, not mine. Mr. Card told me to get every bit of this brass stuff polished before suppertime, though why today of all days is beyond me. It's not as if he was expecting company. Normally he never so much as looks at these things."

"Did he say when he'd be back?"

"No, just not to go home until I've finished the brass, assuming I ever do, and to leave some supper in the warming oven in case he wants a bite later on. Which he probably won't, my guess is he'll stop at the Prettypennys' and get asked to sit down with them. He's been shining up to Mabel Prettypenny, in case you hadn't noticed. Her mother's all for making a match, but Deacon Prettypenny's taken kind of a scunner to Mr. Card, for all he's so rich and handsome. So's young Leviticus Jones, but I'm afraid poor Vitty hasn't much of a chance with Mabel. Not that I've ever heard a word against the boy, which is more than can be said for one or two others I might mention."

Mrs. Plott cast a wrathful glance in the direction of the pigsty, Strongitharm was reminded of his mission. He rushed out the back door and hurried around behind the barn, Mrs. Plott panting behind him with her polishing rag still in her hand. No grunt nor whoofle did they hear, no porcine form did they espy. The rails were down and the pigsty was empty!

The housekeeper tried to wring her hands, but the polishing cloth got in the way. No matter, this was no time for profitless agitation. "Mrs. Plott," Strongitharm demanded, "who else has been here today?"

"Why, just Vitty Jones with a load of brick for that new terrace Mr. Card wants to build."

"Were you outdoors when Vitty came?"

"I was not. I was up to my elbows in brass polish, as you well know. I heard the old truck and thought it might be Joe coming back from wherever he'd been, but it wasn't. I tell you, Mr. Goodheart-"

Mr. Goodheart did not wait to be told, he dashed back around the barn and went inside. He was just in time. The iron pot was now sitting up on a few bricks, the wood chips had been shoved under it and set alight. The smell of melted paraffin filled the air and blue smoke was puffing up out of the pot. As any jelly-maker could have told, the paraffin was at the point of combustion.

Even as Strongitharm snatched the polishing rag from Mrs. Plott to use for a pot holder and lifted the cauldron off the fire, a tongue of yellow-orange flame shot out from it toward the woodpile. Thanks to the minister's swift action, the flame didn't quite reach. He smothered the embryo conflagration with a horse blanket, then carried the smoldering pot out into the dooryard where it could do no harm. He raked the wood chips away from the woodpile and dismantled the improvised firepit, making sure no spark was left to cause further trouble. At last he went back to examine the cauldron. Nothing was left inside but the stink of burnt sealing wax and the charred remains of the wooden letter C.

"So that's why the C was boiling hot," mused Mr. Goodheart.

There was no mystery about how the fire had got started. A fine trail of charring led from the place where the cauldron had stood to a small blob of wax over in a far corner, with a fragment of wick still to be seen. Someone had cut a notch in the candle, tied to it a long fuse, probably a piece of cord soaked in saltpetre, and imbedded the fuse's other end in the heap of dry wood chips. After that, the perpetrator had only to light the candle and go away. By the time the candle had burned down to where the fuse met the wick, he would have been somewhere else, establishing himself an alibi. The wood chips would have heated the pot, the sealing wax that had been thrown in would melt and overheat, as in fact it had done. The woodpile was thus meant to catch fire, the blaze would have spread to the barn walls and roof, to the ell, thence to the house itself.

Pitcherville's firefighting brigade consisted of a nest of buckets, a horse-drawn pumper, and as many volunteer firemen as could be gathered out of the shops and fields. By the time the brigade mobilized and reached the scene, there would have been little they could do except maybe rescue some of the brass pen trays out of the ashes. The pigs had been set free either because the arsonist was concerned for their safety or because it was feared their squealing would alert Mrs. Plott too soon for the fire to get a good hold.

A few bucketfuls of water at the right time could have foiled the perpetrator's evil purpose, but would Mrs. Plott have thrown them? She was clearly in a bad mood today, and not without reason. Joe Minnow had let her down; her new employer was loading her with tasks she'd never had to perform in old Mr. Card's day, making her harness his horse, ordering her to do two days' work in one.

Strongitharm reminded himself to judge not. Maybe Mr. Card hadn't realized what he was asking. Perhaps the new owner was used to having other servants around to share the load. Or perhaps he was used to having none at all. Fine feathers didn't always make fine birds, that trunkful of swell clothes he'd brought with him might have comprised his sole estate heretofore. Mr. Card was certainly pleased to have inherited the farm even though he was no farmer. And to think how close he'd come today to losing it!

Truly the Lord worked in mysterious ways His wonders to perform. Strongitharm was making a mental note for next Sunday's sermon when he spied a glint of clean wood on the fifth rung of the ladder that went up to the loft.

"Well, now, that's funny," he remarked to Mrs. Plott. "This ladder was all right this morning. I'd have noticed. See, here's a fresh splinter on the floor. Joe must have come down in a hurry and caught his heel. It's a mercy he didn't break his neck."

"Joe wouldn't have left that splinter lying there," said the housekeeper. "One thing about Joe Minnow, he's neat as a pin. What would he have been doing in the loft anyway? The hay's all in."

So it was! The odour of paraffin was still too strong in the barn for any smoke from the hayloft to be noticed. Strongitharm swarmed up that ladder sniffing. Once in the loft, he still could smell nothing but paraffin, but he did hear something. Not a mouse in the hay, not a cat after the mouse, more like a stifled groan. Could one of the pigs have climbed the ladder?

The hay had been neatly laid in, but somebody had pushed through it to the corner where Strongitharm had left old Mr. Card's iron pot. There was no other sign of disturbance, he headed in that same direction, and stumbled upon Joe Minnow, trussed up like a turkey gobbler with his own blue bandanna stuffed into his mouth for a gag. Strongitharm plucked out the gag, whipped out his horn-handled jackknife to cut the cruelly tight bonds, and began chafing

Joe's wrists and ankles to get the blood flowing. For an agonizing minute or two, the hired man showed no sign of life, then he sucked in a long shuddering breath and opened his eyes.

"Ooh, my head!"

"Does it hurt?" asked the minister.

"Awful! Who - who are you?"

"Joe! I'm Mr. Goodheart. Don't you know me?"

The stricken man only groaned again and shut his eyes. Strongitharm raised the sore head a little and felt for an injury. There was no open wound and no sign of a fractured skull as far as Strongitharm could tell. However a huge lump at the back was ample testimony that Joe must have received a cowardly great blow from behind. Good shepherd that he was, Strongitharm gathered the semi-conscious man up in his arms and carried him to the ladder. "Mrs. Plott, Joe's hurt. Can you help me get him down the ladder?"

First things first. Sensible Mrs. Plott asked no questions until they'd eased the hired man safely down and laid him on the smokey horse blanket. While she ran in to get some hot tea, the minister continued working on Joe's wrists and ankles. From the looks of those puffy, discoloured hands and feet, Joe had been lying there far too long with the circulation all but cut off. Mrs. Plott burst into tears when she noticed the vicious welts.

"Oh Joe! Joe!"

"Elphima!" For the first time, a gleam of intelligence flashed into Joe Minnow's eyes. "Elphie, is that you?"

"I brought you some tea, Joe."

"Bless you, Elphie. Elphie, don't leave me. Ever."

"If you say so, Joe. Here, drink it while it's hot."

His head cradled in Elphima Plott's checkered apron, Joe Minnow drank from the cup she held to his swollen lips. Strongitharm would have preferred to leave the two alone together, but that must not be. Joe was in no shape to fight should the arsonist come back to determine whether his ruse had worked. The poor fellow ought to be in bed. As to which bed, Joe and Elphie could settle that between them. Strongitharm was a man of heart as well as a man of the cloth. He cleared his throat.

"Joe Minnow, do you take this woman to be your lawfully wedded wife, to have and to hold until -" Strongitharm didn't feel like sticking to the book just now, when death had come so very close to parting these two middle-aged lovers. Joe Minnow had been meant to perish in the fire. Surely the Almighty wouldn't mind if the words got changed around a bit, considering the circumstances.

"Elphima Plott, nee Finchfoot, do you take this man to be your lawful wedded husband?"

"I certainly do, and glad to get him," was the erstwhile widow's brisk reply. "I'd better go make some fresh tea, eh?"

"That would be splendid."

Strongitharm had meant to wind up the impromptu wedding service with a short homily, but Mr. and Mrs. Minnow seemed happy enough without the frills and he himself was beginning to feel that a cup of tea would go pretty good about now. He expressed mild regret that he'd run out of coconut cake, not knowing he'd be performing a nuptial ceremony. Joe said that didn't matter, he'd rather have a bowl of Elphie's pea soup, considering the slim pickings he'd had so far today. His wife went to warm it up and Strongitharm got down to business.

"Joe, do you know who hit you and tied you up? Or when?"

"It's hard to say, Mr. Goodheart. Seems to me I do and then it seems I don't. My head's still not working too good. As for when, it must have been before noontime anyway. I'd bought one of those song sheets with kind of a pretty picture on it that the girls were peddling yesterday at the fair. I'd meant to give it to Elphie at dinner but I can feel it still rolled up in my inside vest pocket. Didn't know the foolish thing would turn out to be a wedding present," he added sheepishly. "Thank you, Mr. Goodheart."

"Don't thank me, Joe. My Father that is within me, He doeth the work. Then you'd been up there most of the day. Were you unconscious the whole time?"

"I kind of drifted in and out. I remember once waking up with a mouse sitting on my nose, staring right down into my eyes. I didn't mind. It was kind of company, in a way. Sometime after that, I heard Vitty Jones's old truck drive up, you know what a racket it makes, and him thumping around down there for a while. Unloading bricks it sounded like. I tried to yell down to Vitty, but that gag was in my mouth and all I could do was grunt like a pig. Say, what time is it now. I got to feed them pigs."

"No, you don't. The pigs - " Strongitharm tried to tell a calming lie, but falsehood was just not in him. "The pigs aren't there, Joe. Somebody opened the pigsty gate and they all ran off."

There was no sense in trying to persuade Joe that the Lord gaveth and the Lord tooketh away. By now the hired man knew perfectly well who must have let out the pigs, and so did Strongitharm.

"But why, Joe? This was a deliberate attempt to burn down the whole place, and you with it. Can you tell me why Mr. Card would deliberately try to ruin himself, just after he'd inherited a good house and farm?"

Joe propped himself up on his elbows, then struggled to a sitting position. He was not a man to take things lying down.

"I don't think Mr. Card had any intention of ruining himself, Mr. Goodheart. He's had an insurance man out here. I heard them talking. He's got the house and barn insured right up to the hilt and then some. Not to pass judgment, but it looks as if Card was intending to lay it on me, claiming I stole the pigs and ran away with 'em after I'd set the fire out of general cussedness. He's been telling around that I'm mean and lazy and can't be trusted. You heard?"

Strongitharm nodded. Joe went on.

"He's been selling things out of the house too, trying to make out he's planning to furnish the whole place new. But he's lying, he don't plan to stay. He's no farmer, never will be. He hates the town, hates the pigs, he don't give a tinker's hoot for nobody but himself. Old Mr. Card told me once his wife had wanted Elphie to have her sealskin coat and her pearl pin, but he never got around to giving them to her, you know how he was in those last years. So along comes this young fellow and takes them away and sells them both without batting an eye."

"It's too bad old Mr. Card never got around to making a will," said the minister.

"Now, that's a funny thing." Joe was really wound up now. "I remember him one time years ago, when Mrs. Card was still alive, driving over to Woodstock and coming back with a blue paper, rolled up and tied with pink tape and a big blob of sealing wax. His wife wanted to know what it was. He told her he'd made a will, he put the paper in the drawer of the parlour table where they kept the deed to the house and some other stuff. And there it laid, as far as I know, till after Mr. Card died and Lawyer Nevins broke the seal. Turned out to be nothing but a blank piece of paper. Just another of the old man's jokes."

"Joe's right, Mr. Goodheart." Elphima was back, carrying a shiny brass tray laden with tea cups, bread and butter, and a bowl of pea soup. "I've seen that paper myself, once when I was helping Mrs. Card spring-clean the parlour. She took it out of the table drawer and held it by the tape, as if she didn't want to touch the paper. 'This is Mr. Card's will,' she told me. 'I hope I never live to hear it read.' And of course she never would have, because there was nothing to read. Mrs. Card would have got everything anyway, so it would have been up to her to make the will. I suppose after she died, old Mr. Card just didn't care what would happen once he was gone. Come on, Joe, eat this soup. It will put heart in you."

"Guess I could use some heart." Joe grinned. "Gave mine to you, didn't I? Oh, and here's a little hunk of nothing I bought you yesterday."

He reached into his inner vest pocket and hauled out a slim roll of faded blue paper, tied with discolored pink tape, and decorated with a great blob of red sealing wax.

"What in thunder? This ain't what I - here, Mr. Goodheart, you better take it. Open it up, for the Lord's sake."

It was the missing will. It left the Card farm to Mrs. Card for her lifetime and after her to their beloved fosterling and faithful helper, Joseph Minnow; except for Mrs. Card's sealskin coat and pearl pin, which were to go to Elphima Plott. No provision whatsoever was made for any distant relative.

"Well, I'll be - jiggered!" The swindled heir stared at the document in total bewilderment. "What in tarnation possessed that - that *cuss* - to pull a stunt like this?"

"His theatrical instincts, I suppose," said Strongitharm. "Mr. Card the younger must have found the real will when he visited here as a boy, rigged up a dummy in a spirit of mischief, and hidden the real will somewhere in the house. After he took possession, he read the old will and decided he'd better grab as much as he could and get away before the truth was found out."

"But why didn't he just burn the will right off?" queried Mrs. Minnow.

"He must have been afraid another copy would turn up somewhere and he'd be left with nothing," said Strongitharm. "I'm afraid this Mr. Card has no higher moral sense than the walrus and the carpenter. They deceived the oysters, you know, and gobbled them up in the end."

"Just as he's been deceiving us," cried Joe, "and trying to gobble up everything he can get his hands on."

"Well said, Joe. His putting the will in your pocket instead of burning it outright shows, in my opinion, a particularly unpleasant turn of mind. Mrs. Minnow, would you be kind enough to take my buggy, drive into the village for the constable, then stop at the parsonage and tell my wife not to wait supper for me? Mr. Card should be along in another hour or two to inspect the ruins so that he can tear back into town and let everybody know he's a ruined man. Joe and I want to be here when he comes. Right, Joe?"

"Right, Mr. Goodheart. In the meantime, if you'll just help me up, I'd better get some mash into the troughs. The pigs should be coming home to supper about now. They know I'd never let them down."

They knew, and they came. So did the constable. And so, to his everlasting regret, did young Mr. Card, lashing his horse to the gallop as he approached the farm, drawing up short in shocked dismay when he found Card Castle intact and a hostile reception committee waiting for him.

The judge and jury were not gulled by Mr. Card's protestations that he'd only assaulted Joe Minnow and tried to swindle the insurance company as a practical joke in the well-known Card tradition. Nobody in Pitcherville, not even Mabel Prettypenny, lamented the dashing bachelor's being shipped off to the county jail. It was generally agreed that any man crazy enough to try pulling the wool over Mr. Goodheart's eyes wasn't safe to be left running loose, anyway.

Night of the Fourth Moon
by *Eliza Moorhouse*

Eliza Moorhouse is the latest in a long line of Okanagan Valley authors to appear in the Cold Blood series. A native of Vernon, Eliza has published numerous short stories in anthologies and periodicals, and has won several awards for her work. Her first published crime fiction, "Night of the Fourth Moon" introduces Grant Calvados, dealer in stolen Oriental antiquities and a character far removed from Vernon, B.C.

NIGHT OF THE FOURTH MOON
by *Eliza Moorhouse*

The double-decker bus wound through the thieves market, passed Happy Valley race track, discharged passengers then continued on to Causeway Bay. Here the bus emptied. The hot breeze rippling the waters of the typhoon shelter left the September travellers longing for rain and coolness.

Greta mopped her face with a tissue and studied Karl, seeking a resolution to their problem. She wanted to ask someone the way back to their hotel, but Karl insisted they weren't lost! Patches of wet appeared under his arm pits. He was using a lot of aggression fighting himself and Greta wished that he would admit defeat and solicit help. Adrift in a strange land, she sensed disaster.

Perturbed by a vague feeling of uneasiness, she wondered if perhaps taking this trip together had been a mistake and tried not to think about Karl's frantic wife, wondering and waiting, back home. Instead, she resurrected the violinist in immaculate black and white highlighted against the polished wood of her piano as they performed on stage with the Chamber Quartet. THAT was the man who had invaded her dreams. Who, then, was this boring man who swore, face red and angry from the Hong Kong heat? The huge onyx ring, once so fascinating, looked ridiculous - out of step with damp cotton shorts.

"We'll get us a cold drink, Greta, then things'll look better."

"Karl?" Where had the fool gone now? She paused, overcome by a prickly sensation at the base of her scalp. They were in an alien passageway. An old woman sitting in a doorstep thrust bare feet into a vat of shrimp. The smell was like rotting manure. Greta stopped and stared down the passageway, at the nuances of light and shadow, the interplay like a macabre symphony. And then she hurried after him, the sense of foreboding stalking her. An open doorway, eyes, the smell of urine, and Karl calling her from somewhere inside: "In here, Greta. There's cold beer and we can have it right now!"

Strange yellow water ran down the sides of decaying bricks onto her white sandals. She felt the terror of the person who is lost and alone. "Karl?" Suddenly he loomed, larger than life, in the doorway. "In here."

They stood at the bar and drank warm, flat beer, Karl and the bartender holding a conversation in pidgin English.

"Let's go now, Karl. It's obvious foreigners don't come here."

"Bullshit. I'm having another damned beer. Two more, okay, Chin?" The oblong-faced bartender nodded and slid two glasses along the counter. "Say, Chin, you helpee us findee our hotel? Hotel. Sleepee place. Can't find."

The bartender wiped his hands on a dubious cloth. "Follow, pliss. Miss Nunn, she know."

Alarmed, Greta tugged at Karl's sleeve. "It's okay," he assured her, "a nun he said. Come on."

The bartender stood aside as they stepped through a beaded curtain. Suddenly Karl reached for her hand and they stood irresolute, staring.

Seated high on a bamboo throne was a woman in a white silk dress. Her large face was moon shaped and the colour of light tobacco. The facial skin had the puckered, dead appearance of ancient cosmetic surgery. Heavy orange lipstick extended into the withered skin on all sides. White hair hung to her tiny shoulders, her eyes riveted. She dropped a kitten into a pillowed basket, where it cried bluntly. Two lovely young women in satin cheongsams watched in amusement from high pillows. Madam Nunn inspected the terrified tourists who'd had the misfortune to wander into her domain.

"It is almost the hour of the rat and I'm tired. Amitabha! What have we here?" In answer Chin, the bartender, gave a long discourse in Chinese.

"A bloody embalmed corpse," whispered Karl. "Let's get out of here!" They edged toward the beaded curtain but the way was blocked.

"My bed is a stone k'ang covered with a mat of soft bamboo. So. It awaits me. What do you want?" Her black eyes studied the onyx ring on the third finger of Karl's right hand. "Speak up! You got dollah-dollah?"

"We have very little money."

"But not on us," Greta hastily added. "We're a bit lost is all. Please, just tell us the way to, uh, the Peking Hotel will be find."

"On Yee Street."

Raucous laughter from the throne, giggles from the icy satin cheongsams. The bartender's mouth quivered in the plum-blue atmosphere. Madam Nunn clapped her hands and the room fell to silence. "Go and tend bar!"

The beaded curtain clicked as the man obeyed. The quiet returned.

The silence was layered with phantom sobs and scented with death. Greta and Karl felt snared by evil and searched desperately for a way out as ever closer, like a locust ferried on the wind, came the man who would spring the trap.

* * *

Grant Calvados turned onto the Cross Harbour approach, stopped at the tollgates then passed into the mile-long tunnel leading to Hong Kong from Kowloon. The recent incident with the China watcher was fresh on his mind. . .

"Ni hao, ni hao."

"Ni hao, Ping. Fine, fine. What do you have?" Grant scanned the grey wastelands of the north Kowloon Peninsula. His mouth settled into a tight line as he scratched one wayward eyebrow. Damn. He'd have to enthuse over the China watcher's interpretation of recent Sino-Soviet relations before getting to the grit.

"In Peking, is said two Soviet diplomats expel for spy job."

Grant contemplated impatiently. "That so. Most interesting indeed. Yes." He looked again toward the wastelands, where in the distance the convolutions of China stretched endlessly. "And?"

"Porcelain. A cup, tiny crack. Good."

Grant's eyes narrowed. "Colour?"

"Green."

Green! His interest deepened. "Glazed?"

Ping nodded. "Shiny. Kuan. Ping know Kuan ware."

Kuan - the white and greenish tinged porcelain, produced during the Sung Dynasty for Court use. Could it be? God, he'd sell his soul! Could such a treasure have survived to lay unclaimed in some dusty market place? "Where?" His voice was hoarse with passion.

"Shop of Lu, Black Tiger Lane."

Black Tiger. . .the narrow street at the top of the hundred stairs. He knew the shop - a discreet collection of illicit antiquities, often broken beyond repair.

"Just one crack you say?"

"Hair crack. Cup good."

He had paid the China watcher generously and on leaving the tunnel made a sudden decision to inspect the cup immediately. He parked at the rear of the shop in a lane hardly designed for vehicular traffic and walked around to the front. He stared at the window display. The faint self-image reflected was hawkish, pock marks above the dark beard proclaimed him a winner in the game of death. In a glance he captured the single piece of Kuan porcelain, its translucency like the eye of the moon. Still, he hesitated. Old Lu would not be glad to see him again; there could be unpleasantness. He toyed with the crisp bills in his pocket and reconsidered - the old man was hanging onto the edge of survival and would welcome the money. Worth a chance. His eyes strayed once more to the tiny cup. He felt an intimacy, reduced his longing to a straight and simple plane wherein only beauty mattered. It was real, he was certain, crafted in one of the thousands of kilns that had sprung up like patchwork throughout China centuries ago. He must touch it. Now.

He entered the shop, ignored the old shopkeeper and stood at the front, gazing at the cup; a moment of peace, a second held in time wherein nothing existed but the exquisite porcelain cup. One spidery crack ran transversely and ended nowhere.

At last he turned to face the old shopkeeper. "How are you, Lu?"

"So! You are back."

"With money, old one."

"It is written, he who treads evil dies many times." The light from the window fell across his face, leaving shadows in the hollows of his cheekbones.

"I have died many times."

"Ah. Then we shall lay forgetfulness." But the old man's eyes held no forgetfulness. A cool, predatory hunger lay behind his dotted pupils.

"The cup is not bad. Cracked badly, but even so. . ."

Lu looked beyond Grant's head, a disturbing cross-match of fear and complacency. Grant turned, following Lu's eyes. A dark curtain across a doorway at the rear of the shop quivered, the toes of sandalled feet suddenly drawn back into the curtain.

Grant spoke softly. "First, the jade paperweight, the one of five virtues."

"Good choice," said Lu, turning toward the window display. "Charity for lustre, wisdom for. . ." When he shifted his long black gown, jade in hand, the man with the dark beard had gone.

Only when he'd manoeuvred the narrow alley and eased through the crowds of Cat Street did Grant allow himself to relax. But the macabre overtones of the shop persisted, suggesting he'd stepped into a trap. Why? Who? Certainly his hunt for antiquities had made him enemies, especially among the illicit dealers of Hong Kong.

He parked overlooking the typhoon shelter of Causeway Bay and absently, like a bewildered tourist, gazed at the water people stretched across the harbour in a labyrinth of junks and sampans. He saw only the tender translucency of the tiny cup. In this game of survival, he could not afford to slip. And if he sometimes felt old at forty-four, ready to head for some placid harbour, the China watcher always got him going again with the sighting of one more treasure for his cache, the House of Harmony. He had taken what didn't belong to him, murdered even, for the treasures he had. He thought lovingly of the jade chess set, the seventh-century Buddhist painting, the rare ivory carvings.

Who knew of the missing cup and that he was back in circulation? The old dealer on Gem Street, for he knew everything. He stared at a patched sail stirring on the water. . .and then there was the China watcher. He bit down hard on his left thumb. Damn! He had to have the cup. He could see it now, beside the pearl fan in the teak cabinet.

What he needed was some naive tourist, preferably a woman, to act on his behalf, offer a handsome sum in supposed ignorance and induce the shopkeeper to sell. If it were done right, whoever had laid the trap would be the loser. He'd have to coach the woman on bargaining, but where to find such a person? His women friends were from the Mad Monkey bar in the Wanchai area, hardly the type to pass as a naive tourist.

Backing away from the area, he headed for Lockhart Road and the Mad Monkey. A Guiness would sit well. Grant Calvados passed under the neon sign and stood for a moment at the elongated bar which ended in a pyramid of blue smoke. The usual tourists were dancing with the cheongsam girls. Shuffling face-to-face on the mean dance floor. Acrylic thrills and sex. A few sailors. Simm the bartender passed him a Guiness and pointed to a vacant table. "Save just for you." Liar, thought Grant, pushing his way through the crowd.

"Hi, Grant, hear you back again!"

He took a long pull of the Guiness and mentally dissected the girl: pots of rouge, kohl-encased eyes, remarkable figure in pink satin. She resembled the rest of the girls, a Mad Monkey clone with a diamond-shaped cleavage.

"Hello, Delores."

She allowed the strap of her pink dress to stray down one arm. Enticing bitch, but not tonight. He couldn't get the porcelain cup out of his mind. "Bring me another drink, same thing."

"Delores get."

He studied the tourists again. Nothing here he could use. Delores hurried back as though she had something on her mind. God. He'd need another drink, listening to her phoney Spanish accent. He grabbed her arm, allowing his fingers to hurt. "This trip I'm Gordon, understand?"

She stared in sultry silence.

"Bend over! No, not your ass, silly bitch. Your face! Bend over this way."

Hurt and curious, she turned and bobbed her breasts over his drink, fishing balls on a stormy sea. He tucked an American fifty into her cleavage. The storm abated. "Upstairs?" she asked with a pleased smile.

"No. Sit down and listen." He leaned back and tried to relax. His tone softened. She had, after all, given him much pleasure. That he was preoccupied was no fault of hers. "Senorita, the other fifty is yours when you return."

"What do I do, Gor-don? For the other fifty?"

"Now listen. Somewhere in Hong Kong, look in the medium-priced hotels, there must be a white lady in trouble. Understand?"

"Trouble?"

"Yes. She could be stranded without money, or she's lost her passport or been robbed - hell, use your imagination. Find out her name, where she's staying and get back here fast."

"I see Simm first."

"Sure, see Simm first. And understand -a lady. You know what a lady is?"

She got up and smoothed her satin dress. "Delores know. White skin, big nose, long skinny feet and brown dress. Lady."

Grant laughed into his Guiness. In a flash, she was gone, no doubt to consult with kitchen staff or bellhops. If anyone could find such a person, Delores could.

When she returned in forty minutes, Grant figured she'd hit the thunder line early and dallied over gin, by the smell of her breath. "Well?"

"A Missus Tor, Hotel Peking on Yee-Wo Street, Gor-don."

Yee-Wo, the street behind Drake Alley. Strange place for a tourist. "You sure? Not Yee-Su? Or Yee-Wat?"

The girl drew back in disgust.

"Okay. Good, senorita. A Mrs. Tor. Anything else?" Little use in asking her how to spell the name. Could be Thors or whatever.

"Lady can't pay for room. Come from Canada. Wear blue dress, skinny feet, long nose, white..."

"Fine, fine. I get the picture."

"I pay cook thirty American dollah."

"Too bad for you." Grant slapped bills onto the table. "See you, kiddo."

Grant manoeuvred his Le Sabre down Drake Alley and parked at the rear of the hotel overlooking a row of shops and shanty houses. The obscure grey building was decorated with broken art-nouveau figurines. The atmosphere was layered in rice, stale beer and unidentifiable pockets of smells trapped by a faulty air conditioner. The man behind the lobby desk had straight black hair above blue almond eyes and a fleshy American nose.

"Good evening. I am a friend of Mrs. Greta Thor."

Having checked the woman out with the bellhop, he was armed with a few facts with which to win the advantage.

"I see. She has an enormous bill. We are urging her to contact the Embassy." He produced a worn ledger and flipped pages. "The bill is high, two thousand Hong Kong."

"Considering Mrs. Thor has been here only five days and considering your low rate. . ."

"I'll recheck." He frowned in concentration, ran a thumb nail down columns of figures. "Ah, apologies. Here we are, then. Six hundred Hong Kong. My eye slipped onto the wrong column. And meals."

"Her husband left three days ago. Doubt that she's eaten much. Here's five hundred. Now, a receipt made out to G. Gordon, and her room number."

The clerk inspected the curious man before him: medium height, slim, dark eyes under springy brows, American nose, soft-textured hair and beard, old pock marks. No, he could not like him nor would he wish to quarrel with him. "Here is your receipt, Mr. Gordon. Room 14."

Grant ignored the dubious elevator and took the marble stairs two at a time. He rapped lightly on her door.

"Go away!"

"I've just paid your bill, Mrs. Thor. They sent me over to help." Let her interpret any way she pleased.

"Oh?" A pause, then, "Oh, thank you." The voice moved closer. "I look frightful. Could you maybe come back?"

"No. Either see me now or never. And I'll reclaim the money left at the desk." Grant scratched impatiently above his left eyebrow. Damned bitch.

A sigh then the door opened a crack. He looked into puffy red eyes, disorganized hair, hands clutching what looked like a bedspread. He nudged his way in and stared. Although a stranger, he knew her intimately: the faithful victim.

"Thanks again for paying my bill. I have this darned headache."

"From crying and not eating, Mrs. Thor. What's happened to your husband?"

"Don't ask!" She went into the bathroom and slammed the door. Lord, he thought, she hadn't even asked for I.D. A dangerous game, taking people at their word.

"Mrs. Thor? Clean up, brush your hair and we'll get ourselves a light supper."

"Uh, okay. There's a dining room downstairs, Mr. . ."

"Here? Good lord, not here."

Seconds later he heard the sound of running water and wandered into the bedroom. The faded finery was of another time:

peach satin lamps, faded mirrors, alcove adorned with a torn velvet curtain. What a dump for two Canadian tourists to wind up in. He examined a photograph of the pair. Greta was pretty with short chestnut hair, ample hips and questioning blue eyes. Beside her was a tall, blond man with a crooked smile who reminded Grant of a sadistic English teacher he'd once had. At last she came out of the bedroom, grabbed a dress from the closet, pulled it over her head and brushed her hair.

They dined in a restaurant near the Star Ferry Terminal. He felt at odds with the red-eyed woman who naively thought him from the Embassy. She ordered a Shanghai Sling with a twist of lime and he asked for a Guiness.

"Are you. . .oh, I shouldn't ask. . ."

He faced her with a fizzing silence.

"Well, I mean - I wondered." The drinks arrived and she toyed with hers. "Are you part Chinese?"

"My mother was Lily Li, the well-known Chinese actress."

"Oh, how interesting. And your father?"

Her sincere interest in his private business bordered on gross impertinence. "My father, who died on the fifteenth day of the fifth moon, was a gems collector."

"I don't understand about the different moons."

"Tonight, for instance is the fourth moon." The death moon, he thought idly.

"Oh. And where was your father from?" She took a huge sip of her drink.

He ignored her and ordered a light supper for both of them. He prayed that she had the finesse to accomplish the delicate, dangerous mission. He would try to relax her and then make his proposal. "I thought it best to order something light, Greta, since you haven't eaten in a while. You don't mind if I call you Greta?"

"Oh, no. And which of the Embassy chaps are you? Oh dear, chaps sound so dreadfully English. My mother is English, you see. My father is from California."

"Just call me Gordon. Now then, Greta, would it upset you to talk about your husband now?"

She carefully speared a bit of celery from her salad. "No, not now. Thanks to you, Gordon, I feel ever so much better. What happened was, we got lost, couldn't find Yee Street where our hotel is. Didn't know then about all the different Yee Streets. Well, we wandered into a drinking place run by a dreadful ugly woman with white hair and a shrunken face. Disgusting." For a moment he thought she was going to cry, but she took a deep breath and continued. "Said I could go but - but I'm to gain Karl's release by. . .oh, Gordon, where on earth am I to get a thousand American dollars by tomorrow afternoon? I can't find the money Karl brought with us."

Grant hid a smile. Madam Outrageous but again! "No problem. I know her quite well. I'll speak to her first thing in the morning. But, isn't there something you're not telling me, Greta?"

"You know that awful person? Oh, Gordon, what a messiah you are! And yes, there is one bit, somewhat embarrassing." She looked away. "Karl is only a very good friend. We met when I filled in as pianist for a chamber quartet. Karl is a natural musician; I'm afraid I have trouble interpreting the music. Anyway, this trip is all the more terrible because. . ." She inhaled deeply, "He has a wife back home and if anything got in to the papers, well, you can see why I haven't gone to the police. That, and being terribly scared."

"I understand. Now just relax. We'll take care of everything for you, Greta. And there'll be a ticket home at the desk for you. You don't mind leaving here tomorrow afternoon? Your friend, Karl, he could be on a later. . ."

"Oh, Gordon! It's my dream to get out of here. I can't tell you. If there's anything, any little thing I can ever do for you in return!" She blushed and studied the floor.

He pushed the dishes aside and ordered coffee. "I don't think - well, by gosh, it's such a little thing. . ."

"Consider it done."

"Ah, here's coffee. All I need, Greta, is for someone to pick up a cup for me." He described it to her in detail.

"Oh, I could do that so easily, Gordon."

"Well, that's great because I'd like you to get it tonight for me. We can call a cab from here."

Her eyes sought the darkness beyond the window, reflected fear and surprise. "Out there, by myself? Where?"

"Oh, nothing to it. The cabbie will take you. Just tell him the hundred stairs. And at the top of the stairs, there's a shop owned by an old man named Lu. Now listen carefully and I'll teach you some bargaining techniques."

But she wasn't paying attention. Her eyes repeatedly strayed to the dark window and he could see that she was already mounting the hundred steps. "I do wish I could go myself, Greta, but they don't like us Embassy chaps buying Chinese antiquities, for some reason. You'd be helping me out enormously."

He handed her five hundred American dollars plus cab fare. "Start bargaining at two hundred and work up, but not right away on the cup. Try something else first."

He followed the checkered cab in his Le Sabre, keeping about a block behind. She had trouble climbing the stairs, had to stop part way to rest. As soon as she got going again, he left his car and followed her. From his vantage point behind a sweets cart, he could see right into the shop. At first things seemed to be going well, but he could tell that she was nervous. It was difficult to discern the shopkeeper's expression, but suddenly Lu got excited and began pointing, his mouth working rapidly. Greta began backing toward the door, shaking her head. Then she opened her purse and showed him the money. Another person came into the shop from the rear, barring her exit. They huddled together and all three disappeared behind the curtain. Grant did not hesitate. He opened the door just as the girl screamed, grabbed the cup and, holding it carefully, ran down the hundred stairs and took off in his car, heading for Kowloon.

What on earth had gone wrong? If only she'd listened! He shuddered, thinking of her fate - the reptile pit old Lu kept under the floorboards in the back of the shop. He'd run into it by accident one night while breaking into the shop.

He parked by the harbour and cached the precious cup in a hideaway under the front seat. His heart was beating rapidly, taking longer to calm now. One more job to do, then he would head home and take a long rest. He had earned it!

Deep in the New Territories, he found the hole in the wire, passed through the frontier and waited by a rocky hill for the China watcher. He felt sad that his old friend would betray him for a few dollars but there was no other explanation. The porcelain cup had been a trap and after careful consideration, he realized that only Ping could have set him up. He dug his elbows into the earth, steadying himself, feeling the rifle stock smooth and cold against his cheek. The China watcher would arrive any moment now.

He felt at one with the dark. There was a feeling of power, of having the world at your disposal. The girl would be dead now, of course, and he would not bother about her friend, Karl. There was no moon and he had to peer intently into the shadows. The top of Ping's pointed hat appeared. Slowly he released the safety and fired. The China watcher lurched forward, spun around and Grant fired again. "Sorry, old friend." He stood over the dead man for a moment, then hurried away, back through the hole in the wire and along the narrow pathway bordering the frontier. He felt cold and tired.

Hours later he reached the Supreme Emperor of Darkness Temple, and home. He walked through the empty, cool corridors and entered a small room. Reaching for the FAX, he sent a message to Madam Nunn. "Mother, I am home. Karl's woman, Greta, is dead. My car is in the safe place. Have it sent here." An answer came in twenty minutes: "Don't you ever sleep? It will be done."

He carried the translucent cup up the stairs to the House of Harmony and set it lovingly beside the fifth century fan. Gone, the smells of greasy duck and gasoline, the gaggle of voices. For a while he wandered in the midst of beauty: a carved lacquer screen, paper-thin porcelain from the Chen kilns, Ming vases and lacquer boxes, Yuan Dynasty figurines and more. None of the treasures had been obtained without cost and, as usual, he began to imagine the faces of the dead peering at him from behind every cabinet and screen. Beyond the open window the moon appeared and hung low in an orange and purple sky. The chess set seemed alive, the galloping knights, pawns fingered silently forward. The shuffle of the queens. The jade flashed orange in the moonlight.

He reached for Mary Ann and injected the morphine intravenously. On his narrow cot now, he felt the surge and began to float in a bubble of peace, away from eyes and faces, away from memories. Up, up into the netherworld, where only fools would dare to dream.

155

The Best of Birtles
by *William Bankier*

William Bankier has been, for thirty years, one of the best and most prolific writers of crime fiction of any length that Canada has produced. Born in Belleville, he has lived and worked in Montreal; on a houseboat on the Thames in London, and now in downtown Los Angeles. Each place has become the setting for numerous memorable tales, including the Edgar Award nominated "The Choirboy." And, as with Birtles, the catalyst for many of them is a dysfunctional family situation and a prime ingredient is music. In 1992, William Bankier was honoured with the Crime Writers of Canada's Derrick Murdoch Award for his outstanding contribution to the genre in Canada.

THE BEST OF BIRTLES

by *William Bankier*

Darius Dolan climbed the iron stairs with another beer for his wife's lover. They were sitting on pillows in the loft with the big windows propped open, watching the afternoon light fade across Old Montreal. "Your drink all right, Lucy?" he asked as he handed the pilsner glass to Raymond Saulnier.

"Don't need another thing." She looked like a doll, red-haired, green-eyed, propped against the needlepoint with her cigarettes and lighter at the ready on the rush matting beside her.

"Play us a tune," Saulnier requested, wiping foam from the black Zapata moustache. "Something in keeping with the mood."

Dolan went to the piano and lifted the cover, leaving dusty fingerprints. While they waited, he pulled his knuckles one at a time and thought about his father. The old man would have asked to hear Chopin. Dolan began to play one of the mazurkas, bending the tempo, extending a trill, putting a lot of emphasis on the left hand. The interpretation was perverse.

When he was finished, Lucy said, "I'm glad I don't feel as bad as you do."

"He's all right," Saulnier said. Before the low-key affair with Lucy Harmon Dolan began, Darius and Raymond had been close. They still worked well together, Dolan organizing the studio sessions, Saulnier coming in as part of the group to play tenor saxophone, and sometimes to vocalize on a jingle.

But it was all changing. Dolan the Anglo could still get work because he had been around such a long time. And he spoke some French and had friends and always paid the musicians on time. Still, the Francophones were moving inward and upward. Raymond Saulnier himself was branching out to front the occasional gig.

The telephone rang. Dolan found the instrument on the floor. He answered and heard Claire's voice. "Daddy, can I speak to Raymond?"

"He isn't here."

"He said he would be. Cut it out."

"Have you rented the safety-deposit box?"

"I said I will and I will. Do you want your precious coin collection back?"

"I want you to have it. I'd like it to be in a safe place."

"Let me speak to Raymond."

Saulnier took the telephone and said, after listening, "That's all right. No problem. Do you want to speak to your parents? *Ce n'est pas vrai.*"

"What's not true?" Lucy asked as Saulnier put down the telephone.

"Claire says you don't love her."

"She's wrong. I resent her self-centered behaviour. And some of her friends are fools. But I do so love her."

"I don't. She just cancelled her lesson." Saulnier was teaching Claire to play the flute. He got up and began assembling a portable screen. "It's dark enough, I think." He plugged in a carousel projector and switched it on.

"Heaven help us, the slides," Lucy said.

One by one, colourful images filled the screen. Saulnier said, "Paris. April." They were looking at a sidewalk cafe. More of the same - a bateau mouche, the Tour Eiffel. Lucy made him hold on child with balloon. Then the scene changed to gulls over water. "The ferry on the way to Dover."

"How many slides do you have, Raymond?"

"More than enough, Darius."

They saw views from the train window on the ride up to London. Charing Cross Station was crowded with tourists. Trafalgar Square. Admiralty Arch. Then, a sad young man with a granite wall behind him and a cap on the pavement at his feet. He was playing a guitar. "I got to know this bloke," Saulnier said. "His name is Stan Kyle. He gave me his card. If you need a guitar player, I can provide his number."

"What we need in Montreal. Another guitar player."

Lucy said, "He looks so mournful."

"He can really play," Saulnier enthused. "Classical stuff. I remember what he told me. He said, 'This used to be a good guitar and I used to be able to play it.' He said he wanted to be Julian Bream. His dream was to play some day in the Albert Hall."

"You tell me your dream," Dolan said. "I'll tell you mine."

The next slide depicted a group of young men crowded around a table in a pub. They were posing, mock-serious, like a Victorian board meeting. Saulnier continued, "This was where we got to know each other. I gave Kyle five quid and he said it paid him up for the day. This pub is around the corner. All these guys showed up later, as I was leaving." He changed slides to one of a double-decker bus.

"Go back," Lucy said.

"Pardon?"

"Can we see that one again?" Click, whirr, and there they were again on the screen, the brave young men in their seedy jackets. "The one on the end. Isn't that Jeremy Birtles?"

"He's dead," Dolan said. But he concentrated.

"We heard a rumour. Look at that face."

The man in question was head and shoulders taller than the others. A snub nose set off innocent eyes. The ginger hair was longer than when Birtles was working as a commercial artist in Montreal and hanging around with Claire Dolan. But it was the disarming smile that confirmed his identity, lips parted slightly to reveal a familiar gap between the front teeth.

"You're right, it's him," Dolan murmured. "The slippery bastard. He got somebody to spread the story so I'd forget about him."

"What happened?" Saulnier asked.

"I kept it quiet for Claire's sake. That man right there," Dolan said, approaching the screen as if he was in charge of briefing a squad of detectives, "stole my silver medallion. It was irreplaceable. I won it when I was 16, first prize at the Manitoba Piano Festival, 1959. A big thing, size of a saucer. Chopin's bust on one side, my name engraved on the other. My father must have turned in his grave when it went missing."

"Took it from your home?"

"And skipped town. At the art studio, they thought he'd gone to Toronto. The police followed up but it seemed he went back to

England. Nothing further came of the investigation. Later that year, word went around that Birtles had died of kidney failure." Dolan sat down. "We believed it. I wrote off the loss."

*   *   *

Dolan asked the cab driver to wait while he ran inside the building on Mountain Street and pressed the buzzer for Claire's apartment. As he bounded up the stairs, she was standing in the doorway with a mug of coffee in one hand and a sticky bun in the other. She put a cheek out for a kiss and made room for him to enter.

"I can't come in. The taxi's waiting."

"That's as good an excuse as any."

"Can we not argue? I'm going on airplanes." He followed her into the vestibule. Over the shoulder of her paisley gown, he could see a proliferation of bamboo and mirrors with advertising on them.

"You'll never find Jeremy," Claire said. "But mother is right, you can use the holiday."

"I've got Stan Kyle's card. I'll telephone him and he'll put me in touch with Birtles."

"Who will immediately go underground."

"Anyway, my absence will give Lucy and Raymond a chance to sort themselves out."

"Ray never loved her," Claire said. "You're worried about nothing."

*   *   *

Dolan had not been in London for ten years. They had extended the Piccadilly Line to Heathrow since his last visit. He rode the train above and under ground to Earl's Court. Outside the station, he dragged his suitcase on tiny wheels around a couple of corners, stopping at a bed-and-breakfast in a converted Edwardian mansion with white pillars needing paint. Derbyshire House. His room was large with a sloping floor. The bed was small with a soft mattress. The bathroom was around the corner and down three stairs.

There was a pub in sight from his window. Dolan went out into a gentle rain, ran to the pub and had a meal of meat pie, sprouts and mashed potatoes. He drank two pints of lager. The food, the smokey room, the people - it was all so perfect that the absence of

Lucy stabbed him in the heart. On earlier trips to London, they had talked about emigrating. Maybe they should have done it. That was mistake number one. The second was when he took the easy way out after the ad agencies began complaining. They started saying Lucy Harmon Dolan was the female voice in too many of the commercials he produced. He should have said he used her because she was the best. For seven years on CBC-TV, she had been the face and voice of The Hit Parade.

But Dolan had not defended her. He backed off because he was insecure over the French/English thing. Then Lucy took him off the hook. Claire was three years old at the time. She said it would be best if she stayed home and looked after the child. So she did. And she never sang professionally again.

Now Claire Dolan was 19 years old, a defiant young woman out on her own. And Lucy was seeking joy with Ray Saulnier. He wanted her to be happy. His absence over the next few days would give them all a chance to assess the situation. It was time for their lives to proceed to the next stage. What would be would be. Maybe Saulnier's accidental discovery of Birtles had been prompted by the hand of Fate.

Sensing the onset of terminal philosophical wisdom, Darius Dolan left the pub and took a long, slow walk in the rain.

Next morning, he telephoned Stan Kyle, dialing the number from the card Raymond had given him. A female voice answered, old enough to be Kyle's mother. From the way she screamed his name, she thought it was time for her son to be out of bed. Kyle came on the line like a disappointed guitar player, dragged from his dream of playing in the Albert Hall.

"Whozis?"

"My name is Dolan. I'm from Montreal." He decided not to unfold the saga of the face in the photograph. "I'm an old friend of Jeremy Birtles. I'm hoping you can tell me where to find him."

"How'd you get this number?"

"You gave your card to my friend Saulnier. He was here last month. Saw you playing in Trafalgar Square."

The voice softened. "I remember. French-Canadian geezer. Looks like a Mexican bandit." Kyle spoke away from the telephone. "Leave it. I don't want breakfast." Then to Dolan, "Why do you want Birtles?"

Dolan used his invented story. "He left some things at a girl's place. She asked me to bring them to him."

"Last we spoke, he was in a room at 23 Inverness Terrace. That's in Bayswater. He's not on the 'phone."

Dolan hailed a taxi for the short ride around the Park to the Bayswater Road. He found Inverness Terrace and walked along uneven paving stones past a succession of residences converted to hotels and rooming houses. Number 23 was a corner house. A man in a turban was pruning roses by the front door. Dolan said to him, "Good morning. I'm looking for Jeremy Birtles. He's my friend and I've come all the way from Montreal to see him."

"Montreal is a fine city. My sister lives there. She teaches political science at McGill University."

"My daughter lives not far from the University. Is Mr. Birtles at home?"

"Mr. Birtles is in number 4. He came in very late last night."

The number was no longer on the door but the outline of ancient paint said 4. Dolan knocked and waited. The familiar voice called, "Who is it?"

Dolan decided to play it as if they were still in Montreal. As if he and the English artist had been all night in the jazz clubs on St. Antoine Street. Lucy had made up the bed in the spare room. Just like old times. "It's me, Jeremy. Open up."

"Darius?"

"Larger than life."

Hasty movements behind the door, then it was flung wide open and Jeremy Birtles was revealed like sunlight from behind clouds. The ginger hair was tousled and the gap-toothed grin was ready for anything. "What a surprise. Do come in!"

The room smelled of linseed oil and alcohol. Dolan saw a mattress on the floor, stretched canvasses stacked against a wall, an open case of bottled beer, a hot-plate with a muddy pot resting on it. "I'm so glad you're not dead, Jeremy."

"So am I. Does that mean something?"

"The rumour in Montreal was that you'd snuffed it."

"I was quite ill last year. Perhaps somebody got that wrong. Find a place to sit. I wish I could offer you something. We'll have to go out for breakfast. Look at you, all plump and prosperous."

There was a stool the size of a goblin mushroom. Dolan lowered himself onto it. "I traced you through Stan Kyle."

Birtles faked a shudder. "Sounds like Interpol. I've been meaning to write you a letter." He turned one of the canvasses and propped it in the light. It looked good to Dolan - a portrait of a broad-faced woman with mahogany hair. "Remember when we were out boozing and I talked about getting out of commercial art? And starting to paint what I want? Well, they got me out of the studios by firing me."

"That's just fine, Jeremy. But you and I have to get something straightened out."

"The medallion. Of course."

Dolan should not have been surprised. He knew there was something of the sociopath in Birtles' make-up. The Englishman had a way of always being on top of whatever was happening to him. Never at a loss. Anticipating the confrontation and defusing it with straightforward charm. "You admit you took it."

"And I was wrong. I remember you showing me your trophies that night. We'd both had a lot to drink. You left the room and I just slipped Chopin into my pocket. It was the wine, I suppose."

"How could you do that? You knew how much that medal meant to me."

"That was the reason. I've thought about it often." Birtles went to the window and raised the blind. He went and sat cross-legged on the mattress. He tugged at the Guinness T-shirt he was wearing to make the fabric cover his knees. "I was leaving town the next day."

"As we discovered."

"I can only explain it this way, Darius. I wanted a keepsake. Something of yours I could take with me. It had to be something of value."

There were birds chirping outside the window. After half a minute, Dolan said, "Is it okay if I reject that phony explanation?"

"You can think what you like."

"I believe you took the medallion because it's big and made of silver and you needed money."

"I would never sell your medallion."

"You've still got it?"

"Of course. But not here. I can't keep anything that valuable in this rubbish tip."

"Where is it?"

"With the few other useful things I possess. At Serena's place." Birtles inclined his head towards the canvas in sunlight. For a moment, both men regarded the painted lady who stared back with an expression of tolerant amusement. Then the artist struggled to his feet. "Let me get some clothes on and we'll go outside and make a telephone call. Serena has this lovely flat in Kensington. You'll like Serena."

* * *

She wanted to see them, but not today. Tomorrow morning, at eleven, they could come for tea or something stronger. "Serena Tennant," Birtles said when he left the telephone booth. "Her parents are rich. They sent her to Roedean. Now they keep her supplied with money and Serena fulfills her end of the bargain by not coming home."

A dozen young men in long red scarves were milling about the entrance to Lancaster Gate underground station. Their aggressive movements caused Dolan to feel apprehensive. He remembered reading about football hooligans on earlier visits to England. "Looks like the riot is about to begin," he said.

"They're Manchester United supporters. Here for the game against Wimbledon this afternoon." Birtles tried to pry open Dolan's face with a bright-edged smile. "We could travel down to Plough Lane and see the match."

"Is it far?"

"Half an hour on the District Line." The artist glanced at his watch. "We can nip in here to the 'King's Head' and throw down a couple of pints to ease the journey."

It was all coming back. In Montreal, the arrival of Jeremy Birtles had always been a breath of fresh air. He had seemed a risky person, even before the theft of the medallion. But there was something irresistible in his enthusiasm. We know guns are lethal, Dolan told himself. But what man has never lusted after the thrill of hefting one?

"Let's go for it," he said, leading Birtles into the pub.

They came out of the station in Wimbledon and began walking to the football grounds. They were part of a straggling army, most of them supporters of MUFC. Hoarse chanting erupted ahead and behind. At the corner of the Broadway, a youth raced past them, shirt-tail flying, and broke speed records veering down the slope of Hartfield Road. Twenty yards behind him, a uniformed officer, hatless, ran in pursuit. They were passing 'The Prince of Wales'. "The clever thing to do," Birtles said from the pub entrance, "is to give this crowd time to get inside the park."

"You're on," Dolan agreed.

He carried overflowing pints to a corner table. Birtles said, "Ta!" and "Cheers!" Then, "Tell me all the gossip from Montreal."

"It's changing. Still beats Toronto as a place to live. But I've done my work in English for a lot of years. Could I start working in French? Probably not. I'm history in that sweet town."

"Come and work in London."

"I could never make that big a move. I'm too old."

"Think about it. Lots of Canadians work here." Birtles winked. "And tomorrow you'll know Serena." When he came back from the bar with two more, he asked, "How's the family?"

"Claire moved out last year. She's in that old building at Mountain and Maisonneuve. Across from the sidewalk cafe."

"I remember."

"She and Lucy could no longer get along. Two strong-minded women in the same house."

"Is Lucy still singing?"

"She should. It might calm her down. Raymond Saulnier wants to use her in commercials." The beer was beginning to talk. "Raymond Saulnier wants to use her every way he can."

"Uh-oh."

"No big deal. Lucy and I had a lot of good years. Now she's getting ready to go on to something else."

"As should you."

Dolan made a face. "This old horse is out to pasture." But looking around the crowded pub at the women with their eyes and smiles, he felt as if he could start over.

They arrived at Plough Lane after half-time. They found room on the terraces at the Wimbledon end and stood pressed in closely with a crowd of several hundred. All swayed in a slow, sensuous wave from side to side, hardly aware of the game on the field. And as the throaty singing arose and drove all other thoughts from his mind, Dolan linked arms with Birtles and a stranger and they sang with surpassing joy like the devout in a great cathedral - "Walk on, walk on, with hope in your heart. . ."

*   *   *

Serena let him in. Dolan moved past her into a cool vestibule. He saw mahogany and oak and mirrors and silver. A vast, unframed painting nearly filled a wall between casement windows flung open with white curtains sucked out across painted sills.

"Is Jeremy here?"

"Jeremy can't make it." She was older than he expected, and more attractive. Her hair had been cut short since the Birtles portrait. Dressed in beige slacks and a loose white blouse, she presented a long curved neck and shoulder that had Dolan looking for a spot to sink his teeth. The green eyes were calm as twilight, and they flooded him with understanding. "I'm drinking gin. Would you rather have coffee?"

After the late carousal with Birtles, he was feeling seedy. But he heard himself say, "Gin is fine. What happened to Jeremy? I was with him last night."

"Vintage Birtles. He showed up here at eight o'clock this morning. Which went down badly with your hostess, I can assure you. Jeremy has decided to fly to America. Just like that, whim of the day. Stopping off first in Montreal." She brought Dolan his drink in a heavy crystal beaker. "He has friends there who can help him out with some money. I started him off with air fare. Then it's on to the West Coast."

Through one of the windows, Dolan could see Kensington Gardens with people in deck chairs scattered across the grass and rainbow-coloured ice-cream vans parked on the High Street. He said, "Then it looks like he's left me high and dry."

"Can you bear it?"

"No pain so far." He decided to get business out of the way. "Did Jeremy tell you? I'll want to pick up my medallion."

"Sorry?"

"The silver medallion you're keeping for him. It belongs to me. I won it in a piano competition." As he spoke, Dolan realised yesterday's suspicions were now confirmed. Birtles had made up a story on the spur of the moment. So he was not surprised when Serena said, "I have nothing of his. Has Jeremy been a naughty boy again?"

Dolan told the story. Because she was so simpatico, he found himself dwelling on the early days in Winnipeg when he was spending all his time practicing, attempting to please an unpleasable father. "This makes me seem like a damn fool," he concluded.

"You're not the only person he's taken advantage of."

She sat beside him on the chaise lounge. He was feeling comfortable in the elegant room. "I think if I ever saw him again, I'd want to kill him. He tells you what you want to hear. He diverts you."

"Please don't be angry. It's a waste."

"It's been so many years. Then by this fluke, I get back in touch with him. And he says no problem. I've got your medallion. But he was jerking me around. And he's gone again."

"You must be a good pianist."

"Used to be. I'm more of an arranger now. A composer. Of sixty-second commercials." He finished his drink. "You should hear the theme from Jiffo Cleanser."

"I'd like to hear you play."

There was a piano on the other side of the room. He was surprised at how eager he was to perform for her. He concentrated on walking slowly to the instrument. It's tone was the best he had encountered since the competition when he was sixteen. The late-night partying, the topping up of alcohol this morning - Dolan's inhibitions vanished. He did not even try to decide what to play. Powerful bass chords thundered from his left hand as one arpeggio after another took him through a series of key changes. Then he was playing 'Stella By Starlight' as if it had been written by Franz Liszt. He was cocktail pianist in the classiest bar in the universe, entertaining an audience of royalty from monarchies past and present. The pyrotechnics were shameless. His arms ached when he finished.

"Bravo! Darius, that was brilliant. Play some more." She brought them both another drink and sat on the bench beside him. "You are my Chopin and I am your Georges Sand."

He drank and played again, shocked by the fleeting brush of her lips across his cheek.

They went out for lunch at two o'clock. He was stiff with gin but in control. She took him to a small restaurant on a side street within sight of the Albert Hall. "I heard of a guitar player who dreamed of playing there," he said. "He's a busker now. In Trafalgar Square."

She had the knack of keeping him talking. It was like a three-hour session with a sensuous therapist. "My father never came to visit me in Montreal. After mother died, I offered to fly him east from Winnipeg and install him in his own apartment."

"He was set in his ways."

"He despised my work. He refused to recognize that I've been a success in the music business." They were drinking red wine. He refilled their glasses from the second bottle. "There was never any guarantee I would have made it as a concert pianist. We have to go where life leads us." He remembered standing in the doorway of the old house, expecting his father to come and say goodbye. The taxi was waiting to take him to the airport. The driver sounded the horn. "Dad?" The wingback chair framed that stubborn head with its halo of white hair.

Serena said, "I'm glad life led you here, Darius."

*   *   *

It was on his second night sleeping at Serena's place that Dolan sat bolt upright in bed, recalling something he had told Birtles.

Serena whispered, "Are you all right?" She was grey shadow. Dawn's light hesitated between half-closed drapes.

"I know what he's up to. I told him my daughter is living alone. They used to date. I reminded him where her apartment is located."

"Why would he go there?"

"Because she's vulnerable. And he's an opportunist."

"Jeremy is a thief. Does she have anything worth stealing?"

In his mind's eye, Dolan saw the collection of gold coins in their leather and velvet case. Twenty-five of them worth close to $350 each. Case and contents would bring nine grand, easily. He told Serena about it. "When she moved out last year, I turned them over to her. She's been talking about a safe deposit box. But she hasn't done it."

At breakfast, he said, "I'm going to have to leave." To telephone Claire and try to warn her would be a waste of time. Whether Birtles had arrived or not, she would hear nothing against him. The only course was to head the man off.

"I never thought this was forever, Darius."

"When I get it sorted out, maybe I can come back."

She hid behind the teacup she was holding. "I hope you're worrying over nothing."

*　　*　　*

He rode a taxi from the airport all the way in to Centre-Ville. The late lunch people were having one more drink at the sidewalk cafe as he went inside Claire's building across the street. She had not answered the telephone when he dialed her number from Mirabel. His ring held a key to the apartment. He let himself in.

"Claire?" The place was airless. He went to the tall window between the bookcases and raised it shoulder high.

Her bedroom was far neater than she had ever maintained her room at home. The sofa-bed in the living room was unfolded and made up. A suitcase on the floor overflowed male clothing. Birtles! If confirmation were needed, a book of matches on the end table bore the identification, 'The Prince of Wales, Hartfield Road, London SW19'.

Dolan felt his anger rising. The guy was unbelievable. He had taken that day of comradeship and turned it immediately to his advantage.

The coin collection! Dolan knew where Claire kept it. There was a small cabinet at the bottom of the oak bookcase near the window. In it, she stored a number of precious artifacts she did not want to leave lying around the room. He knelt by the window, pressed the door and felt it spring open. Inside he saw a stack of letters bound in ribbon and a toy plastic doll in a heart-covered dress. But the leather case was not there.

Dolan's eyes were at window level. Below, on Maisonneuve Boulevard, he saw a familiar figure crossing from the cafe. It was Jeremy Birtles, hands in pockets, jacket flapping behind him. Since he was staying here, Claire must have dispensed another key. Dolan got to his feet and drifted inside the bedroom. He was not sure how to handle the situation. Birtles was a lot younger and probably stronger than he was. It was too late to call the police.

Footsteps on the stairs. Key in the lock. Door opening and closing. Birtles moved through the room, snuffling, clearing his throat. The telephone clicked off the cradle. Dolan ventured a glance into the room. Over the back of an upholstered chair, he saw the Englishman's shoulders and curly head. The dialing went beyond seven digits. He was taking the opportunity to run up some long-distance charges.

"Hello, Keith? It's Jeremy! How are things in glorious San Francisco? No, I'm not. I'm in Montreal. I'm settled in with the daughter of an old geezer I ran into in London. You bastard, we're just friends. The old geezer won't soon be back because I set him up with Serena. I did! That should be good for a fortnight. Don't worry about money, I'll be bringing some with me."

Dolan looked around for a weapon. He was having trouble seeing. He was blinking flashes of light. There was a bronzed horseshoe on the window ledge, a souvenir of some playground competition. He grasped it in his right hand and hearing Birtles put down the telephone, took quick steps through the doorway.

He came out of the bedroom as the Londoner got to his feet. The reaction was spontaneous. Birtles stepped back when Dolan rushed at him, the horseshoe raised. He lifted his arm to shield his head. Dolan was screaming, "You thieving son-of-a-bitch. . .!"

The window ledge caught Birtles behind the knees. He fell backwards, striking his head against the raised sash, doubling over and sliding through the aperture to fall three floors to the sidewalk.

As Dolan stood away from the window and out of sight, people holding glasses were beginning to leave the cafe and move tentatively into the street.

*   *   *

Not wanting to surprise Lucy with Raymond Saulnier, Dolan telephoned the house. "Hi, it's me."

"Where are you?"

"Claire's place." Quickly, he described what had happened - the pursuit of Birtles from London, the confirmation of his theft of the gold coins, then his accidental tumble through the open window. "Maybe I'd better call the police."

"Wait a minute. Did you touch him? Was there a fight?"

"No. He was taken by surprise."

"Then just come home. We'll talk about what you have to do."

Dolan left the building by the back door. He walked down to Ste. Catherine Street and hailed a cab. He was home in twenty minutes. Lucy had coffee ready, he could smell the fresh brew as he came inside. She held her arms open to him, their first embrace in quite a while. When he was seated at the kitchen table, she said, "You don't have to do anything. Claire didn't even tell me Birtles was in town. We've been having zero contact. The guy is notoriously erratic. He flies in here from London, who knows what personal problems are troubling him? He's not the first depressive to jump from a high place."

"But that isn't what happened. He was getting set to go to San Francisco."

"Having stolen your coins."

"I should have searched his suitcase. But he probably disposed of them already. He told his friend he'd be arriving with money."

"Forget him, Darius. Don't even tell Claire you were there."

It would save a lot of hassle if he could live with it. "How's Raymond?"

Her eyes flickered. "He's been working a lot. Rehearsing an album." She sipped coffee. "How was London?"

"I did what English people do. I got drunk at a soccer match."

"It was brilliant of me not to go."

"I missed you quite a bit."

The Dolan's began to have quiet pleasure. They divided the morning paper, discovered new outrages in the community and shared them, reading aloud. Darius got hungry. He opened a tin of refrigerated biscuits, put them in the oven and, eight minutes later, served them with butter and jam. There was not much wrong with the moment. The argument for keeping quiet about Birtles took on weight.

Claire arrived within the hour. She let herself in at the side door and entered the kitchen with a closed-up face. "Daddy, you're here. I thought you were in London."

"I came back."

"Well, I have an announcement to make. Raymond and I are getting married."

"I knew it," Lucy said. Her face was drained of blood. "I could tell."

"He's twenty years older than you are," Dolan said.

"So?"

"I think you'd better wait."

"You can't give me orders."

"Something has happened."

"Darius, what's the difference?" Lucy said.

It seemed now that he was always going to confess. It was happening sooner rather than later. "I saw Jeremy at your place."

"When?"

"An hour ago. I went there from the airport. It was exactly what I was afraid of. The bastard has stolen my gold coins."

"No he didn't."

"And when I confronted him, he tried to get away. Claire, he fell out the open window. He's dead."

Claire sat down at the table. She had her mother's jaw, the determined mouth turned down. "Is this some trick to break me up with Ray?"

"It's what happened."

"Did you two have a fight?"

"I never touched him. All right, I was going to. He stole my medallion years ago. And now he's done me again."

"The coin collection?" Claire reached forward and put a hand on her father's arm. "I gave it to Ray. He's using it for short-term collateral on a loan. He had to give cash to the studio where he's making his album. I'll have the coins back, end of next month."

While Dolan said nothing, Claire listened to her mother. They could not bring back Jeremy, whatever was told to the police. Involving her father in an inquest which might lead to a trial would not help anybody. She agreed to go home now, discover the sad accident, and let events take their course.

She had been gone from the house for less than a minute. Darius and Lucy were still looking at the floor when Claire came back inside, took a gift-wrapped package from her handbag and gave it to her father. "I forgot. Jeremy gave me this to give to you. He thought he'd be gone before you got back from London."

Dolan broke tape. He unfolded gold foil wrapping. The weight told him what it was before he took the lid off the box. There, in a nest of tissue, lay the medallion. He saw the bust of Chopin. He turned it over while the women watched in silence, and read his name and the inscription on the other side.

There was a piece of note-paper folded square under the medallion. He broke it open and saw the flowing script of a trained artist. Dolan read the message aloud.

"Dear Darius: I hope this comes not too late to make things right. I could have told you the truth in London, but it would have come out sounding shabby. Isn't the truth often like that? I did sell the medallion to a man in Montreal. My idea was to come here and steal it back from him, if he still had it. Which he did, and I did. But it was all so indefinite, how could I have told you what I had in mind?

"Anyway, here you are with your beautiful prize. And I've had a great few days with your charming daughter, my old friend Claire. And now San Francisco calls. I must be sure to wear a flower in my hair.

"Isn't it fine, the way things work out in the end? All the best, Birtles."

Double Bogey by *John North*

Toronto writer, computer systems consultant and golf enthusiast, John North scored with his Arthur nominated story "Out of Bounds" in Cold Blood III. In this, his third published story, he returns to the golf course, which has never seemed so chilling.

DOUBLE BOGEY

by *John North*

John Friesen didn't look worried as he repeatedly bounced the golf ball on the face of his driver - but he was - very worried. While he appeared absorbed with keeping the club and ball moving in unison, his mind was miles away from the golf course and the Hospital Appeal pro-am. He had triggered an irreversible train of events and belated second thoughts were a waste of time.

While many of his fellow professionals resented the hours spent humouring amateur partners, he relished this type of charity event where three amateurs and a professional competed as a team. It released him from the day-to-day routines of the workshop and provided an opportunity to promote his repair service as well as the customized golf clubs he made. It also enabled him to keep up with local golf happenings and gossip and even, sometimes, win some money in the simultaneous pro-only competition.

Suddenly he flipped the Titleist high into the air and caught it behind his back. The small group of spectators clapped politely and then moved back to allow the three amateurs from the group playing behind through to the elevated fourteenth tee. John looked to see where their pro was, and saw him talking to a young woman on the edge of the thirteenth green. There always seemed to be a delay on this hole and a glance at the green 180 yards away told him that there would be least five more minutes to wait before his group could resume play. Each member of the group ahead had marked his ball on the putting surface and the foursome was now engaged in confusing itself with conflicting advice on the likely lines of the various putts.

*At two o'clock the climate control monitoring program
running in the microcomputer had changed the setting
of the thermostat and the heating system had responded.
The temperature in the room was approaching thirty
degrees Celsius - the maximum setting of the thermostat
over the workshop bench. Under the same bench a
small crack in the seam of the metal kerosene drum had
already leaked enough of the fluid to create a small
pool.*

John walked over to his teenage caddy who was leaning on the golf
bag and spitting at a soft-drink cup near the litter basket. "Practicing
for a career in professional baseball, are you?" John asked. "Make
sure you work on your slider as much as you do the expectorative
aspects of the game." He unzipped the side pocket of the golf bag,
removed the portable phone and walked off the tee. The caddy
gazed blankly after him.

He made two calls, and on each of them hung up before the
answering machine could pick up on the fourth ring. Karen was
probably out shopping and the lack of response to the second call
reassured him that Don hadn't changed his plan and made one of his
infrequent visits to the office. As he folded up the phone he noticed
that a mini-cam from the local television station was aimed in his
direction. He smiled automatically at the camera and turned to
Sharon Villa, the sports reporter, who stood beside it.

"How come you're working?" he said. "I thought you'd be on
this side of the camera today." John had made a set of golf clubs for
Villa and knew her as an avid and knowledgeable golfer who played
whenever she had the chance.

Sharon smiled at him. "That's great, Frank," she said to the
cameraman. "Just a few shots of groups coming onto the last green
and then we're through. Take a break. I'll meet you back at the
clubhouse in half an hour."

Sharon turned back to John. "I wish you were the News
Director," she said. "I was all set to play until Bob got instructions
from on high. Seems that the wife of one of the station owners is a
mainstay of the Hospital Appeal and she felt that some in-depth
coverage might generate additional revenue for the charity. As the
station's designated golf expert I was assigned. Anyway, how's the
game going?"

"Much the same as any pro-am," John replied. "Three keen, but nervous, occasional golfers who are trying too hard to play shots they'd never attempt at their own courses. As a team we're eight under par, with another couple of birdies on the way in we should finish in the money."

"Lots of luck," said Sharon. "You'll need to be closer to twelve under, Bob Albion and his team of sandbaggers is ten under after the fifteenth ."

John laughed with her. Albion was a well-known golf fanatic who belonged to two local clubs. He could be relied upon to enter each and every available golf tournament within a three hour drive of the city. He was notorious for his desire to win, and for some of the stunts he had pulled to do so. He was also John's landlord, and if the rent he charged for the renovated barn that housed the golf business was any indicator, he could easily afford his hobby.

"What was the point of taping me on the phone? I thought you were here to cover the golf."

"I had a long shot of you doing the ball bouncing act on the face of your driver and I thought the mobile phone would make a great contrasting shot. The modern and traditional aspects of the venerable game." Her voice assumed a serious voice-over tone.

"Well if you use the clip on air, be sure to mention that John Friesen is a respected local club maker and repairer whose craftsmanship and expertise can only improve your game and lower your handicap. I can always use some new business."

A shout from the tee indicated that John's group was waiting for him. He glanced at his watch as he walked back.

In the workshop, liquid continued to drip from the kerosene drum and potentially incendiary fumes were spreading through the room. In the office area the phone bell had been switched off and the incoming call was terminated before the answering machine could kick in. The microcomputer hummed gently on its stand and the program now running was due to execute its next command when the internal clock registered three o'clock. The "Housekeeper" program had been changed earlier in the day when the clock had been checked and reset.

The other members of his group had already hit by the time John joined them on the tee. One ball was on the back of the green - about as far from the pin as it was possible to be without leaving the putting surface. The other two were in the deep bunker at the front left of the green.

With the wind blowing briskly from behind his right shoulder John asked the caddy for his six iron. He teed up the ball, looked at the pin on the front left of the green long enough to establish the line of flight, and took a couple of slow practice strokes. He settled over the ball, took an easy swing and started the ball towards the right-hand edge of the green. As he had intended the ball rode the wind and swung gently towards the pin. It landed just short of the green, bounced once, rolled towards the flagstick and stopped three feet short. One of his best shots of the day.

John bowed mockingly to the other golfers on the tee, winked at Sharon and then started towards the green. His excited partners congratulated him on the shot while he wondered, for the millionth time, why he couldn't consistently hit shots that good. He knew that the margin of excellence between himself and tour players was extremely small and that on any given day he could turn in rounds as good as any of the well-known tour pros. What he knew he lacked was the tenacity to do it day in and day out, and enough desire to make the sacrifices necessary to push him over the competitive edge.

Four years ago he had come to terms with his future. He resigned from his position as club pro to establish his own golf club business. He didn't want to spend the rest of his life selling shirts, slacks and sweaters; giving lessons doomed to be forgotten within hours; and playing against the members while trying hard to make it look like a fair contest. He realized he wasn't of tour calibre and that he was better at making clubs than hitting them. In his future competitive golf would be a remunerative hobby rather than a career.

In the workshop the kerosene drum had reacted to the rising heat by expanding very slightly. The tiny increase in the size of the crack that had been made earlier in the day allowed more liquid to dribble down to the floor. The ensuing pool eventually overflowed the slight depression in which the drum sat and a small stream of

*fluid trickled towards the interior partition separating
the workshop from the office. There it disappeared
through a crack in the floor.*

John's present dilemma was caused by money, or rather the lack of it. His initial dream of his own small independent business had been rudely shattered as soon as he and Karen started to plan the project in detail. Even with their joint savings and a loan from her parents they were barely able to get together enough cash for stock and raw materials, let alone to rent and equip a workspace. They soon realized that the choice was between abandoning the idea of striking out on their own or looking for a partner with capital. After asking around some of their friends and members at the golf club they had been introduced to Don Partick, a young accountant who had inherited a sizable legacy when his parents died in a car crash. Partick was a social golfer who played only a few times a year and who made it clear that he had absolutely no desire to become involved in the technical side of the business. He had checked John's plans and reputation carefully and was convinced of his competence, diligence and honesty. Partick admitted that golf was not the reason for his participation. He simply preferred the role of instant independent entrepreneur to the grind of junior associate in a multinational accounting conglomerate. With no misgivings on either side the partnership documents were signed and the business was born. John's current problem, however, remained financial. Although the business generated more income than he had originally estimated, splitting it with a partner kept him perpetually poor.

*Below the floor the kerosene flowed along the metal
edge of the partition wall to form a larger pool in a
depression in the concrete foundation of the building.
As luck would have it, the pool formed just underneath
the area where the solvents were stored and close to the
point at which the natural gas line entered the premises.*

In the first year the partnership had worked well. John had immersed himself in the technical aspects and had spent countless hours developing suitable working space, selecting stock, testing and lining up operating supplies for the repair work, and establishing and cementing links in all areas of the local golfing community.

Don's training and business contacts had been invaluable in getting the venture off the ground, and his infusion of capital had enabled them to present a prosperous and progressive business image. His initial insistence on quality had gone unquestioned by the busy John, and the result had been such items as the smart premises, expensive stationery, and essential business trappings - such as the oversize desks, the black leather chairs and sofa, the fax machine, an office computer that even regulated the environment of the building, and the portable phone John now carried in his golf bag. Despite his misgivings about the scale of the expenditures, John had gone along with Don's wishes, since he was the source of the money.

> In the office, the internal clock in the computer triggered another sequence of commands. The first command activated the power to the workshop exhaust fan and the second one erased the program the machine had just run. The computer had barely executed the erase sequence before the effects of the first command were felt.

After a slow but satisfactory first year, business had picked up, and both partners were pleased with what they had accomplished. However, as year two progressed problems began to emerge. John was kept increasingly occupied with the golf end of the business while Karen became more vocal about the time he spent at work and enduring a lower living standard then she had anticipated. Their tentative plan to start a family was no longer a topic of conversation. Meanwhile, Don's initial enthusiasm waned and his visits to the shop grew further apart. He came in only when he had to and clearly saw his role as a passive investor rather than a working partner. It was apparent that Don's main interest was in what the business provided for him rather than what he contributed towards its success. He saw his share of the operation as a framework for a lifestyle, and as a way to provide the tax-free peripherals essential to support it. Don's detachment and lack of participation made it easy for John to resent his partner's share of the growing profits. Don had moved from saviour to albatross.

While John walked onto the green to mark his ball he sneaked another glance at his watch. It must have happened by now - if all had gone well his problems should be almost over. He and Karen would be able to start over and nobody would have lost out.

The exhaust fan never switched on. The electrical wire to its motor had been unclipped from the wall and rerouted to floor level where it passed through a plastic bottle sitting on a floor heating vent. There was an inch of liquid in the bottom of the bottle which bulged slightly from the pressure of the fumes within. The points at which the wire entered and left the bottle had been sealed with a caulking compound, and inside the bottle the wire had been stripped of its insulating plastic, scraped to a narrower diameter and had several thin strips of paper wound loosely around it.

John looked over the long putt of his amateur partner. The ball was two inches off the edge of the green, sixty downhill feet from the flagstick over a slick green with at least two changes of direction. John knew the man would be pleased to get down in three from there, but gave the optimistic support he was supposed to provide. "Leave the stick in," he said. "Give it a good rap, though. What do you think - aim about a foot from the right-hand edge?" His partner nodded nervously and then jabbed at the ball. From its initial path and velocity the ball looked as if it would pass at least two feet to the right of the cup and run right off the green. However as it sped across the green it tracked inexorably towards the left and began to look as if it would pass close to the hole after all. As if drawn by a magnet the ball closed in on the flagstick and as John prepared encouraging remarks about the line being good even if the speed was wrong, the ball slammed into the flagstick, popped up several inches in the air and dropped into the cup. There was a moment of complete silence and then the whole team exploded into a round of congratulations and back-slapping. Once the excitement had died down John quietly sank his own short birdie putt to count in the separate competition among the professionals.

When current flowed into the wire leading to the fan, events happened so fast that they seemed virtually simultaneous. The wire heated up and began to glow red at its narrowest point. The paper started to burn igniting the gasoline fumes in the plastic bottle. As the bottle exploded the liquid gasoline in the bottom caught fire and the fumes from the pool of kerosene burst into flames. While a fireball enveloped the area of the workbench a tongue of flame ran along the kerosene trail to the crack in the wall, along the metal base of the wall, and ignited the pool of fluid trapped on the foundation. The ensuing explosion set light to the contents of the storage cupboard and broke the gas main resulting in two further explosions that leveled all the internal walls and severely damaged two of the outer ones. Large sections of the roof fell in and the flames, fed by the gas line, leaped dozens of feet into the air.

The improbable putt seemed to galvanize the team and they gained another two strokes on par over the next three holes. As the game progressed John tried to shake off his preoccupation with what should be taking place at the workshop. He had given it his best shot and it was too late to do anything about it now. His basically honest nature had caused him severe qualms about setting the fire, but as the scheme had evolved it seemed to provide a win-win situation. He and Karen would be better off, Don would suffer no financial loss, and the landlord of the building would be compensated by his insurance. Defrauding the insurance company was wrong, but it was a victimless crime and the relatively small amount of his subsequent claim wouldn't even be noticed on their corporate balance sheet. The fire would provide the excuse to sever the unsatisfactory partnership with Don, and furnish enough cash to indulge Karen in some long overdue luxuries before he re-established the business with himself as the sole proprietor.

The last drum of solvent had exploded in the ruins of the workshop. The oily black smoke from the boxes of rubber golf club grips was sucked skyward along with the cleaner fumes generated by the burning wood of the furniture and fittings. Occasional tongues of flame still flared from the rubble as pockets of combustible material caught fire. The burnt timbers from the fallen roof and walls collapsed even lower as the material underneath burned away. Two cars and a truck stopped on the nearby road, and the occupants leaned on the vehicles as they watched the fire. The siren from an approaching fire truck could be heard in the distance.

At ten minutes to four they arrived at the eighteenth tee to learn from one of the spectators that the Albion group had finished at twelve under par - one stroke better than their score. The last hole, a downhill par five with a long dogleg around some tall trees, might provide a chance to catch Albion's team. When his three partners had hit their tee shots towards the corner of the fairway John took the driver from his bag. He decided to go for broke and try to carry the corner. He took a smooth hard swing at the ball and was rewarded as it disappeared from sight over the trees. It should be in excellent shape for a shot to the green.

The firefighters continued to pump water onto the soggy black remains of the structure. Parts of the uneven rubble held small pools of water that reflected the afternoon sun while other areas steamed intensely as the heat underneath vaporized the water. The roadside spectators had now grown to the point where a policeman was having trouble keeping the traffic moving.

The four golfers reached the corner of the trees having discussed every possible way they could beat, tie or fall short of the score posted by Albion's team. They found two balls in the fairway at the corner of the dogleg and a third in the ditch on the right edge. John's caddy came back to report that his ball had cleared the trees and was in the centre of the fairway. The two amateurs played high iron shots over the trees and short of the pond that guarded the front of the green.

A black water-logged mess was all that remained of a thriving business. The fire was completely extinguished, and the firefighters were putting their equipment back into their trucks. The gas company had turned off the gas lines and the police had managed to persuade the last of the bystanders to leave.

When the group arrived at John's ball they were all excited. Not only had it cleared the trees but had taken a favourable bounce on the firm fairway and left a shot of one hundred and forty-five yards with an excellent angle to the flagstick. Behind the green the flagpole on the clubhouse lawn drooped languidly in the still air. He shook off the eight iron the caddy held out and reached for the nine iron. As he took a last glance at the green to align his shot he noticed a police car pull up to the clubhouse and park under the portico. He took several deep breaths to try to settle down, but he rushed the backswing and hit into the ground well behind the ball which vanished to a watery grave in the exact centre of the pond.

John was furious at his lapse of concentration and the poor execution of such a routine shot. Probably the arrival of the police car had nothing to do with him and all he had managed to do was deprive himself of some prize money. He immediately apologized to his partners and handed the club back to the caddy who was trying unsuccessfully to stifle a smirk of misplaced satisfaction.

The first amateur managed to hit to the green, but his ball rolled down the slope and into the trap beyond. Unless the other player could hit close to the pin and sink a birdie putt for a tie, it looked as if the best the team could hope for would be a par and second place - one stroke behind Albion's team. Realizing the fate of the team was in his hands the nervous golfer was having trouble selecting a club. John put the pitching wedge in his hands and placed a reassuring hand on his shoulder. "Hit it hard and aim for the centre of the green. Anywhere on the putting surface gives us a chance for a birdie and a tie."

"Close only counts in horseshoes and grenades," said the golfer. "I might as well hole it out for a clean win."

"Go for it. You can do it," encouraged John. One of the other golfers, with a more pragmatic outlook, mumbled something about John's mouth and God's ear.

A short fast swing started the ball climbing towards the right corner of the green. At its highest point over the pond it began to curve gracefully towards the left hand side of the green and the flag. The entire group held their breaths as the ball plummeted towards the green, bounced once and disappeared into the hole. The happy amateur had scored the first eagle of his life and stood stunned as the rest of the group rushed over to congratulate him. When the excitement had died down John dropped a ball close to the pond and pitched onto the green about fifteen feet from the pin. As the group walked on the cart-path around the pond, the spectators around the green gave them a round of applause. Up at the clubhouse John could see the club manager pointing his group out to a man in a grey suit. John's par putt stopped on the edge of the hole. He tapped in for the bogey and joined his waiting partners. While the group signed their scorecard on the edge of the green, the man in the suit went over to the police car and spoke briefly into the radio. John shook hands with his partners and agreed to meet them in the bar in a few minutes.

He gave the caddy his car keys and told him to clean the clubs, put them in the trunk and then meet him in the locker room. The policeman who had pulled a small black book from his jacket pocket waited and approached John as the caddy shambled out of earshot.

"Mr. Friesen?"

"Yes?"

"Inspector Bristol, Township Police. I'm afraid there's been a bad fire at your workshop. We tried to contact your partner, Mr. er..." He glanced at his notebook. " ... Partick, and when we couldn't reach him we called you. Eventually we sent a car to your house and your neighbour told us where you were."

"What happened? Is the damage bad?"

"Pretty bad I'm afraid, sir. The whole place was completely destroyed. It looks as if there was an explosion and then a fierce fire. The firefighters said there was almost nothing left when they arrived. Right now though I'd like to know if anyone was likely to have been in the building."

"No, everyone was away today, thank God. Our receptionist is away on vacation, my partner is down in the city meeting with our lawyers and I have been here all day. I'd better get cleaned up and then go out there. Is there anything you want me to do?"

"In view of the explosion and the possibility of arson, we've asked the fire investigator to check the site over. However, he won't be able to get there for a couple of hours. I'd appreciate it if you could keep clear until he's finished. There's nothing you can do at the moment, sir. I expect you'll be wanting to get in touch with your partner, landlord and people like that. I assume you were insured."

"I hope so," said John nervously. "Don takes care of the business side of things, but I expect he put it through Russ Thompson's agency - I know he handles the insurance for our company cars."

"Well that's all we can do for now, sir. If you could drop in at the police station sometime tomorrow, we can tie up any loose ends and I'll give you a copy of the investigator's report. The insurance company will probably want it later."

"Thanks very much for letting me know," said John. "I'd like to take a look at the damage on the way home, if that's okay. I'll certainly call in at the police station tomorrow morning."

"No problem, Mr. Friesen, so long as you just look. I'll warn our man at the site to keep an eye open for you, and I'll expect you tomorrow."

They had walked up to the clubhouse as they talked. Bristol drove off in the police car and John went in search of his caddy. Forty minutes later he was ready to leave. He had turned in the scorecards, showered and changed, paid his caddy, informed the organizers he could not stay on for the dinner, congratulated his jubilant team-mates on their unexpected victory and made his excuses to leave what promised to be a prolonged celebration. He swung the van out of the parking lot and headed for the workshop. Even though the excitement was long over and the fire trucks had departed, traffic still slowed on the highway to look at the police car and the area of charred devastation. When he pulled into the muddy ruts and puddles of the small parking lot, a policeman climbed out of the cruiser parked near the entrance. John wound down his window and stared aghast at the ruins. It was unbelievable. The building had been completely flattened to the point where no part of the debris was more than waist high.

"Mr. Friesen? Inspector Bristol warned me to expect you."

"Yes, that's right."

"I'm afraid you'll have to stay away from the actual ruins until the inspection team has had a look at the site. Not that there seems much left for them to look at."

John could not believe the extent of the destruction. When he had planned the fire he had expected a charred building with the contents destroyed. He certainly had not anticipated anything on this scale.

Accompanied by the policeman he skirted the ruins in silence. When they'd finished he shook his head in disbelief, thanked the constable and climbed into the van. If he'd known the result would have been like this he would never have had the courage to do it. He hoped Albion had enough insurance to replace the building - it needed rebuilding not restoration. He drove slowly off the site and the policeman returned to the police cruiser to await the inspection team.

When he arrived home he saw that Karen's car was not in the garage. Their neighbour, Mrs. Poole, was sitting on the rocker on her porch. He had known her a long time. She had lived there since he was a child and in the intervening years she had become a trusted friend. His parents had died several years earlier and since then she had almost become one of the family.

He waved and walked across her lawn and she put down her book as he approached.

"How was the golf? You don't look very happy."

"Oh the golf went well enough, but the police came to tell me that the workshop had burned down."

"Yes. They came here and I told them where to find you. They came about an hour after Karen left. Apparently the Cancer Society needed a last-minute replacement for one of their volunteer drivers. She said she'd be gone for a couple of hours to drive a patient to the clinic in the city. She should have been back by now though."

"You know what those out-patient clinics are like. Sometimes you're in and out of there before you know it, and other times it seems to take forever. This must be one of their slow days."

John walked slowly across to his house and wondered if there were any traces of arson. During the next hour he made several attempts to call Don and kept looking out of the window for Karen. She still had not returned by the time it became dark enough to switch on the lights and he called Don's number again, only to get the answering machine.

John wasn't much of a drinker, but he made himself a large scotch and water and sat by the empty fireplace with it. His mind kept replaying the picture of the burned-out workshop. He shook his head in irritation and wondered where Karen was. She should have been home hours ago. He walked into the kitchen and looked on the list of phone numbers taped to the wall. He tapped out the number against "Cancer Soc. (Mrs. Stoner)" and the woman who answered was very surprised to hear from him. Mrs. Stoner had scheduled no runs to the clinic that day, and she assured him that she had not phoned Karen. He took a deep pull of his drink and phoned several of her friends. None of them had seen her, or heard from her, that day. He made one more call to Don's answering machine, hung up in disgust and returned to the den to replenish his glass.

Several drinks later he had still not been able to reach Don, and his worry about Karen's whereabouts had swung from concern to anger and back to concern again. He made a sandwich and ate it while he watched the coverage of the fire and the pro-am on the local news program. He was surprised at how he looked on TV. While the medium made some people look deranged, it seemed to flatter him. He was even liked the sequence of him using the cellular phone despite Sharon Villa's somewhat breathless remarks about him being a high-tech golfer on the move. At least she had mentioned his name and that of the now-defunct business. He switched off the set and glumly stared at the screen. When he found himself thinking in cliches such as "what's done is done" and "it would probably work out best for all concerned", he drained his glass, cleared up the kitchen and went to bed.

While John tossed and turned in an uneasy sleep Inspector Bristol was hard at work. He too had watched the TV program of the pro-am but his reaction was very different. Several minutes after the golf finished Bristol was still sitting in his armchair. The TV now showed a supposedly adult comedy show but Bristol was thinking about what he had just seen from the golf course. The phone interrupted his musing and he turned off the TV before answering it. The report from the fire site inspection team caused him to get his jacket and return immediately to the police station.

Much later when he returned home for the second time Bristol had interviewed the chief investigator from the inspection unit, brought his Superintendent up to date and issued several series of orders to members of his team. He decided not to contact John Friesen until the morning when both would be more refreshed and one of them would be far better informed. Rather than stick around the station and needlessly supervise his capable staff Bristol opted for the rest he would need to get him through tomorrow. He also had a whisky before turning in, but in his case it was only one and his sleep was immediate and restful.

Bristol was in the office at six-thirty the next morning reading the results of the inquiries he had instigated the night before. By seven o'clock he had scanned each of the reports and finished one mug of coffee. He was just settling down to a second mug and the careful re-reading of the reports when the desk sergeant appeared in the doorway.

"Excuse me, Inspector. Mr. Friesen is here and would like to see you urgently."

"Sure. Show him in would you and bring him some coffee. He's going to need it." Bristol stacked the reports he had been reading and placed them face-down on the desk.

"Good morning, Mr. Friesen. Have a seat, please."

He got no further since John started speaking immediately he entered the room. "It's Karen, she didn't come home last night. My wife, I mean. She's disappeared. I've brought in a picture of her. She's never done this before. You must help me find her." He sat down abruptly in the chair facing the desk and stared at Bristol.

"Take it easy, sir. The Sergeant's getting you some coffee. Then we'll get it all sorted out. When I asked you to call round this morning, I hadn't exactly expected you this early in the day."

There was a brief knock on the office door and the Sergeant returned with a round plastic tray bearing a mug of coffee, a jar of creamer, sugar, a spoon and a small plate of digestive biscuits. Without saying a word he placed it on the corner of Bristol's desk and left the room.

Bristol gestured towards the tray and waited silently while John fixed his coffee. By the time his visitor had taken his first sip, Bristol was ready.

"I'm afraid I have some more bad news for you, Mr. Friesen. We now believe that your wife and partner perished in the explosion at your workshop yesterday. Last night the team of investigators found two badly burned bodies in the rubble. Later examination of a wedding ring and an identity bracelet found at the site indicate that the bodies were those of your wife and your partner." He forbore to mention that the two bodies had been discovered unclothed and joined permanently together in death among the burnt remains of the office sofa.

John was stunned. "What? Karen and Don? I don't believe it. There's no way!" He slumped back in his chair and most of the coffee spilled in his lap.

Bristol pushed a box of tissues across the desk. "I'm afraid there's no mistake, Mr. Friesen. I'm very sorry."

"It must be a mistake," John insisted. "Don was at a meeting. Karen didn't even have a key. How could they have been there? Whatever were they doing there? The place was closed yesterday..." He stopped abruptly. Don's meeting in the city, Karen's phoney phone call from the Cancer Society, his all-day commitment at the pro-am and the times involved coalesced into the most likely explanation. When the realization of what must have occurred struck him John went white and shrank in the chair. Bristol must know about the arson and John was the obvious suspect.

As Bristol assessed the reaction to his news there was another knock at the door and a constable entered and handed Bristol a folded piece of paper. He opened it and glanced at the contents, then nodded to the constable who left the room.

"There's no doubt about the identities, I'm afraid. We've been trying to check with local dentists. Both your wife and partner were patients of Dr. Crystal and his office has just confirmed that their dental charts match the teeth of the two bodies." He waved the piece of paper he had just received.

"I'm sorry to have given you such a shock, Mr. Friesen. Look, let me get you another mug of coffee while you dry yourself off and collect your thoughts." He took the mug from John's unresisting hand and swiftly left the room. By now John had decided that he should say nothing until he was able to speak to his brother Jim, a lawyer.

Bristol delayed his return to the office by checking his phone messages, returning a call to the Superintendent, and visiting the washroom. When he arrived with the refilled coffee mug five minutes had elapsed. John had used several of the tissues to soak up coffee from his trousers and was leaning on the desk smoking a cigarette.

"I helped myself to one of your cigarettes, I hope you don't mind. I quit six years ago, but just now what I needed more than anything else in the world was a smoke."

"No problem," Bristol replied. "I've tried to give up several times, but I just can't break the habit. It's my way of coping with stress, and if anyone deserves a cigarette it must be you."

John drew heavily on the cigarette. "I just don't know where to start. It's all too much," he said. "Yesterday my only problem was my golf swing, but now I've got to cope with funeral arrangements, wills, settling the business, the landlord, and God knows what else."

He looked as if he was about to burst into tears and Bristol tried to divert his attention. "Is there anyone I can contact to help you with all this?" he asked.

"My brother Jim is a lawyer, he'll know what to do."

"Do you know his number, Mr. Friesen? I'll call him."

John searched through his wallet until he found Jim's business card. "He'll probably be at the office by now, he always was an early riser."

Bristol took the card and dialled, John stared out of the window as he tried to think what to do. He was vaguely aware of Bristol's telephone conversation.

"He'll be here in about thirty minutes, Mr. Friesen. As you heard I just gave him a brief outline of what has happened."

Friesen was relieved that his brother was coming. Jim probably dealt with this sort of thing all the time. He would keep John on track and make sure he did all the bits and pieces necessary. Bristol didn't seem to have any suspicion that the fire was deliberate or that he had set it. He needed time alone to think.

"I wonder if I could use the washroom?"

"Of course. Let me show you where it is."

Fifteen minutes later they were back in Bristol's office. John had combed his hair and washed his hands and face. The left leg of his trousers was damp from his further efforts to remove the coffee stain. He looked, and felt, much better and had decided to say as little as possible. Bristol leaned over the desk to offer John another cigarette.

He accepted reluctantly. "You realize, of course, that you've just rekindled my addiction. I think I'm a smoker again."

Bristol laughed. "That's not my only recent bad deed, I'm afraid. I have a confession to make. Last night I had you figured for one of the most cold-blooded and calculating killers I had ever encountered."

John suddenly sat very still in his chair. Bristol was toying with him. He tried to breath normally. How could Bristol suspect him of deliberately killing anybody?

Bristol gave another self-conscious laugh. "I have an unfortunate tendency to look for complicated solutions to crimes I'm investigating. I know from experience that the most direct solution is usually correct, but it doesn't stop me. It's probably the result of reading too many detective stories. Last night I saw the TV coverage of the pro-am and the segment about you carrying the phone in your golf bag. This was only minutes before I heard about two bodies found at the fire and the tentative identification. I wondered if you'd taken out massive insurance on your wife and then murdered her with a bomb triggered by a telephone call."

John stared at him. He was beyond speech. Bristol must know the truth. Why didn't he just arrest him?

"Even if anyone thought of a bomb set off by remote control with a telephone call, you would have a perfect alibi. On a golf course - miles away from a phone. Who would think of a cellular phone in a golf bag unless, like me, they saw you on TV in that exact situation? Simple, eh? Just get her to the office on some excuse, make the call and set off the bomb."

John didn't trust himself to try and speak. He was sure the policeman knew the truth. He just stared at Bristol who wondered if he had gone into shock.

"The investigators looked for evidence of arson as a matter of routine, but didn't spot any of the obvious giveaways. There appears to be no sign of foul play, and they said the fire and explosion started in the workshop, nowhere near a phone. That, by the way, is another thing that went against my theory - the total devastation at the scene. That fire and explosion could only have been the work of a demolitions expert or one of those freak occurrences that you read about only in textbooks."

John still said nothing. Maybe Bristol didn't suspect him. He continued to stare blankly at the Inspector. How could Rosemary and Don deceive him like that?

"Anyway, just to be sure, I checked with the phone company about calls from your portable phone. They showed that calls were initiated to your home and office during the times you were on the course yesterday, but neither was completed."

"I was trying to save money by hanging up before the answering machines cut in," John said. "I didn't realize they could trace calls like that. It's just as well I have nothing to hide."

Bristol smiled. "Anyway, before I abandoned my master criminal scenario I made one more call to Russ Thompson about your insurance coverage. He said that your partner had arranged the usual business types of coverage, but that you had terminated the insurance coverage on your wife last year. That's where my theory finally collapsed and I had to recast you as victim rather than culprit. I owe you an apology."

Bristol stood, came around the desk and stretched out his hand. "There will be an inquest, of course, but unless there are any unexpected developments, it looks as if we shan't have to bother you again. Oh, by the way, here's a copy of the preliminary report from the fire investigation team."

John shoved the report into his jacket pocket before he reached out to shake the policeman's hand. He thanked him for his concern and left the office.

As he walked slowly towards the main door to wait for Jim he thought about Karen and Don and the irony in the timing of their illicit meeting. He realized he had inadvertently hit the jackpot. Although his original plan had completely misfired (he cringed at the unintentional pun), all his business problems were solved along with a family one he hadn't even been aware of. He was apparently free of suspicion and able to start his life again enriched by experience. He wondered if Bristol would be so sympathetic if he knew about the terms of the partnership insurance Don had insisted on when they started out. The cost of maintaining it had been a bone of contention, but the windfall of the unanticipated $250,000 survivor's benefit would go a long way to making some of his unexpected challenges easier to handle.

The Lady From Prague by *Eric Wright*

Eric Wright, one of Canada's most honoured crime writers, has twice won the Arthur Ellis Award for Best Novel, and twice for Best Short Story. His eight novels about Toronto cop Charlie Salter have earned him an international following. An executive member of the International Association of Crime Writers, Eric has a particularly fine ear for the kind of all too plausible drama played out in this story.

THE LADY FROM PRAGUE

by*Eric Wright*

I saw her almost as soon as she spotted me, though she may have been watching me through the glass. She came hurrying through the big double doors apparently on her way to the lobby, but half a dozen times in her progress she glanced slightly sideways to where I was sitting in the corner by the tiny bar. She circled the room rapidly, then stopped before the exit door, turned and hurried down the step to pause in front of my chair.

It was a big room, created out of some leftover space when the building was converted into a tourist hotel, and the natural route from door to door was down the centre, but there was a kind of runway round the perimeter, one step up from the main area and separated from it by a low rail. When the lounge was full, it made for an easier throughway from door to door, but in the present deserted state of the room it was an unnatural path to take. My antennae were quivering long before she spoke.

There were only two other people in the lounge, a middle-aged, cautious-looking couple drinking coffee on the far side of the room. I had noticed them by the desk when I collected my key and summed them up as a couple taking a cheap three-day break, probably from up north, Leeds, perhaps. The hotel was about half-full of people like them; the other half were mainly European tourists.   There are many such hotels in the Bayswater area, cheap tourist accomodation, cheaper still if you buy a package from an airline. This one had been converted from a former residence for single middle-class business ladies, and the lounge must have been where they held the weekly dances. I found it a pleasant place to read a paper or to have a snack before bed-time, because it was nearly always empty. The bar was no more than a cupboard tended by an East Indian lady who served coffee and pastries from her own stock, but she would bring you anything from the restaurant if you asked her.

The woman was about forty, I guessed, dark, attractive, slightly dishevelled as if she had just run for a bus. She was carrying a small, new-looking attache case which she put down on the floor beside the armchair facing mine, well inside my "space" when there were thirty other chairs to choose from. "Can I please?" she asked in a very thick accent, pointing to the case. Then she started towards the door, fumbling in her pockets, pantomiming someone preparing to make a phone call.

Now I had to make my first decision, rather sooner than I had expected. I should say now that I am a writer, mainly of detective stories, and I am always on the lookout for incidents I can turn into plots. When you travel alone things happen to you, probably in my case because I give off a receptive air, and I have had my share of entanglements in other people's lives. I welcome them, always ready, of course, to disentangle myself from the maniacs or the plain boring.

There was the woman on the ferry crossing over to Calais twenty years ago, for instance. I had chatted to her enough on the crossing to find out she was making her first excursion to Paris for which she had saved for a year, so that when she twisted her ankle badly as she was going ashore, I ended up spending two very pleasant and totally innocent days with her in a Calais hotel while she recovered, even borrowing a wheelchair from the hotel to take her for walks about the town. We talked steadily and freely in the way one does on board ship, not expecting ever to see one's companions again, and on the evening of the second day she told me a story of her discovery that her father was illegitimate and that her real grandfather was a Norwegian ship's captain whom she intended to track down one day, a story that I used almost intact twenty years later.

Then there was the girl on the railway platform in Copenhagen whom I watched from the train taking passionate and grief-laden leave of her man, and then saw, a few hours later, obviously deeply in love with another man in the dining car. The only way I have been able to make sense of that is by asssuming the existence of twins, and the world doesn't need another "twins" story. But I'll find a way to use it some day.

And just to round off these examples let me cite the middle-aged lady with the row of flat curls on her forehead and triangular diamond-studded glasses on a chain, whose opening remark to me in the ship's bar on our first night out was, "My husband and I live like brother and sister." I never followed it up, but it made a good opening to a story in which a character does follow it up and finds that the remark is much more complicated than he thinks.

All these incidents and many more have provided the fuel that stokes my word processor. My point is that it is important not to be careful, or nothing happens. You can always disentangle yourself when it becomes clear that the encounter is getting sticky in one form or another. This time, though, a decision had to be made in much less time than usual, for in London one must be wary of unattended baggage. As she circled the room, and until she put her case down, I was already slotting her into a Hitchcock-like encounter, but the attache case changed things. I had a second to decide (she had already turned away), but a great deal can be thought, if not actually framed in sentences, in a second. The first possibility was that in a very short time, unless I moved quickly, I would be found littered around the room in unidentifiable fragments. But the room was empty apart from the couple from Leeds and surely not significant enough of itself to make a worthwhile terrorist target. That decision made, I moved on to the next. Now the emptiness of the room and the circularity of her progess towards me lent some weight to the possibility that the attractive, dishevelled lady in the green leather suit and silk blouse with two buttons undone was on a different mission entirely, one I thought I could handle. It occurred to me that there was another dimension to her behavior with the attache case, that she must know the effect on a stranger in a London hotel of asking him to guard a case, and that she was testing me.

I nodded and stayed where I was.

She returned too quickly for someone who had had to use a pay phone in a London hotel lobby, and threw herself into the armchair, giving me a harrassed smile. Then she jumped up and fumbled some more for change, eventually putting together enough coins to buy herself a small bottle of mineral water from the lady at the bar. She sat down, poured herself a glass, sipped, pushed back her hair, jerked her open blouse this way and that across her breasts, moved her case closer to her feet, smiled at me, sipped again, all the time watching me with her sideways air. Then she said in her thick accent, "You are English?"

"No," I said.

"I hate the English."

"I'm Canadian." Once more my brain was in motion. If I had replied 'yes', what would she have done? But some instinct on her part, prompted perhaps by my button-down collar, still not common in England, had made her guess accurately.

She nodded four or five times. "I hate the English," she said, as if to make sure I had heard.

It was a demand for me to enquire why, but I resisted it. The first thing I wanted to confirm was that she would not be put off by politeness or indifference. If she pursued the subject then I could be pretty sure it was me who she was interested in, not the English. The most likely possibility at this stage was that she was about to pick me up. I was wary, of course, but once I had gathered my wits I could find little risk in seeing how she went about it. There was a slight chance that she was mad, that she would suddenly leap up and scream that I had attacked her; she looked distraught, but, I judged, not out of control.

There was a limit to how far I would let her go, not out of any fear for myself, but out of consideration for her. I have been in the situation before of having an attractive woman in a strange place come on to me—who hasn't, and why does it never happen in Toronto?—and if you are at a resort hotel or on a cruise ship, sheer decency requires that you let her know quickly if she is wasting her time, that your wife is on her way. You can enjoy the opening encounter, but there is a point at which her investment in you will become an embarrassment when she finds out she has been wasting her time, an embarrassment that could turn to anger. On a cruise ship she might retaliate by telling the other passengers that you ...well, whatever.

If she is a professional, then it is that much more important, for her sake, to break off quickly so that she can scout a more likely prospect and not lose too much work time.

We hadn't reached that point yet. For the few minutes that she had been there, and for a few more yet, I had a right to appear puzzled. I had listened politely but given her no encouragement. And she was attractive. I wondered how much she charged, if that was the case. She had certainly worked out an original technique. I kept in mind that she might yet be a lady in distress.

I glanced across the room as she rooted in her bag, conscious that the middle-aged couple from Leeds were watching, and I smiled slightly at them, sort of indicating that what they were thinking was probably true, but I was in control of the situation. They looked away immediately. I could almost see the woman's lips move. ("Don't get involved, Henry.")

"He invite me here," the dishevelled lady said. "Invite me. Here. I pay for hotel, everything, he say. I pay all money." She lit a cigarette and put it out immediately. If this was an act, she was performing brilliantly. Perhaps it was true.

"Then he say, is cancelled," she continued. "But I have no money! No matter. Is cancelled."

"Who," I asked, "is he?"

"Big man with factory. He come to Prague, tell me, come to London. I give you job. Then he cancel."

"It happens," I said.

But she was not interested in conversation. "Filthy English." She added a few words in her own language. "I have no money. Nothing."

"Back to Prague?" I asked.

She leaned forward and put her hand on my knee. "You English?" she asked again, and squeezed hard as if searching for the answer there. She shook her head in answer to her own question. "You stay here?" she asked.

Here it comes, I thought. I said I did.

"You have room by yourself?" She leaned forward and I got a whiff of perfume, dark and heavy.

"Yes I have my own room."

Suddenly she burrowed in her purse again and brought out a wallet. "Look," she said. "Filthy English. All my money. Gone. I have nothing to eat today. Yesterday, one omelette. One. That is all."

I judged she was leaving her options open. She was a professional, pretending to be an amateur who was obliged through circumstances to offer herself for the price of a bed, in which case she would be asking for money in the morning. Or she really was a lady in distress. Then why didn't she go to the embassy, or to the police? No, getting into my room was just step one. I had no intention of leaving the lounge with her, of course, but it was too soon yet to say so. As far as possible, I wanted to get the whole of her plan.

"Can I buy you a meal?" I asked, pretending that her last remark was the whole point of the encounter. It seemed a fair price to pay for the story I would get out of it.

She went into a flurry of shrugs and nods to convey that she was embarrassed, but she was also hungry. "I will have omelette," she said. "All the other food here is..dirt, English."

I walked over to the bar and gave the woman the order, adding two cups of coffee. I looked over to tip the wink to the couple from up north to let them know I wasn't being suckered, but they had gone.

While we waited for the omelette and I waited for her next move, she gave me an expanded but even more garbled version of her predicament. All I could get out of it was that a glass manufacturer on a visit to Prague had employed her as an interpreter, and subsequently asked her to come to England and work for him as a translator. She had paid her own fare from Prague, and he had assured her she would be taken care of when she arrived. But when she got to London there was no one to meet her, no message, and her calls to the factory in Birmingham had gone unanswered.

It was a good story, even possible, but I didn't believe a word of it, mainly because I had been to Prague when it was under the old regime, and the interpreters for our party were all excellent linguists. This lady could barely make herself understood. She was now overplaying her part ludicrously.

"What are you going to do tonight?" I asked, as if I hadn't heard her question about my room. According to my rules, I should not have asked her this. It was time to leave, while I could still pretend ignorance of her real purpose, and she could look for someone else. But I wanted to let her know that in enquiring about my room, at least, she was wasting her time.

I could not penetrate the look she gave me, but I guessed that she was calculating the lack of progress that my question implied. Then she smiled. She kicked off her shoes, curled her feet under her and smiled with an unmistakeable openness. "I make you afraid," she said.

This was irritating. "Of what?"

"Perhaps you don't like me. Perhaps some English woman has cheated you. You have no money?"

So there it was. I was still holding open the possibility of a Czech lady in distress, but now she brought all the sexual hints together in her smile.

It was time for me to go to the lavatory and not return, a slightly mean trick but I should not have let things get this far. And then she said, "You think I am prostitute? I am not prostitute. I have no money." She began to cry quietly. "I did not ask to sleep with you. Oh, God, no."

"Then what did you mean?" I asked.

"I thought, you have a room with two beds, I could have the other one, just for tonight."

"How do you know what kind of room I have?"

"This is tourist hotel. All rooms have two beds. *Sleep* with you! Oh, God, what is happening to me?" She pulled herself together and stood up. "Now I go." She stood up and looked bleakly around the room.

"Where to?" I asked.

"Somewhere. It is not cold." She looked at her watch. "If I have money, I could get single room, like you. I don't want your bed, Englishman. Keep your bed."

She almost had me, but a sudden sideways shift of her eyes, the same gesture she had used when she circled the room, held me back. I had just been about to give her the fifty pounds she needed for a room but that little gesture made me see it all. She was not a tart, of course. This was the end of the con. This was exactly the feeling in me she had been working towards, and I felt so cheered by seeing through it that I wanted the encounter to end on a slightly better note for her than it was doing. I thought of a gesture which would allow her to leave with the impression that I had not had the faintest idea what she was up to, that she had been defeated by my stupidity. I dug for my wallet. "Here," I said. I offered her ten pounds. "For breakfast."

She looked hard at me, perhaps considering a gesture of her own. But ten pounds is ten pounds. "I have to take it," she said, almost to herself. "I have no money. Goodbye, Englishman."

It had taken her an hour, and she had earned ten pounds. Worth it to me, but hardly to her, I thought.

The lobby was empty as I walked through to get the elevator, and so, too, was my room when I got to it, stripped bare - my clothes, the travellers cheques from under my mattress, even my alarm clock.

The police, when I began to tell them where I had been while my room was robbed, were very interested in the Czech lady, even supplying me with details about her appearance that I hadn't noticed. "But she was with me the whole time," I protested. "She had no time to come up here. She had nothing to do with it."

"Coincidence?" the sergeant asked. "Did you see anyone else about in the lounge or in the lobby, sir? A couple maybe, middle-aged, respectable-looking?"

"They left about an hour before I did."

"Plenty of time," he said. "Half an hour would be enough. They're very good, those two. Those three, I should say. Don't forget to get a refund on your travellers cheques. If you call in at the station, we'll give you a document to get you home. If you don't mind my saying so, sir, it's as well to be careful when you're travelling alone. We do our best but we can't protect all you Americans from...adventuresses." He smiled. "There's too many of you and not enough of us. And she's not always Czech. Sometimes she's French. Once she was a Russian. Goodnight, then, sir."

Plumbing the Depths
by *Alison Cunliffe*

Alison Cunliffe's second published story reflects her love of the Caribbean and deep sea diving. A Toronto journalist, her first story appeared in Cold Blood III and was widely praised by reviewers across the country.

PLUMBING THE DEPTHS

by *Alison Cunliffe*

A diver was up and it looked like trouble. Pete Ryan hollered for his wife. "Dinghy's got to go out, Meg!"

Pete scanned the barely swelling seascape anxiously, knowing that Meg could haul the dinghy up to the big boat and get it ready for a rescue run faster by herself. Thank heavens the Free Press was securely anchored in a safe, sheltered bay. No worries there.

Pete tried an okay sign, arms swinging wide and then clasping in a circle over his head. No response. Plenty to worry about there. The diver, Kathleen Vega, it looked like, was thrashing at the surface, face mask jammed up on her forehead in one of the classic signs of a panicked diver.

Pete slid down the ladder to the swim platform of his 65-footer and leaped lightly into the runabout he always towed behind. Meg had already started the engine and was untying the tow line even as Pete slipped the little dinghy into gear.

They could hear Kathleen screaming despite the throaty put-put of the dinghy's motor. "Tom! Tom! Oh, my God, where's Tom?"

Another head surfaced, off to the right, a riot of long, blonde curls rumpling around her as she thrashed just a little more than the best divers do at the surface. Pauline Alexander. "Have you seen Tom? He went racing for the surface ... "

"It's okay, Pauline. We'll find him." He resolutely ignored her after that. Kathleen was the problem. The little boat glided ever closer to her.

Pete's voice deepened and slowed into his best calm-panicked-diver rumble. "It's all right now, Kathleen. We've got you. Can you make it if we tow you back to the boat?"

Right voice, wrong message. Kathleen's thrashing grew more frenzied.

"Damn you, no. No tow. I want Tom. I've lost Tom. I've got to find Tom."

Pete caught Meg's eye wordlessly and she nodded. He blessed the day he'd found this wonder who knew what he needed almost before he knew himself. Pete gave the dinghy's motor just a shot of gas and settled his weight as far over the side away from Kathleen as he could manage. He had to counter-balance the weight-shift to come and still be able to get back to his helm without a second's delay.

The dinghy glided to within inches of Kathleen. Meg, muscles toughened from years of hauling anchors and shifting 40-pound scuba tanks, had Kathleen under the arms and up and over the side of the boat in a flash.

As soon as Pete could move without letting his little boat capsize, he reached out to grasp and heave on the top of Kathleen's scuba tank. She tumbled fully into the boat in a tangle of thrashing fins and sprawling arms.

Pete tuned Kathleen out after that, knowing Meg would handle the woman. He squinted into the Caribbean sun, scanning the sparkling waves for Kathleen's husband, the man she was supposed to have been diving closely with as a buddy pair.

Pauline, he noticed, was already within a few fin strokes of the boat, swimming strongly and cleanly on her own. He hadn't seen or heard her husband, Gary, surface, but there was his fluorescent pink hood, one of his defences against frequent ear infection, moving steadily toward the Free Press.

Bud Rowan, the fifth passenger on this charter, was bobbing gently in the waves, scanning the ocean around him. Thank heavens they'd all been diving closely together. Pete didn't insist on it, but he was always happier when his entire group of divers looked out for each other, rather than splitting up into the buddy pairs he did insist on.

"Pete! I think Tom might be in trouble. I saw him reach for his J-valve rod for more air and then ... Over there! I think I see something!"

Pete soon spotted the glint Bud was pointing at. Not good. Pete should have been able to see a head sticking out of the water.

He knew Tom's equipment well. Pete would see sun bouncing off bright chrome like that only if the man was face down and flat out on the water.

As the dinghy came closer, Pete recognized the old-fashioned steel tank Tom Vega insisted on using. Closer still. No doubt at all now. It was Tom. Pete swallowed hard. The man's floating body was too still, and face down so that Pete could see all of the scratches that the air tank strapped to Tom's back had collected, from top to bottom, on this and other dives. Tom should be yelling for help. But Pete, strain as he might, could hear nothing but the slap of gin-clear waves, the murmur of his dinghy's small motor and Kathleen's strangled sobs.

Pete tried not to think as he searched his vessel for the length of tough cotton canvas he knew he'd tucked away somewhere. A decent covering for the dead. It was all he could think of to do.

Meg was feeding their stunned passengers, who were arguing half-heartedly about who'd found the most rare shell or the most beautiful sea fan on this trip. A few of the finds had decorated the table until Meg banished them and distracted them with food instead. Pete hadn't been able to eat. Neither had Kathleen. She was below in the tiny cabin she and Tom had for the week. She was sleeping, thanks to the tablets some doctor had once prescribed for Meg during a now-forgotten family crisis. And Pete was trying not to let it register that he was making a body bag for what used to be a living, breathing man, a man he'd liked sometimes and disliked others, but a man who had the right to go on making people like him sometimes and not others. Trying not to shout, Why me? Trying not to say over and over and over again: We've never had a serious accident. We run a good ship, a safe ship. Our divers don't get hurt.

Not good enough. Not safe enough. A diver wasn't just hurt. He was dead. Pete Grant wanted desperately to know what had gone wrong, whether he could have done something to stop this tragedy before it happened.

Pete had dived with Tom, years ago when the man first started coming down to the Caribbean for a yearly fix of sun, sand, sea and plenty of pampering on the Free Press. Pete tried to dive with all his passengers. There was no better way to assess their skills and just how careful he had to be with them. The answer with Tom was: very careful.

Tom, Pete remembered, talked a good dive, deeper, longer and boasting of seeing bigger and better sea-life than anyone else could spot. And the man certainly had experience, more than 200 dives, Pete knew from a sneak peak at Tom's dive log.

But Pete suspected he was about to dive with a very nervous buddy almost as soon as he joined Tom in the open gearing-up area at the back of the boat and started helping the man find and get into his equipment for that first, get-acquainted dive.

"Didn't we tell you we had plenty of the new aluminum tanks on board?" Pete asked, handing Tom's smaller, steel model over to within easy reach.

"Sure," Tom said a little breathlessly. "But I love this old thing, even if it doesn't hold as much air."

Pete thought it was odd but didn't comment. "I don't see your pressure gauge. Might it be in your luggage down in the cabin?"

"I don't use one. I learned to dive with the good old J-valve, and it's still good enough for me."

Pete really didn't approve of that. He'd learned to dive with that method himself, but he didn't like it and he'd switched to the pressure gauge almost as soon as they became available. The principle of the J-valve was fairly simple. The diver needs to know when he's getting short enough on air that it's time to end the dive. You can't tell just by time. How much air you use depends on how hard you swim and how far beneath the surface you go, even on how comfortable you are because a scared diver can breathe very heavily indeed.

J-valves like the one on Tom's tank were an early answer to the problem. He'd run out of air on his dive and reach around behind to pull on the bottom end of a rod attached to the unreachable valve behind his head. That would open the valve and release the small amount of extra air that had been locked away from the main part of the air tank.

Pete frowned. "I can rent you a pressure gauge, if you like. Heck, I won't even charge you."

Tom smiled that devil-may-care grin that seemed to be able to charm men and women alike within a 50-foot radius of its warm gleam. "Thanks, but no thanks."

"Suit yourself." But Pete still didn't like it. Too many people get scared when they run out of air, even if they're trained to pull that rod and get more. And scared divers are half-way to big trouble.

Pete passed over the man's regulator without comment. That piece of equipment was not boat issue either, but there was little surprise in that. Most of Pete's passengers brought their own regulators. Pete took his own whenever he travelled. He liked the feel of his own mouthpiece, and he liked knowing just how much air the device would deliver under what conditions. And he didn't like to take the chance on a poorly serviced air-supply mechanism standing between him and the compressed air in the tank strapped to his back.

He usually took his own buoyancy compensator with him, too. He strapped on the inflatable jacket with a comfortable smile that faded as Tom donned a small, inflatable ring around his neck and ran the strap from front through his legs to back to hold it in place. The inflatable devices Pete had rented at times never quite seemed to fit properly, and it spoiled a dive if you had to try to get used to just how much air had to go into an unfamiliar device to let you swim effortlessly, neither sinking nor rising. But this guy had to be a real nutbar about original equipment if he subjected himself to this.

"Guess you love the horse-collar, too."

"Sure do. It's all what you get used to I guess."

"Have you ever tried one of these jacket BCs? They're incredibly comfortable after feeling that horse-collar jamming into your chin when you're bobbing around on the surface. And they hold your head higher out of the water so it's easier to get all your air from the snorkel, even in rough waves."

"Yeah, I tried one once, in the pool. Just didn't like it. Stick with what you know, you know?"

Pete shrugged uneasily, and did one last buddy check on Tom.

"Whoops, Tom, you forgot your weight belt. If you promise not to spread it around, I'll tell you about the time I forgot. Couldn't get down to save my life until I did a duck dive. Wouldn't you know it? Meg noticed and I didn't hear the end of it for two months!"

Tom grinned sheeplishly and reached into the open box that held his equipment. The belt was old and worn, and even the lead weights strung through it showed the scars of many a bang into a coral head.

"You bring your own weight belt, too?" Pete shook his head, smiling. "You're the first passenger I've ever had who brings this much equipment. If everybody did maybe I could make a decent living out of this business!"

Tom laughed and so did Pete.

"Just before we go down, I want to add one order, Tom. Bring up any shells you really like the looks of, interesting pieces of sponge or coral. But no black coral. That's absolute. We won't be deep enough to find any on this dive, but I like to make it clear to everybody on my boat that I won't tolerate souvenir hunting with something that's getting so scarce. And make sure that whatever you do bring up, you're prepared to clean. Meg has a set of dental instruments you can use. They're perfect for scraping away some of the encrustation that'll stink to high heaven as the shell ages out of the water, not to mention the critter inside.

"But we both get pretty upset about people who kill the critter and then decide the shell isn't worth the trouble of cleaning after all."

"Okay, Pete, I understand. I promise."

The dive was a great one, once Pete got over worrying about his buddy having to duck dive below the surface. Even with his weight belt securely in place, Tom was breathing so hard, filling his lungs so full, he couldn't just dump the extra air out of his horse collar and slip easily to the depths. But he seemed to relax once they were floating easily in a school of flashing yellowtail just a few inches above the forest of delicately fingered staghorn coral.

Pete shook the memories off sadly and reached for his sailor's palm. Better get this sewed up and stowed out of sight before the rest of the passengers started wandering out to the back deck. The first few stitches weren't too bad. With a few more, though, Pete was brooding about the man who was never going to dive again, never cover up being nervous until he could finally fly effortlessly through the water, never complain again that Pete took him only to dive sites where the depth and the current were suitable for beginners. He'd never know that magical feeling again when you get your buoyancy so right you're flying in a slow-motion dream of beauty coming alive with waving fronds and brilliant colours and the teeming, endless variety of life under the sea.

The sewing needle jammed into the sailor's palm dropped out of his nerveless hand as he freed it for the next stitch. He tried to bend over to pick it up. Instead he ran for the rail and bent over it to be violently sick.

Pete sighed and settled back in his armchair for a long pull on his beer. He eyed the stout door between the galley and the passengers' lounge-cum-dining-area appreciatively. With a wife like Meg, if you wanted company and comfort, you had to find it in the galley. When he'd finally realized that, he'd done a little redesigning inside his boat.

The result was a sanctuary he felt he deserved at the moment. He'd pulled himself together long enough to radio the police to expect the victim of a fatal diving accident when the Free Press pulled back into port. They'd sounded suspicious. Had he been taking care of his passengers as well as he should? Police didn't like accidental deaths involving tourists. It was bad for the industry the islands depended on so heavily. Pete didn't like the situation himself. It hadn't been easy to pull himself together long enough to wrestle the body down below.

He could hide now for a while and find a strange sort of peace in watching Meg throw herself into her favourite form of therapy. He winced, though, as his wife flung herself cross-legged on the floor in front of the pots cupboard and started removing the contents. Three casserole dishes, a frying pan and a steamer surrounded her on the floor before she emerged triumphant with a cake pan.

That door between the galley and dining room hadn't just been for privacy. The paying customers would never understand the mess that Margaret Ann — he always thought of Meg that way when he wasn't too pleased with her — could make of a kitchen when she was in the midst of a cooking frenzy.

Sometimes it was tough living in the close confines of a sea-going motor yacht with a much-loved-one who could drive you crazy as no one else could. Most of the the time it was worth it. Yes, life a lifetime ago had had its own attractions. Their home in Whitby was within easy commuting distance of Pete's police desk and Meg's job as a feature writer at the Toronto Star. The pay cheques were steady though the long, shifting hours were awful and the work was an endless new challenge. But the Caribbean called. Pete and

Meg fled without a regret but with many a nervous twinge to a diving charter business in the spectacular, untouched outward reefs of the Caymans that they'd come to love so well.

Fifteen years of yearly vacations with Doug Doyle and Sue Freeman on their R/V Sea Wolf – "research vessel," a designation aimed more at the tax man than the truth – hadn't been enough for either of them. And so Ryan Oceanics Ltd. was born. And the 65-foot R/V Free Press was christened.

"You had it made, Doug, and you didn't even know it," Pete muttered, eyeing the pots and dishes scattered from one end of the galley to another.

Pete's therapy sessions rarely resulted in worse than a two-aspirin hangover. Meg's unfortunately, resulted in a floor-to-ceiling mess and a thorough disinclination to clean up afterward. Somehow that had become Pete's job.

Pete took a swallow of beer and cleared his throat. "What are you making?"

"What's that, dear?" Meg cracked an egg into what seemed to be the fourth egg-whipping bowl on the counter.

"I said, what are you making?"

"Brownies," she said absently.

Pete eyed the littered counter helplessly. "That's all?"

"Well, I put together a lobster salad for tomorrow at lunch. With that home-made garlic mayonnaise you like so well. It might be too rough on the crossing back to port to cook. And I thought while I was at it I might make some veal cordon bleu to finish in the microwave next week."

No wonder passengers complained they gained 10 pounds per trip, even though they swam to exhaustion. No wonder his own middle was spreading uncomfortably.

Pete cleared his throat and moistened it with another swallow of beer. "So, what do you think?"

Meg whipped her egg even harder until he was ready to swear the poor thing would beg for mercy.

"I think you did the right thing, anchoring for the night. Half the passengers would probably be sick in the 12-foot swells they said we'd have on the crossing back to port if we'd gone today."

"No, what do you think about Tom?"

Meg was creaming the butter and sugar for the brownies now. Pete figured they'd be the lightest, airiest chocolate sins he'd ever ingested.

"I think it might be murder."

Pete dropped what was left of his beer. Meg handed him a cloth calmly and he wiped the upholstery dry. They'd said the coating would resist stains and moisture. Looked like for once a salesman hadn't lied.

The aftershock of Meg's bombshell rumbled in his brain. He reached for another beer, snapped the can open and leaned against the counter.

"Okay, Margaret Ann. I'll bite. What on earth makes you say a fool thing like that?"

Meg slapped down the fork, butter, sugar and all.

"Motive? We saw that two years ago, and for that matter on every other trip Tom's ever taken on this boat. Method? I don't know, but I bet if we looked long enough we could find it. Opportunity? There's nothing so easy in the world as killing your dive buddy. Look how many people manage it every year when they're trying not to."

"Diving's a perfectly safe sport, Meg, you know that."

"If you don't panic. If you do..."

"I know, Meg, I know. I took the course, too. You're out of air, you panic, you fly for the surface, all those air bubbles get trapped in your body. One, just one, that's all it takes if it expands in a vital place and cuts off the blood flow."

Pete could almost feel it happening in his own body. The terror. The lungs locking shut. The air in those locked lungs expanding as the diver raced upward for more air and swam desperately, dangerously fast through water packed into itself with a pressure that decreased with every inch closer to the surface.

Pete swallowed. "Poof. Embolism. Dead diver. Or badly hurt, anyway. But it could have been an accident. Kathleen was in hysterics. And you know what a nervous diver Tom was, for all he tried to hide it. He's exactly the kind of diver who'd get into trouble and panic and kill himself."

"Kathleen is a good actress." Meg rummaged angrily in her oversize freezer. She pulled out a roast of beef, three chicken legs and the glassily staring kingfish Pete had caught on their last crossing from Florida. Finally came the walnuts she'd been seeking. She tossed the meat back in the freezer. Pete tried to be grateful that she always replaced her frozen messes, if not the rest of the chaos her cooking created.

"You saw how they all surfaced fairly close together and at about the same time. If somebody did something to make Tom panic, it could have been any of them." Pete took a long pull on his beer and thought more about that. It certainly could have been any of them. And they all had reasons in their own way ...

"Kathleen as his buddy should have been closest to him, best positioned to do something. But I've dived with them, too," Meg added sourly. "Kathleen never struck me as a particularly good buddy about staying close. And she should have with the way he was about diving."

"Oh, you noticed that, too."

"Sure, every time I filled his air tank, it was down to the J-valve reserve and just about drained dry. Hers was always half full or more. That guy was sucking back a lot of air when he was down."

"Okay, so he was nervous, and Kathleen may not have been as close to him as she should have been. Gary, Pauline and Bud were probably closer if they were diving as they usually did. But you said Kathleen had a motive. You mean that mess with Bud and Sally two years ago?"

Pete started at the savagery with which Meg cracked her first walnut, and then another, and then another. Her voice, finally, was deceptively soft.

"I might have been inclined to murder you if I'd caught you..."

She might at that.

Pete had to laugh. The situation had been so bizarre. Tom had flown down to the Caymans five days after his honeymoon. Kathleen didn't dive, not then. And she must have figured sitting in a boat waiting for heads to break out of the water three or four times a day was not her idea of a good time. She might have changed her mind and come anyway if she'd known what else other than diving was Tom's idea of a good time.

Tom obviously hadn't minded leaving his blushing bride at home for this sacred tradition of Free Press vacations in the first week of October every year for a decade. His business partner, Bud Rowan, was with him, and Bud's wife Sally. There was another couple, too, but Pete couldn't for the life of him remember a single thing about them. Pete wasn't surprised when Tom started making a play for his partner's wife. He'd managed flirtation or full-blown affair on every other Free Press trip.

This one got him into rather more trouble, though. Bud was none too happy when he decided late in the game to join his wife and Tom on their night dive under the pier. When Bud got there, they weren't doing much diving. They were wearing smiles along with their scuba gear and very little else. There was nothing in the water currents that should have pushed them together in that particular way.

Bud was not very happy with the situation. Sally didn't get back into her cabin with him for the rest of the trip. She sweated and worried on a couch in the lounge. If Tom snuck up a few nights to join her, Pete tried not to notice. But it wasn't easy. Tom emerged from the water that night with a nose huge, swollen and reddening brightly enough to light up the entire after deck. Meg had a little nurse's training. She was able to tape the poor appendage up quite well until a doctor could take a look at the break. But nothing could get that swollen nose into a mask. Tom was out of diving for the duration. Even if his nose had fit, the swelling would have made it impossible for him to blow air into his ears to equalize the awesome pressure changes as a diver goes deeper or more shallow in the water.

Tom was soon too frantic to have any thought of diving anyway. Bud, status as betrayed friend easily overcoming that of business partner, decided to let Tom's equally betrayed and very newly wed wife back home know just what had been going on.

Kathleen boiled for three days. Then Pete made her acquaintance, via an emergency phone call, patched through on open radio waves via the Cayman Air Sea Rescue Association.

"You're sure it's an emergency, Sparky?" These calls were expensive, very expensive.

"Yeah, Pete, just get him up to the radio. I don't want to try to cope with this – lady – myself any longer than I have to. Just tell him it's about his marriage. Oh and that she's going to shoot his Rolls Royce, break his favourite golf clubs in half, drown his dog and pour every drop of his Chivas Regal down the sink."

Pete found his boat hailed as the Free Love for months after that. He couldn't really blame the avid audience that heard every detail.

The verbal massacre lasted an hour and a half. Whew! Hundreds of dollars for a browbeating. Pete comforted himself with the thought that Tom owned his own refrigeration and heating shop.

He could pay. And he wouldn't want word to get around that he'd stiffed a poor charter boat captain for a $500 phone call. If Tom were smart, he wouldn't want word of this phone call to get around at all. Not at home with his business associates, anyway.

It had been too late to worry about Cayman gossip, that was for sure. Every VHF-radio-equipped boat within five miles of the Free Press had heard all the gory details. And the next year, when Tom came back, Kathleen came with him and a regulator of her own.

"Okay," Pete said, "so Kathleen had a motive. He treated her pretty rotten. But for Christ's sake, that was two years ago. Why would she wait this long to do him in?"

Meg shoved a pan of brownies into the oven.

"Because she's probably finally realized he'll never change, he'll always run around on her whenever he can get away with it. And maybe because it took her until last year to get him to make her a partner in that business he has. She gets the whole shebang now."

"No, she doesn't. Bud's still a partner, too, so Kathleen had a quarter, I guess, and now that Tom's dead she's got half. And Bud gets to run the show. He'd like that."

"He might at that." Meg blinked in thought. "He might indeed. Tom was saying at dinner last night Bud had some plans. Tom didn't like them, of course, but it seems Bud has been claiming the business has been running downhill and Bud is sure he knows what to do about getting it back into shape."

"Doesn't Gary have some connection to the company, too?" Pete asked, trying to remember more about the tall, thin passenger who seemed to be memorable for very little more than his very bad jokes and very pretty wife.

"That awful pink hood. Some doctor told him reducing the temperature change in the water would help cut down the ear infections. I can't seem to make him understand it's my vinegar, water and special ingredient formula that does it when he's diving with us."

"He should be listening more to you," Pete smiled.

"Well, I've been doing a lot of listening when I can get him to let me put the drops in his ears. He's a supplier for Tom's company. He doesn't seem to have been too happy with Tom, and I don't think it's all because of Pauline, either."

"What's Pauline got to do with anything?" Pete thought of her blonde curls and habit of staring straight into your eyes when she talked to you. It reminded him of another passenger with fall-into-infatuation-with-the-captain syndrome. Pete immediately set out to make sure he stayed out of her way.

"Pete," Meg said gently, "you're hidden up there in your wheelhouse most of the day, where people out front are right under your nose, and they know it. Me, I spend half the day back here cooking. The window's shaded. Lots of people don't seem to realize I have an eagle's eye view of what's going on."

"Tom and Pauline had a thing going on?" Pete realized he should have known. But he'd thought Tom would have more sense than to carry on the affair tradition under his wife's nose.

"Well, something was going on. They didn't exactly fornicate in front of my very eyes. But they didn't hold back all that much either when they knew Gary and Kathleen were napping between dives."

Pete contemplated a third beer until Meg quietly, firmly caught his eye.

"Okay, so we've got suspects. Heck, maybe even Pauline if she started to not like the way the romance with Tom was going. But we don't have any proof that anyone other than Tom himself did anything other than panic."

"Well, then, you'll just have to find the proof, won't you dear?"

Pete wasn't all that convinced. But he locked up Tom's dive gear before he went to bed, just in case the equipment had something to say that a killer wouldn't want to have heard. It could have been an accident. Any one of his passengers could have engineered an accident. All of them had reason to do it. Pete had the five days it would take to get back to port before the police would get into the act. But this was his world that had been violated. He didn't want police botching up the cleansing. He was determined to find the solution himself.

Pete poured a rum punch to better ruminate with and sank back in his easy chair. Margaret Ann was making soup, unfortunately. Two weeks worth of leftovers festooned the counter and the stock pot had originally been buried behind fully three-quarters of the contents of the pots cupboard. The three-quarters now filled most of the counter and half of the floor.

"If you were going to murder a dive buddy and make it look like an accident, how would you do it?" Pete asked.

"Get him drunk the night before," Meg said promptly with scarcely a skip in her onion chopping. "Then I'd diddle with his depth gauge and get him down to, oh, maybe 180 feet. Between narcosis and hangover, he'd be handing his regulator to the fish with no interference from me at all."

Pete chuckled. "Remember that chamber dive we did? Air pumped into that cramped little cylinder so hard that you get all the nitrogen narcosis, all the rapture of the deep that you'd get diving at 150 feet. We were looped to the gills. Weird, isn't it?"

"I remember," Meg grinned. "Instant party time. I remember you rolling on the floor, getting tangled up in all our feet. You had a fit of giggles because you'd dropped a pen and it bounced into the side of your shoe. I don't know what's more ridiculous: that you found it that funny, or that we did, too. But that's narcosis for you."

"Yeah. Remember that six-foot-six cop who said he and his buddies drove up to the clinic most Saturday nights to party at 250 feet and walk out with no fear of a hangover?"

Meg laughed and Pete did, too. But Meg soon sobered and turned to stirring her soup. Pete poured himself another rum punch. And another. He had reason the next morning to wish he'd done a chamber dive to get high.

The nagging headache didn't stop him from pouring over poor Tom's dive gear, though. Pete was pretty sure the cops waiting in port wouldn't find anything wrong. Pete was a very experienced diver, and he wasn't finding anything.

Old or not, Pete couldn't find a damn thing wrong with either the old-fashioned horse collar Tom insisted on using or the small air bottle used for inflation as the diver went deeper and needed more air to keep him neutrally buoyant. Pete even sniffed the air in the mini-bottle and the collar. No problems there, either.

Strange, though, that Tom hadn't tried to use the air left in the mini-bottle during his panicked flight to the surface. Or maybe not so strange. Panic-stricken divers had been known to do far more foolish things.

The larger air tank Tom had strapped to his back had quite a few scratches that looked new. So did everyone else's. Pete had some painting to do before the next charter to pretty up the equipment he offered his passengers. All the divers must have crammed themselves into a few interesting coral caves before the accident. And from the way they surfaced so close together in both time and space, they must have been quite close together under water just before Tom did his last screaming run for air on the surface.

Pete checked the air pressure on the tank. Six hundred pounds per square inch. Not too surprising. The reserve, depending on conditions, could easily vary by a few hundred pounds per square inch.

What was surprising though, was that the J-valve was still in the up position. Somehow Tom hadn't released his reserve air. He'd run for the surface, gasping for air, locking his lungs in his panic and trapping those deadly, expanding air bubbles in his bloodstream.

The rod Tom should have pulled to release his reserve was in place, right where it should have been, within easy reach of a diver used to reaching for it. It looked fine: a little rusty from corrosive seawater, a little abraded from close encounters with hard coral. In fact the J-valve itself showed a few scratches on its underside. Tom must have been banging himself around in some really tight spots. Odd, that. Some divers glory in seeing what tiny nooks and crannies they can wiggle in and out of. Nervous divers usually don't. But Tom was just the kind of won't-admit-it diver who could be talked into trying almost anything that made him nervous.

Still, there was nothing, absolutely nothing to prove that murder had been committed.

Or was there? Pete had to think about this. Think a lot. Why would Tom, for all that panicky divers can do strange things, not pull that rod to get that extra air? Or reach for the little bottle that inflated his horse collar? Pete headed for the galley. And beer. And Meg.

They finally figured out how it could have been done. Pete tried it with a spike doctored a little with his metal file. Then he snorkelled down to the reef for a likely piece of coral and doctored it with his dive knife. Yup, that could work.

The rough part was proving it. Meg put out a selection of hors d'oeuvres that needed no attention but were guaranteed to get every watering mouth gathered in the dining room.

"Anybody want to discuss murder?" Pete said.

The babble drowned everyone out for a long minute.

"It was an accident, it must have been," Pauline finally managed to say. "We were maybe a hundred yards away and Tom came out of a tight coral overhang, and we saw him shoot for the surface. God, I could see his eyes, big and staring. It was awful. Kathleen was following him, so we thought they were going to be okay." Pauline's blue eyes drowned in glitter.

"Gary, is that what happened?"

The man sighed. "I don't know. I was worried about Pauline. I didn't see Tom. I just looked around and Pauline was gone, in the seconds since I'd last checked on her. I'm sorry. I know we were supposed to be diving in a threesome with Bud, because he didn't have a buddy, but I forgot about him altogether when I couldn't find Pauline. So I surfaced and saw her swimming toward the boat. I didn't even know anything was wrong."

"Like I told you that day, I did," Bud said heavily. "I saw Tom reach for his J-valve rod and then run screaming for the surface. Kathleen followed him, too fast for safety, I thought. I don't know, maybe not. I tried to get over there and grab them, make them slow down, but I was too far away. So I came up and just started looking. I knew something was wrong." Bud buried his face in his hands. "He was my partner. He was a jerk in some ways. Anyone who knew him knew that. But he was a good man, too, always able to make you laugh."

"Something," Pete said softly. "Something."

Meg interrupted, voice cracking with harshness. "Where were you, Kathleen, when all this was going on?"

"Right where I should have been," Kathleen said calmly. "Right behind my buddy." Her voice cracked theatrically. "Right behind my husband."

Pete let it lie for a day. He had to start heading back to the Caymans and he couldn't concentrate on exposing a murder when he had a boat full of passengers to shepherd safely through swells thankfully settling down to six-footers on the way back to port and police.

Besides, letting it sink in that he might know what had been done, how, and by whom, just might make it easier to scare the murderer into doing something foolish.

The boat was on auto pilot, so he had three-quarters of his attention free to check and double-check his facts, conclusions and strategy.

That night, safely anchored, he found he just couldn't wait any longer. Especially when he found Kathleen alone on the rear deck trying so hard to look grief-stricken and woebegone that it made him want to be sick.

"We know how you did it," he said conversationally.

"What? What are you talking about?"

"No one was watching the pair of you very closely, were they, Kathleen? You led him into that coral cave, knowing how nervous he'd become, knowing he'd never refuse you the dare. You made sure you both stayed in there until he was low on air and would be reaching for his J-valve rod any minute."

"He always got nervous in tight places, you know that. It's not my fault he wouldn't stay out of them."

"I've got to admit it was smart, Kathleen. You couldn't know for sure he'd be frightened enough to lock his lungs and embolize. You couldn't know it would kill him even if he did. You could just stack the odds in your favour, helping to make sure he wouldn't be alive to testify about what you did."

"Pete, you can't mean any of this ..."

"Oh, but I do. You see, I found this in your luggage." He brandished a thin piece of staghorn coral. "You couldn't resist keeping this, could you? To gloat over?"

"Pete, that's ridiculous. We've all been bringing up souvenirs."

"Not souvenirs like this one. There are some rather strange grooves in this one. I've checked. They could have been made easily with a dive knife. They just happen to fit the width of that J-valve that Tom couldn't release. The scratches on the underside of that valve ... It'd be awfully hard to get scratches there no matter how tight the coral cave was, Kalthleen. And these scratches, they line up perfectly with the ridges in this piece of coral."

"Pete ..."

"Just before you finally led him out of the cave, when you were sure he'd be on his last gasp of air in the tank, you jammed this piece of coral in to the J-valve to make sure the valve couldn't open. You ..."

Pete should have been expecting it. He wasn't. Kathleen leaped for the fragment of coral and threw it overboard. Pete dived over the side, clothes, shoes, wallet and all. He lost his wallet, had to find it the next day in sunlight and with an hour and a half of air and searching time strapped to his back. But he caught the piece of coral two inches away from the bottom.

He came up dripping. "Meg!" he hollered. He needn't have bothered. Meg already had Kathleen in a steel grip, only half-way down the swim ladder toward a desperate dive into the sea and an attempt to flee to the nearby uninhabited island.

Pete shook salt water out of his eyes.

"Did you feel anything for him, Kathleen, even a little bit, when you jammed this coral in? Could you breathe when he pulled and pulled on that rod and the coral refused to let the lever drop down and release that precious air? Did it hurt even a little when you followed him so fast for that first five or 10 feet that you could yank the coral out and no one would know? Were you scared he'd survive, and be able to tell us what you'd done?"

Kathleen's green eyes glinted. "You can't prove a thing," she grated.

"I'm not so sure," Pete said, reaching hard for calmness.

Pete and Meg sat in court, holding hands, after he testified and all the way through until Kathleen was convicted. Pete wanted to got out for dinner after. Meg said no. Meg said, in fact, they had to get back to the boat, fast. She had to cook.

Last Resort by *Peter Sellers*

In addition to editing and appearing in the Cold Blood series, Peter Sellers' short fiction has been published in Mike Shayne Mystery Magazine, Alfred Hitchcock Mystery Magazine, Hardboiled, and the anthologies Criminal Shorts and Northern Frights. In 1992, his story "This One's Trouble" was nominated for an Arthur Ellis Award. And, together with William Bankier and James Powell, he was honoured with the Crime Writers of Canada's Derrick Murdoch Award.

LAST RESORT

by *Peter Sellers*

Barker was late getting away again and he drove all night. He stopped once at the side of the Massachussetts Turnpike and slept in the car for an hour and a half, then he pressed on. He drove much faster than the 55 mile an hour limit, but he didn't figure there'd be many state troopers out looking for speeders at four o'clock in the morning. He made it to Hyannis just as the sun was coming up.

He parked his car at the Kennedy Memorial and sat on one of the stone benches watching the day begin. Seagulls swirled above him, landing on the beach and the grass, struggling crabs clenched in their beaks. A middle-aged couple jogged past and waved and a few minutes later a woman strolled by in the company of a large black lab. After half an hour, Barker went back to his car. He knew Harris well, so he knew he'd be awake.

Barker drove slowly the last few hundred yards to Oceanview. He passed Veteran's Park to his left and the bird sanctuary to his right and followed the road as it curved to the west. Oceanview was right there. Two four unit buildings at the water's edge. Their situation was perfect. Ocean to the south, beach to the east, bird sanctuary to the north and, to the west, large private homes. Even on the crowded Cape, Oceanview gave you the impression of solitude.

Barker had been right. Harris was up. He was standing on the low stone wall near the steps that led down to the small private beach, a steaming mug of coffee in his hand. The wind tossed Harris's blond hair and blew the steam wildly to the side. He turned when he heard Barker's car tires crunch over the gravel. Barker parked next to a German-made car that also had Ontario plates and climbed out.

226

"You want a coffee?" Harris asked as Barker drew up beside him. "You look like you could use it."

"Thanks. I could also use a couple hours sleep."

"Pulled an all nighter again, eh?"

Barker shook his head. "One of these days I'll get away in time and make it here at a civilized hour. Like just in time for a cocktail."

"Buddy," Harris said, "you're on vacation. It's always time for a cocktail."

Barker had that first drink of the day in the unit he'd be using for the next week. It was the southernmost second floor unit of the southernmost building. It had an unobstructed view both south and east and Barker thought he could happily stay there forever. He sipped the spiked coffee slowly. Harris had laced it with a stiff shot of brandy and Barker could feel the tension from eleven hours of driving easing out of his shoulders. It was good to be back.

"So how's the ad biz?" Harris asked with a chuckle. "Crazy as ever?"

"Oh yeah," Barker said, although he didn't want to talk about work. "What about the resort game?"

"Resort," Harris laughed. "'Bout the same. Half full this week, half empty next."

"You got all eight units open yet?"

Harris shook his head. "Two are still out of commission, but I hope by next season."

"Can you hang on?"

Harris shrugged. "Dunno. It'll be tight. The bank says they won't loan me any more." Then he smiled. "But I'm still in there swinging."

"Many of the regulars here?"

"Some. The Snells. A couple of kids, Ellie and Don, who claim they're married but I got my doubts. Jessica Smith's here, too."

"With her husband?"

Harris nodded and grinned. "He's up in Boston at the moment, but he'll be back."

"That wouldn't be who you're thinking of swinging at?" Jeremy Smith was the manager of a bank in Boston, but Harris had always said he didn't feel right about approaching him for money.

"I have to do something," Harris said. "It's awful tight."

Barker figured that was an understatement. Harris had bought Oceanview in a weak moment and in a hurry. Burned out by too many years in the ad business, too many impossible deadlines and too many unreasonable clients, he'd jumped in the car one morning and headed across the border, ending up on Cape Cod. He'd never been there before and it was love at first sight. It was still early in June when he arrived so finding a place to rent for a week wasn't a problem. He found Oceanview early that evening and paid cash in advance for one of the available units. Five days of staring out over the ocean, walking on the beach and sipping cold Stroh's was working hard to undo the knot in his stomach. On the sixth day, he found out the whole place was about to go up for sale. The owner told Harris he'd thought about going condo with it, but decided to unload it instead and just retire. Harris thought about it for a minute, then said simply, "I'll buy it."

They discussed it for a long time, but Harris's mind was made up. And the same tenacity that made him so good at defending his ideas back at the agency made him stick to this idea too. The real estate agent drew up the papers, Harris agreeing to pay the full asking price with no conditions. He arranged for a deposit through a local bank and then headed back to Toronto to sell his house and make all the other arrangements.

The Toronto real estate market collapsed the week Harris put his house up for sale. It stayed on the market for months and, when it did sell, it was for much less than he'd dreamed possible. Right from the start, Oceanview put Harris in the hole.

But it was what he wanted to do. He told all this to Barker as he was cleaning out his office, disposing of the detritus of fifteen years in advertising. For eight of those years, he and Barker had been partners. At one time, according to one of the industry magazines, they were among the top three creative teams in the city. Now that was over.

Harris drew up a map and promised to hold one of the units for Barker for two weeks in July. He said Barker would love it too, and he was right.

It wasn't until Harris was almost back on the Cape, everything he was taking stuffed into the trunk and tossed carelessly on the back seat, that he realized he'd never even looked at the second building.

When he did, half an hour after the deal closed, his heart sank. The building he'd stayed in had been recently renovated, badly he was to discover later, but the other had not. It still boasted lead plumbing ready to burst in several spots and wiring that had been untouched since construction. The plaster bulged from the walls and the wind whistled through cracks and gaps.

Now Harris understood why no one had lived there during his stay. The owner had said it was just a slow time of year and it was better to have all the guests in one building.

Already stretched to the limit, Harris couldn't afford to repair the units right away and he wasn't able to do it himself. He limped along from one payment to the next for five years, slowly putting away enough cash to bring the new building up to standard one unit at a time. Now only two remained to be done, but there was no more money to be borrowed. Harris was more worried than Barker had ever seen him.

"So who's that from the old country?" Barker asked from the window.

"The Ontario plates? Guy named Merrill. He's a contractor, handyman type. Been here a week already and he's doing some work for me. He's working on Jessica, too. You'll meet him later."

Barker nodded and yawned. "I think I'm gonna sack out for an hour or two. Got my key?"

Harris fished it from his pocket, tossed it to Barker and went to the door. When Harris had gone, Barker dropped on the bed and it was almost cocktail hour by the time he woke up.

*　　*　　*

Barker stood on the deck of Harris's condo and looked out across the ocean. He sipped his beer and watched the windsurfers zig-zag across the snapping whitecaps off the public beach.

"Nice to see you again," a voice said not far from his left ear.

Barker turned to look at Jessica Smith. She was wearing a light summer dress that the wind plucked at and lifted coyly, like an adolescent trying to catch a glimpse. Seeing the flashes of long tanned leg, Barker could understand why. She looked better than he remembered and he remembered she looked awfully good.

"Too windy," she said. "Let's go in."

Barker hung back for a few seconds, watching the colourful sails scooting back and forth in the distance against the choppy green of the water and the crisp blue of the sky, then he went in too.

Most Saturday nights, Harris had as many guests as cared to come into his place for a casual drink. Barker had seen such gatherings with as many as fifteen people and as few as Harris and himself sitting on the deck watching the ocean and getting quietly crocked. It was a continuation of something Harris used to do in his agency days in Toronto when, every Friday at four, he hosted Happy Hour in his office. Then, though, it was strictly BYOB.

There were eight of them this time. Jessica was standing next to Ian and Betty Snell, both doctors from New York who were Oceanview regulars. There was a guy on his own, talking with Harris, who Barker took to be Merrill. And there was a young couple who seemed oblivious to anything except each other. They didn't look married to Barker, either.

Barker went up to the Snells and they shook hands. Barker enjoyed talking with them, particularly Ian, who was always anxious to discuss advances in medical research and surgical technique with anyone who'd listen.

Ian was about to fill Barker in on a new development in post mortem identification when Jessica came over and placed a hand on Barker's arm. "I was hoping you'd be back," she said.

Barker sipped his drink. "I was hoping the same thing," he said.

"That I'd be back?"

"That I would. How's Jeremy?"

"He's Jeremy. Business could be going better. The economy has taken its toll, but things certainly could be worse." She paused, then added, "They may get that way soon. Harry asked him for money, you know." She frequently referred to people in the diminutive, which Barker found curiously insulting.

"Did Jeremy go for it?"

She shook her head. "Harry's too bad a risk, unless Jer's intention was to give him the money so he could eventually foreclose and then buy the property back from the bank for a song. But Jeremy's too ethical for that." She said it as if ethics were sort of like scabies.

Barker noticed that Merrill was watching Jessica carefully from across the room. He looked to be about thirty with dark eyes and well defined cheek bones. It seemed that a guy just like him showed up at Oceanview every year. The same time as Jessica. "So who's this guy Merrill?"

"He's from Toronto, too," she said softly. She pronounced every syllable carefully, unlike a native who'd slur it out as Trawno.

"Some kind of handyman?"

"Mm hmm. Very. He took care of a little plumbing problem for me last week when Jer was back in Boston on some crisis or other."

"It's nice to have helpful neighbours." Barker finished his drink. "I've gotta go into town and pick up some groceries. You need anything? Or does Merrill have it covered?"

"You're wicked," she said.

"That makes two of us."

*　　*　　*

Barker hit the Stop 'n Shop and walked out with four bags of groceries. Then he went to a nearby liquor store for half a dozen bottles of wine and four six packs of Miller. Finally, at a hardware store he picked up a bunch of things Harris needed. He figured he'd spend the next morning putting in a couple of dimmer switches and popping a washer into a leaky faucet and then, if there wasn't too much wind, he'd try his hand at windsurfing.

He dropped by at Harris's and gave him one of the six packs.

"Nightcap?" Harris asked.

"Sure." Barker took the opened beer and drank it from the bottle. "So what's the story with our Jessica and this guy Merrill?"

"You always cut right to the chase," Harris laughed.

"The question is, though, who's chasing who?"

"She's just playing her little game while Jeremy's in Beantown. He'll be back tomorrow and she'll cool her jets."

"She said you asked him to bail you out and he turned you down cold."

Harris shrugged. "There's still a chance. I think he liked the idea a bit, and I'm going to try him again when he gets back. I don't know what else to do."

"You'd do anything to keep the place."

Harris spread his arms wide. "Look around. I'd kill somebody to keep it."

"Kill somebody?"

Harris thought for a minute, then said, "Well, maybe I'd punch 'em real hard."

231

*　　*　　*

The next day the wind blowing in from Nantucket and Martha's Vineyard was harder than ever and, after taking care of the chores using some tools Harris had borrowed from Merrill, Barker decided windsurfing was out of the question. He was just throwing his beach gear into the car when Jessica walked up to him.

"Where you going?" she asked.

"Thought I'd drive up to Marconi Beach for the day." He slammed the trunk.

"Want company?"

"What about old Jer?"

"He won't be back till tonight. Hang on, I'll get my things." She ran inside, reappeared a few minutes later with a big shoulder bag, and climbed into the front passenger seat. Barker started the engine.

She popped a Chet Baker tape into the cassette player and sang along. "Let's get lost, lost in each other's arms..."

"I bet you say that to all the boys," Barker said.

She laughed. "Only to you."

"What about Merrill?"

"Are you still on that kick? There's nothing between me and Merrill, and I've never been unfaithful to Jeremy. Besides, I've only ever thought about that with you."

"Flatterer."

*　　*　　*

As they climbed down the wooden steps to Marconi Beach the wind fell away, blocked by the high bluffs. On the sand it was very hot. They walked a long way down the beach, away from the families with kids and the young lovers, and Barker spread out a towel.

He'd packed a lunch and they ate it looking out over the water at the horizon. Every so often a sail would appear, slicing through the brilliant, infinite blueness of the sky and then it would disappear again like a mirage. They walked along the beach, the surf rolling in and soaking them to their knees. Once, a wave washed a starfish up on shore in front of them and Jessica picked it up, feeling how soft and pliant it was.

"It's still alive," she said, and she reached out to gently drop it back in the water.

"It'll probably just get washed back up again," Barker said. "Then some seagull'll have it for lunch or a kid'll take it home and pin it to a cork board."

"At least this way it'll have one more chance. Who knows how it'll turn out."

At three o'clock she said, "We better head back. I want to be there when Jer gets home."

As it turned out, she was too late.

* * *

When Barker pulled into the Oceanview parking lot, they could see Jeremy's car. And as they got out, they could hear Jeremy's voice carried on the wind. It was loud and very angry.

"God damn it, I told you before I left that it was out of the question. Don't you understand that? Out of the question. No can do. Impossible. Now I'm here to enjoy my vacation and if you don't leave me alone and stop bugging me about this, we're packing up and you're giving me back the rest of our rent money. And I'll litigate you into the ground to get it."

Jessica looked at Barker over the roof of the car. "Whoops," he said.

Jeremy came around from the front of the condo, head down and nostrils flaring. He glowered at Jessica. "Where the hell have you been?" Opening his trunk and hauling out an elaborate brown leather suitcase, he went on, "I wasn't here two minutes and he was on me like a bad smell. Jesus." He puffed inside and slammed the door behind him. Jessica followed without a word.

Barker went looking for Harris. He found him standing by the low stone wall looking out at the ocean.

"What the hell was Smith so steamed up about?" Barker asked. "Did you ask him for dough again?"

Harris shrugged.

"You never did know how to pick your spots, pal. It's like trying to sell an ad to a suit who's just got reamed out by the client for something he didn't do. You'd barge right in and try anyway and you always got shot down."

"Not always."

"Mostly. He probably had a lousy day in Boston. He probably had a lousy drive back. He was probably figuring Jess'd be waiting for him with his slippers and a beer. He was in a lousy mood. And you just dove right in."

"I can't wait anymore. I'm dying on the vine here. I don't see any other way. If he won't help me out I may as well torch the place for the insurance money." Barker shuddered at the image and Harris kicked sand and stones in front of him as he walked back through the parking lot.

As Harris walked away, Merrill drifted out of one of the untenanted condos, brushing plaster dust off his trousers in great grey clouds. "Hiya," he said as he saw Barker walking towards him. He was younger than Barker and he had more hair. It was blond and wavy and had bits of plaster in it. "Boy, Harry's in a bit of a state." Somehow hearing Merrill use Harris's diminutive irked Barker a lot. "I guess it was having Jessie's old man light into him the way he did."

"You heard that, eh?"

Merrill nodded and chunks of plaster flew out of his hair like shrapnel. "Hard not to. I'm redrywalling the top floor and doing a little work to the plumbing and with the windows open and the wind blowing in it was like they were standing in the next room." He reached into the open trunk of his car and took out a battered metal tool case and a plastic hardware store bag. "Saw you coming back with Jess. What a doll. Good thing her old man came back when he did, 'cause another day or two and I couldn't've been held responsible for what happened. She's something, wouldn't you say?"

Barker didn't say and Merrill's brilliant smile faded a little. "No offence, of course," he said. "Anyways, Harry's got himself a hell of a place here, once I get it fixed up for him, that is," he chuckled. "I sure hope he can hang onto it. Well, back to the salt mines." And he hefted the tool box and the bag and headed back inside.

Barker watched him go, and still didn't say a word.

*　*　*

The wind died down early in the evening.

Jessica invited everybody to a barbecue to celebrate the fact that Jeremy was back. She corralled Barker into lighting the barbecue, an old charcoal burning relic that took a couple of quarts of lighter fluid and a pack of matches to ignite. Huddled over it in the lee of one of the buildings, Barker longed for a gas model. But finally it caught and he left the coals to grow hot as he pulled up a few deck chairs and brought down a dozen beers.

Jessica came with the steaks and the swordfish and Don and Ellie separated from one another long enough for her to make a Caesar salad. Merrill brought a bottle of California wine that had dust on it. Barker figured he coated it with plaster dust just to give it that vintage look. Harris brought foil wrapped potatoes and Ian and Betty Snell brought a pie that each claimed the other had baked. Jeremy brought his bad temper.

There were enough people there, and enough to drink, that everything was relaxed and mellow. The food was good and, Barker admitted reluctantly, so was Merrill's bottle of wine. The sky darkened quickly and Barker marvelled again at the number of stars you could see on the Cape at night. Vainly, he hunted out the various constellations but gave up after finding one of the dippers. He wasn't sure if it was the big or little one.

A couple of times, he also noticed Merrill's hand drifting over to Jessica's leg and she pushed it away as casually as she could with a quick glance at her husband. Barker wasn't sure whether Jeremy noticed or not. Once he missed it because Harris was talking to him, using a lot of urgent, clenched fist gestures and Barker couldn't tell if it was just falling night or if Jeremy's expression had darkened.

Sometime after ten the party broke up. Jessica was the first to leave, asking Jeremy if he'd like to walk with her a little. His reply was curt and clear. He was going to bed. As he stalked away he turned to Merrill and growled, "Say the hell away from my wife."

Merrill's smile glowed in the darkness. "Screw you," he said.

When Jeremy was gone, Jessica started off alone. Then, by ones and twos, everyone else gathered up what they'd brought and trundled off into the darkness.

Barker picked up his empties and folded the deck chairs, throwing some water on the coals to make sure they were out.

*   *   *

An hour later, Barker was sitting on the deck with the outside light turned off, his feet resting on the top railing and a mug of tea in his hand. He could hear the invisible ocean lapping on the shore. He had just about decided that he'd found Orion's belt when he heard the screaming.

It was coming from the building to the west and it was definitely a woman. Then the door to the Smiths' unit flew open and a figure raced out of the doorway, still screaming. Barker could tell from the voice now, and from the wild mane of hair flowing in the dim light that spilled out of the still open doorway, that it was Jessica and she was running toward the ocean.

Lights began snapping on in other windows. Knocking his tea to the floor, Barker jumped from his chair, darted down the stairs and headed toward the screaming figure who disappeared into the darkness.

He caught up to her at the edge of the beach. She had stopped running and was just standing there weaving back and forth and keening, like a woman who's just been told her fisherman husband won't be coming home from the sea.

Barker grabbed her by the shoulders and she slumped against him so he had to hug her to keep her from collapsing entirely. "Jess," he said, "what is it?"

She was racked by a series of moist sobs and Barker started her back toward the buildings, her half walking and him half dragging her. Others were running to meet them now. Harris got there first, followed by Merrill, then Ian Snell. It struck Barker funny how a woman screaming brought the men out. It must be some primal thing that stirred in them, perhaps enhanced by eating meat seared over an open fire not two hours before. He wondered where Don was, though. Probably too wrapped up in Ellie to be aware of anything else.

They started to take her back inside, but Betty Snell met them in the doorway and shook her head. "Not here," she said. So they lifted her up the stairs to the Snells on the second floor. Betty followed and the men left her with a still sobbing Jessica and went back down.

Jeremy Smith lay on the floor of his livingroom, blood in a puddle around him and splattered on the walls and furniture. He was without a shirt and there were puncture marks on his back where someone had driven something into him repeatedly and violently.

Ian Snell grabbed a blanket off the chesterfield and tossed it over the body. Harris almost made to grab it back, then stopped and simply muttered, "Jesus, the carpet's already ruined. Did you have to use up a perfectly good blanket, too?" Snell didn't hear him. He was already on the phone to the police.

*   *   *

The cops got there fast. They took control of the crime scene and then, as soon as the Medical Examiner pronounced Jeremy Smith dead, the forensic crew went to work crawling around with vacuum cleaners and toothbrushes like Molly Maids bucking for a promotion. They dusted everywhere for latent prints and studied the splatter marks on the walls and the floor like fortune tellers gawking at tea leaves.

Barker was standing outside, apart from the rest of the guests who milled around talking nervously among themselves. He was looking at the sky again, hunting for constellations.

A man in a well tailored suit came walking toward him.

"Find anything?" he asked.

"Excuse me?" Barker replied.

The man pointed into the air. "Up there. Find any constellations?"

Barker shrugged. "Just the Dipper," he said. "And I think maybe Orion."

"Not yet," the man said. "Only see Orion in the wintertime." He looked up at the sky in silence for several seconds, then he turned fully to Barker. "My name's Tyler. I'm in charge of this investigation." He flashed a shield in front of Barker's face but it was too dark to read it.

"Ask away."

"You knew the deceased?"

"We've been down here at the same time for the last four years."

"Ever since Mr. Harris bought Oceanview?"

"That's right."

"Can you think of any reason why someone would want to kill Jeremy Smith?"

Barker shook his head. "No."

"I understand Harris and the deceased had an argument earlier today."

Barker wondered who he'd heard that from. "People have

arguments all the time."

Tyler ignored that. "Do you know what it was about?"

"It was about money. Harris wanted Jeremy to refinance Oceanview and Jeremy refused."

"They'd had this conversation before?"

"Yes."

The questions continued for about ten minutes, Tyler flipped his notebook closed, thanked Barker and moved away. Barker went inside and was in the kitchen making tea when he saw the body come out of the Smith's, carted by two ambulance attendants. Then the Medical Examiner came out followed by the cops, and they all drove away.

As they pulled out of the parking lot, there was a knock at Barker's door. It was Ian Snell.

"Jessica's okay," he said. "Betty gave her something to calm her down and she's sleeping. Betty'll stay with her and when she wakes up we'll see if she needs any more attention."

Barker nodded. "If there's anything I can do."

"Not at the moment." He opened Barker's fridge and took out a Miller. "I had an interesting chat with the guy they use as a Medical Examiner."

"Uh huh."

"Yep, he's a local doctor they use on cases like this. For heavy duty forensic stuff they send up to Boston, but he can pronounce death and do basic autopsies and things like that. He gave me a look at the body. A lot of wounds. We counted about 27, a good dozen of them post mortem."

"Did they find the knife?"

"Wasn't a knife. Most of the wounds were round, like the killer used a skewer or something. But there are a few that didn't penetrate very deep, mostly the post mortem ones so maybe the killer was getting tired or something, and they aren't round. They look more square. Like maybe he used two instruments. Put one down, picked the other one up. We'll know more when the stuff comes back from Boston. Anyway, whatever the murder weapon was, they didn't find it." He drained the beer and slapped the empty down on the counter. "Thanks. I'll keep you posted."

*   *   *

Barker had just walked out of a shoe store on the main street in Hyannis with a new pair of Rockport's under his arm when he saw Snell and the local M.E. shake hands and go their separate ways.

"Hi," Barker said. "Any update?"

Snell smiled and shook his head. "Not much. And they haven't exactly moved forward very far on tracking down the murder weapon. They have a room full of forensic experts up in Boston stabbing pot roasts with any pointed object they can get their hands on. No match yet."

"They'll turn something up eventually."

"I think what's driving them nuts partially is that they've picked up some microscopic metal fragments that seem to indicate the same weapon made all the wounds."

"So they've got a square peg round hole problem," Barker chuckled.

Snell nodded. "They just haven't been able to find what they're looking for."

Barker looked thoughtful for a moment and then said, "Maybe that's because they don't know where to look."

"Pardon me?"

"Oh, just thinking out loud. See you back at the place." He turned and walked slowly back towards the ocean.

* * *

Barker was standing in the Oceanview parking lot waiting when Snell pulled in.

"Ian," he called. "Come with me. I want to show you something."

They climbed the stairs to Barker's deck and went inside. Barker led the way to the kitchen. A large, thick filet stood on the cutting board.

"Look at this," Barker said.

He picked up something that lay next to the steak and, holding it like a knife, he stabbed it into the meat and pulled it out again, the raw meat sucking at the blade as it withdrew. It left a neat round puncture.

"Now, look at this."

Carefully, he pressed the same instrument about a quarter of an inch into the beef and took it away. The hole was square.

Snell whistled. "What is that?" he asked.

Barker held it up so Snell could see. It looked like every other screwdriver he'd ever seen, except that the head of it was square. "It's called a Robertson screwdriver," Barker said. "They use them all over the place in Canada. I borrowed this one from Merrill. They come in four or five different sizes and I bet if the cops are put onto it they'll find a match pretty quick."

Snell took the screwdriver from Barker and studied it carefully. "Learn something new every day. So are you going to educate the cops now?"

"Why don't you tell your buddy the M.E. Let him be a hero."

*　　*　　*

They arrested Harris around three o'clock that afternoon. Barker watched from the deck as Harris's door opened and he came out in handcuffs, escorted by Tyler and two officers in the blues of the Barnstable police. They put him in the back of a squad car and drove slowly out of the lot.

The phone call came half an hour later. Harris sounded calm but intense. "I need you, pal. Come as soon as you can."

Barker was patted down before they let him in, then he and Harris sat across a small table from one another on moulded plastic chairs. A cop with a large pistol in an open holster stood by the door.

"I'm scared," Harris said. "You gotta do a couple things for me."

"Anything."

"I need a lawyer. All I know around here are a couple of real estate guys and I don't want somebody court appointed. I want the best there is."

"Did you do it?"

"How stupid do you think I am? Get me someone from Boston or something. Somebody good. Get me whoever the Kennedy's use." His shoulders drooped suddenly and his head fell forward. "Just get me out of here."

"What are you gonna use for dough?" Barker asked. "I mean, I can lend you a few bucks but..."

"Thanks but I don't want to borrow your money."

"Then take a court appointee."

"God damn it, I don't want some second rate jerk who passed law school with a C minus. Do they have the death penalty in this state? Get me someone good. I'll pay somehow."

"How, for Christ sake?"

Harris didn't answer for more than a minute, then he said quietly, "I'll sell the place."

"Aw, Jesus," Barker said, "there has to be another way."

"You tell me what it is."

"A bank?"

"They wouldn't loan me a penny to fix the place. You think some lard ass banker is going to loan me big bucks to hire a lawyer to defend me on a charge of killing another lard ass banker? Gimme a break. Look, call my real estate agent and get her looking for a buyer."

Barker looked thoughtful, then said simply, "I'll buy it."

"Huh?"

"I'll buy it. Then when you get kicked loose from here the place'll still be there. I'll work up an offer today. After I call some Boston lawyers."

Harris's eyes welled up. "Thanks," he said. "Bring the offer as soon as you can. Now please get me a lawyer. Jesus, I'm scared."

*　　*　　*

After leaving Harris, Barker had called a friend of his at a Boston agency and got the names of several key attorneys. One of them was sitting in that little room with Harris right now, mapping out a defense.

Then Barker had called a real estate lawyer in Hyannis and had an offer prepared. He'd deliver it to Harris later on. Finally, he'd called back to Toronto to start the arrangements for selling his house and arranging the rest of the necessary financing.

It didn't look good for Harris, now that the cops knew what the murder weapon was. They knew one just like it was missing from Merrill's kit. They knew that Harris had borrowed it. They knew about Harris's financial situation. They knew about his violent argument with Jeremy Smith. It may or may not have been enough to convict him, but either way the decision could be a long time coming.

Now, Barker sat on the deck in the sunshine. A cold bottle of Miller stood open on the wooden railing, next to his feet. The sky was very clear and the sun sparkled on the water. He raised his glass in a toast and said, aloud but softly, "Well Barker, think you'll do well in the resort game?"

"No idea," he answered himself. "But I'm certainly willing to take a stab at it."

He laughed loudly and looked down at the sea wall where Jessica sat, the soft wind caressing her golden hair.